The
DAILY TELEGRAPH
Book of
Contemporary
Short Stories

The
DAILY TELEGRAPH
Book of
Contemporary
Short Stories

Edited and with an introduction by
John Coldstream

This anthology first published in 1995
by HEADLINE BOOK PUBLISHING

A HEADLINE REVIEW paperback

10 9 8 7 6 5 4 3 2 1

ISBN 0 7472 5078 2

Typeset by Keyboard Services, Luton, Beds

Printed and bound in Great Britain by
Cox & Wyman Ltd, Reading, Berks

HEADLINE BOOK PUBLISHING
A division of Hodder Headline PLC
338 Euston Road
London NW1 3BH

Contents

Contents

Acknowledgements

Acknowledgements are accorded to the following for the rights to reprint the stories in this anthology.

'Stirring the Pot' © Tom Sharpe 1994; 'Baglady' © A. S. Byatt 1994; 'Simon' © Patrick O'Brian 1994; 'Shreds and Slivers' © Ruth Rendell 1994; 'Forward to Fidelity' © Alan Judd 1994; 'Marriage Lines' © Penelope Lively 1994; 'The Wilderness Club' © Shena Mackay 1994; 'A Winter Admiral' © Michael Moorcock 1994; 'Beautiful Things' © Maggie Gee 1994; 'Humphrey's Mother' © Penelope Mortimer 1994; 'The Ghost of the Rainforest' © Barry Unsworth 1994; 'Dressing Up' © Angela Huth 1994; 'Hotel des Voyageurs' © William Boyd 1994; 'Grace' © Jane Gardam 1994; 'Headless' © Brian Aldiss 1994; 'Twenty Years' © Doris Lessing 1994; 'Legacy' © Frank Ronan 1994; 'Not Shown' © Penelope Fitzgerald 1994; 'The Beetle' © A. L. Barker 1994; 'Crying in a Bucket' © Christopher Hope 1994; 'Ta for the Memories' © Deborah Moggach 1994; 'Back to My Place?' © Max Davidson 1994; 'Happy Hour' © Rose Tremain 1994; 'Poor Toni' © Allan Massie 1994; 'Parker 51' © Lesley Glaister 1994; 'Pepper and Leo' © George V. Higgins 1994; 'Graceland' © William Bedford 1994; 'Lippy Kid' © Hilary Mantel 1994; 'The Voice of Mo' © Paul Bailey 1994; 'Down the Tube' © Lucy Ellmann 1994; 'Shared Credit' © Frederic Raphael 1994; 'The Lantern at the Rock: A Ballad in Prose' © George Mackay Brown 1994; 'Forward to Fundamentals' © Michael Carson 1994;

Acknowledgements

'Drawn From Life' © Justin Cartwright 1994; 'Mist' © Richard Adams 1994; 'Desert Island Discs' © Victoria Glendinning 1994; 'Growing Away' © David Cook 1994; 'Goodbye to Yonkers' © Berlie Doherty 1994; 'Confession' © Clare Boylan 1994; 'The Kitten' © Carlo Gébler 1994; 'Space Invaders' © Elizabeth Berridge 1995; 'Late Luck' © Matthew Sweeney 1995; 'Second Fiddle' © Bernice Rubens 1995; 'Performer, Performance' © William Palmer 1995; 'Vermin' © David Profumo 1995; 'Sea Lion' © Douglas Hurd 1994; 'The Roman Candle' © Donna Tartt 1995

Introduction

---◆---

'The art of the glimpse.' It is hard to imagine that William Trevor's succinct definition of the short story will be bettered. It is no easier to remember a time since the 1930s when that art has seen a greater flowering. 'The glimpse' is meeting not only with respect but also with immense popular acceptance: witness the presentation earlier this year of the W. H. Smith Literary Award to Alice Munro for her 1994 collection *Open Secrets*, and the sustained appearance among the bestsellers of both *The Matisse Stories* and *The Djinn in the Nightingale's Eye*, successive volumes by A. S. Byatt, one of the contributors to this book. And only a snob or a churl would decry the popularity of Jeffrey Archer's *Twelve Red Herrings*. At last it seems possible to give the lie to the all-too-common howl that there is no market for the short story.

Perhaps some credence should be given to the theory of the thirty-second soundbite and the preference for the brisk engagement, rather than the prolonged association with a novel, as favoured by an earlier generation. At a time when some of the most eagerly awaited fiction weighs in at 500-plus pages and forsakes narrative in favour of self-indulgence, there is more pleasure to be found in creativity distilled to its essence – a complete, fulfilling experience delivered in less than half the time it once took to transmit *The Late Show*.

The stalls in that market appear to be on the increase, too. Apart from the continuing support of BBC Radio, women's magazines and some small-scale literary journals, there is now a quarterly publication called *Raconteur*, in which the celebrated mingle with the unknown and which in the spring combined with the *European* to present a prize of £10,000, no less, to the best new story.

Oddly enough, a legacy from another of Robert Maxwell's newspapers must be saluted here. One of the fondly remembered features of Cap'n Bob's ill-fated *London Daily News*, which had a brief life in the late 1980s, was a new weekly story occupying a full tabloid page. So when, at the end of 1993, it was decided to produce in the Saturday edition of the *Daily Telegraph* a twenty-four-page tabloid section dedicated exclusively to Arts and Books, the opportunity to revive the experiment, this time for a national – indeed, a supranational – audience was too good to miss. How would novelists respond to the challenge of giving satisfaction in as little as 1,600 words and certainly in no more than 2,000? Sometimes, particularly in the early stages, against a tight deadline?

About six months – representing a couple of dozen stories from some of the best writers in the British Isles – was the initial goal. In the event, the response both from the invited authors and from the readers of the newspaper was so positive that the series was extended to a year, then to fifteen months, by which time a further decision to change the format had been taken and, for reasons in part technical and in part tactical, the short story as a regular ingredient ceased. There was a feeling that, although a number of our principal writers had yet to contribute, we should 'quit while ahead' rather than allow the standard to become diluted by inferior work. Even so, there would of course be special occasions or appropriate seasons when an outstanding story would find a place in the new-look section.

In the pages that follow, you will find ample proof of how magisterially, darkly, wittily and sometimes shockingly the challenge was met. You may never again swallow a mushroom with quite the same confidence; you will undoubtedly experience a *frisson* the next time you find yourself alone in a shopping mall; and as for buying a ticket in the National Lottery . . .

A. S. Byatt believes that the *short* short story of the kind represented here is a quite different animal from the story of 8,000 to

Introduction

10,000 words, in which more than one idea can be developed in more than one direction. Any great novel, she says, can afford to make up to twenty big mistakes which the reader will overlook; but to make one mistake in a short story is to kill it stone dead. After all, we are dealing with something far closer to a poem than to a novel; something which requires precision, accuracy and great control.

I am sure you will relish watching some masters of the craft at their work as much as we enjoyed setting them to it.

John Coldstream
Literary Editor
Daily Telegraph

May 1995

Stirring the Pot

Tom Sharpe

Tom Sharpe was born in 1928 and educated at Lancing College and at Pembroke College, Cambridge. From 1963 to 1972 he was a lecturer in History at the Cambridge College of Arts and Technology. In 1986 he was awarded the XXXIIIième Grand Prix de L'Humour Noir Xavier Forneret. He is married and lives in Cambridge.

It was an unusual advertisement. DEAF MUTE REQUIRED FOR CHAIN-SAW WORK. ESN TEENAGER PREFERRED.

'I'm buggered if I'm putting that in,' muttered Mr Potter, the advertising manager of the *Lexham Gazette*, when he saw it. 'Major Grail again, I suppose?'

Miss Bleyne nodded. 'Comes of him being a recluse. He's out of touch with the present.'

'Out of something. Next time he comes in, tell him to wait for me.'

'I'll try, Mr Potter, but he's ever so difficult. He says he's like Time.'

'Time? What on earth does he mean by that?'

'I think he means he waits for no man.'

Mr Potter looked at her suspiciously. There were moments, more frequently of late, when he had the impression Miss Bleyne was taking the mickey. He went upstairs to consult the editor.

'Unholy Grail's at it again,' he said, thrusting the offending copy on the desk.

Mr Wellstead ignored it. 'What the hell does banausic mean?' he asked.

'Banausic? That's not in the advert.'

'It's in this letter from Miss Roach about the horrors of hunting,' he said and looked at the advert.

'Fairly offensive,' he said. 'Still, it could give us a good headline.

MAJOR RISKS LIFE OF TEENAGE HALFWIT ought to raise circulation nicely.'

Mr Potter shuddered.

'In the hands of a teenage moron it could do other things. We could be seen as accessories before an exceedingly nasty fact.'

Mr Wellstead considered this slight problem.

'All right, check it with Ponson first for liability,' he said. 'If he gives it the say-so, we'll print.'

Mr Potter went out and, ignoring the solicitor's office, headed for the bar of the Ram. Mr Ponson was in his usual place with a brandy and water, marking the racing page of the *Telegraph*. Potter sat down beside him.

'And what can I do for the *Lexham Gazette* this bright and cheerful morning?' Mr Ponson asked.

'Wellstead wants your opinion about Major Grail's latest.'

'Seems a bit odd to me,' said Mr Ponson, when he'd read the advert. 'The Mad Major must intend cutting down Warden's Wood.'

'Using a simple-minded deaf mute with a chain-saw?' said Potter.

'Got to find someone to do it.'

'I daresay, but why the deaf mute?'

Mr Ponson applied himself to the problem.

'See what you mean,' he said finally. 'The poor devil couldn't exactly scream for help if he did himself a mischief, could he?'

'Don't,' said Potter, visualizing a scene of speechless carnage.

'Only trying to weigh up the pros and cons,' said Mr Ponson, and signalled for another brandy.

'Can't you just come down on the side of the cons?'

'It's rather an interesting point of law all the same. Wellstead's worried about liability, is he?'

'Circulation,' said Potter. 'Thinks we're competing with the bloody *Sun*. Anything to push up sales. If it weren't for Lady Bartrey, we'd have full-frontals on page three. Her and the vicar.'

'Full-frontals of La Bartrey and the vicar? What a horrible thought. Now that would lead to an action under the obscenity laws. I'd advise Wellstead to forget it.'

'Yes,' said Potter, thanking God the editor hadn't yet thought of it and wondering at the same time if Mr Ponson added brandy to his early-morning tea. 'Can I tell him to forget the chain-saw massacre too?'

'The what?' said Mr Ponson, still occupied with the dreadful vision of Lady Bartrey full-frontal.

'The Major's advert,' said Potter, stifling a 'For God's sake'.

'Oh that. I must say I can't see anything legally wrong with it. Quite harmless. Stands to reason no one's going to reply. Can't if they're educationally subnormal. Won't be able to read it in the first place and couldn't write a letter even if they did.'

Mr Potter went back to his office despondently. 'The old soak says we can go ahead,' he told Miss Bleyne. 'All the same I think we'll shove it in under Agricultural Implements to be on the safe side. No one looking for a job is going to see it there.'

'If you say so, Mr Potter.'

That was Tuesday. On Thursday he came in from lunch to hear Mr Wellstead shouting into the phone on the floor above.

'Mr Wellstead's ever so angry,' said Miss Bleyne.

'I can hear that,' said Potter, as the editor told someone he wasn't going to be called an insensitive swine.

'I can't think what it's about,' said Miss Bleyne. Potter could.

Two minutes later Mr Wellstead burst through the door.

'I suppose you enjoyed listening to that?' he shouted. 'I suppose you think it's funny to hear me called a . . .' He checked himself and glanced at Miss Bleyne. 'All right Potter, I'll discuss this in my office.'

Potter followed him miserably upstairs.

'Now then, you blithering idiot, do you know what you've just done?'

Potter swallowed drily. 'Not precisely.'

'Then shall I tell you?' said Mr Wellstead.

'Am I to take it Major Grail is somewhat put out?' said Potter hoping to delay the explosion. The editor advanced on him.

'Major Grail? The hell with Major Grail. That was the RSPCA. They've had a flood of complaints about that insane advert. My phone hasn't stopped ringing.'

'The RSPCA? Surely you mean the NSPCC?' Potter began but the editor silenced him.

'No I don't. If you put teenage morons with chain-saws in Pets & Livestock you get the . . .'

'Pets & Livestock?'

'Dogs, Cats, Rabbits and assorted Pets,' Mr Wellstead yelled. 'So why in God's name . . .'

'But I thought . . .'

But Mr Wellstead was past listening. 'Thought? Thought?' he bawled. 'You didn't think. You aren't capable of thought. You wouldn't know a thought if it was stuffed under your snout on a bleeding plate.'

Potter thought about handing in his resignation. Mr Wellstead forestalled him.

'Let me tell you this, Potter. If you want to keep your job, you won't even try to think. You'll do exactly what barking lunatics like Major bloody Grail and I . . . You'll do what I tell you to. Is that clear?'

'Yes,' said Potter and looked hopefully at the door. But Mr Wellstead hadn't finished. 'Some damned official from the Education Department calls me up and dresses me down like I was some sadistic monster,' he continued before correcting himself. 'As though I was. She's even got me talking like an ignoramus. Said we had set a terrible example of uncaringness for the educationally challenged.' He paused and looked at Potter almost pathetically. 'Why the Pets & Livestock section, of all places?'

'Hang on a moment,' said Potter and went downstairs.

Miss Bleyne fiddled with her nail file. As usual she had nothing to do. 'I just thought it would look more cuddly like, in with bunnies and hamsters instead of with turnip cutters and the muck spreader old Mr Foulless has been trying to sell.'

Potter went back upstairs and explained this to the editor.

'She may be right at that,' Mr Wellstead admitted. 'I can't begin to imagine what that Education cow would have said if we'd put a mentally challenged dummy down as an Agricultural Implement.'

That was Thursday. On Monday the editor was even more distraught.

'You look awful,' Potter said intentionally when he met Mr Wellstead in the car park.

'You'd feel awful if you'd spent the early hours being shouted at by a madman in New York.'

'God,' said Potter, regretting his unkindness.

'Exactly. God,' said Wellstead. 'The Almighty's taking a personal interest. And we all know what that means, don't we, Potter?'

Potter nodded dumbly. Mr Wellstead went on.

'Wanted to know what the hell I'd done to provoke all these complaints to head office. Nearly a thousand faxes, letters galore, phone calls. You name it. The works.'

'A thousand faxes? I don't believe it. Not a thou . . .'

'Of course it's not true,' said Mr Wellstead. 'But when did truth matter to God?'

'You'd think he'd be pleased with an outcry. Always gone for it before in his national dailies.'

'The proprietor's forte is not consistency. Nor is taste. Remember his Christmas Message last year; "Dig the Dirt on the Virgin Birth"?'

'Christ,' said Potter. 'No wonder they call him the Digger.'

'Pay dirt pays,' said Mr Wellstead. 'Now get out. I want to think.'

Downstairs Potter picked up *The Times*. There were days even now when he dreamt of getting a job on a respectable paper. Anything to get out of Lexham. Idly he turned to job vacancies and instead found the Obituary page. Opposite him Miss Bleyne went on pretending to type. It was then that he saw the small notice. He read it through several times.

'Miss Bleyne . . .' he began and stopped. There was no point in asking her directly.

'Yes, Mr Potter?'

'Do you ever get bored, Miss Bleyne? I mean frantically, almost terminally bored?' he said. She looked at him curiously and said nothing. 'I only ask because Major Grail's just died in Switzerland after a long illness bravely borne.'

Baglady

A. S. Byatt

A. S. BYATT was educated at York and Cambridge and taught at the Central School of Art and Design and at University College, London, before becoming a full-time writer. Her novel *Possession* won the Booker Prize and the Irish Times/Aer Lingus International Fiction Prize in 1990. Her other fiction includes *The Shadow of the Sun, The Game, The Virgin in the Garden, Still Life* and *Sugar and Other Stories*. She was made a CBE in 1990.

'And then,' says Lady Scroop brightly, 'the company will send cars to take us all to the Good Fortune Shopping Mall. I understand that it is a real Aladdin's Cave of Treasures, where we can all find prezzies for everyone and all sorts of little indulgences for ourselves, and in perfect safety: the entrances to the Mall are under constant surveillance, sad but necessary in these difficult days.'

Daphne Gulver-Robinson looks round the breakfast table. It is beautifully laid with pearl-coloured damask, bronze cutlery, and little floating gardens in lacquered dishes of waxy flowers that emit gusts of perfume. The directors of Doolittle Wind Quietus are in a Meeting. Their wives are breakfasting together under the eye of Lady Scroop, the Chairman's wife. It is Lord Scroop's policy to encourage his directors to travel with their wives. Especially in the Far East, and especially since the figures about Aids began to be drawn to his attention.

Most of the wives are elegant, with silk suits and silky legs and exquisitely cut hair. They chat mutedly, swapping recipes for chutney and horror stories about nannies, staring out of the amber glass wall of the Precious Jade Hotel at the dimpling sea. Daphne Gulver-Robinson is older than most of them, and dowdier, although her husband, Rollo, has less power than most of the other directors. She has tried to make herself attractive for this jaunt and has lost ten pounds and had her hands manicured; but now she sees the other

11

ladies, she knows it is not enough. Her style is seated tweed, and stout shoes, and birds-nest hair.

'You don't want me on this trip,' she said to Rollo when told about it. 'I'd better stay and mind the donkeys and the geese and the fantails as usual, and you can have a good time, as usual, in those exotic places.'

'Of course I don't want you,' said Rollo. 'That is, of course I *want* you, but I do know you're happier with the geese and the donkeys and pigs and things. But Scroop will think it's very odd, *I'm* very odd, if you don't come. He gets bees in his bonnet. You'll like the shopping, the ladies do a lot of shopping I believe. You might like the other wives,' he finished, not hopefully.

'I didn't like boarding-school,' Daphne said.

'I don't see what that has to do with it,' Rollo said. There is a lot Rollo doesn't see. Doesn't want to see and doesn't see.

Lady Scroop tells them they may scatter in the Mall as much as they like as long as they are all back at the front entrance at noon precisely. 'We have all *packed our bags*, I hope,' she says, 'though I have left time on the schedule for adjustments to make space for any goodies we may find. And then there will be a *delicious lunch* at the Pink Pearl Café and then we leave at two-forty-five *sharp* for the airport and on to Sydney.'

The ladies pack into the cars. Daphne Gulver-Robinson is next to the driver of her Daimler, a place of both comfort and isolation. They swoop silently through crowded streets, isolated by bullet-proof glass from the smells and sounds of the Orient. The Mall is enormous and not beautiful. Some of the ladies have been in post-modern pink and peppermint Malls in San Diego, some have been in snug, glittering underground tunnels in Canadian winters, some have shopped in crystal palaces in desert landscapes, with tinkling fountains and splashing streams. The Good Fortune Shopping Mall resembles an army barracks or a prison block, but it is not for the outside they have come, and they hasten to trip inside, like hens looking for worms, jerking and clucking, Daphne Gulver-Robinson thinks malevolently, as none of them waits for her.

She synchronizes her watch with the driver, and goes in alone, between the sleepy soldiers with machine-guns and the uniformed police with their revolvers and little sticks. Further away, along the walls of the Mall, are little groups and gangs of human flotsam and jetsam, gathered with bags and bottles around little fires of cowdung or cardboard. There is a no-man's-land, swept clean, between them and the police.

She is not sure she likes shopping. She looks at her watch, and wonders how she will fill the two hours before the rendezvous. She walks rather quickly past rows of square shop-fronts, glittering with gilt and silver, shining with pearls and opals, shimmering with lacquer and silk. Puppets and shadow-puppets mop and mow, paper birds hop on threads, paper dragons and monstrous goldfish gape and dangle. She covers the first floor, or one rectangular arm of the first floor, ascends a flight of stairs and finds herself on another floor, more or less the same, except for a few windows full of sober suitings, a run of American-style teeshirts, an area of bonsai trees. She stops to look at the trees, remembering her garden, and thinks of buying a particularly shapely cherry. But how could it go to Sydney, how return to Norfolk, would it even pass customs?

She has slowed down now and starts looking. She comes to a corner, gets into a lift, goes up, gets out, finds herself on a higher, sunnier, emptier floor. There are fewer shoppers. She walks along one whole 'street' where she is the only shopper, and is taken by a display of embroidered silk cushion-covers. She goes in, and turns over a heap of about a hundred, quick, quick, chrysanthemums, cranes, peach-blossom, blue-tits, mountain-tops. She buys a cover with a circle of embroidered fish, red and gold and copper, because it is the only one of its kind, perhaps a rarity. When she looks in her shopping bag, she cannot find her camera, although she is sure it was there when she set out. She buys a jade egg on the next floor, and some lacquered chopsticks, and a mask with a white furious face for her student daughter. She is annoyed to see a whole window full of the rare fishes, better embroidered than the one in the bag. She follows a sign saying 'Café' but cannot find the café, though she trots on, faster now. She does find a ladies' room, with cells so small they are hard to squeeze into. She restores her make-up there: she looks hot and blowzy. Her lipstick has bled into the soft skin round her mouth. Hairpins have sprung out. Her nose and eyelids shine. She looks at her watch, and thinks she should be making her way back to the entrance. Time has passed at surprising speed.

Signs saying Exit appear with great frequency and lead to fire-escape-like stairways and lifts, which debouch only in identical streets of boxed shopfronts. They are designed, she begins to think, to keep you inside, to direct you past even more·shops, in search of a hidden, deliberately elusive way out. She runs a little, trotting quicker, toiling up concrete stairways, clutching her shopping. On one of these stairways a heel breaks off one of her smart shoes. After a moment she takes off both, and puts them in her shopping-bag. She hobbles on, on the concrete, sweating and panting. She dare not look at her watch, and then does. The time of the rendezvous is well past. She thinks she might call the hotel, opens her handbag, and finds that her purse and credit cards have mysteriously disappeared.

There is nowhere to sit down: she stands in the Mall, going through and through her handbag, long after it is clear that the things have vanished. Other things, dislodged, have to be retrieved from the dusty ground. Her fountain-pen has gone too, Rollo's present for their twentieth wedding anniversary. She begins to run quite fast, so that huge holes spread in the soles of her stockings, which in the end split, and begin to work their way over her feet and up her legs in wrinkles like flaking skin. She looks at her watch; the packing-time and the 'delicious lunch' are over: it is almost time for the airport car. Her bladder is bursting, but she *must go on*, and must go *down*, the entrance is down.

It is in this way that she discovers that the Good Fortune Mall extends maybe as far into the earth as into the sky, excavated identical caverns of shopfronts, jade, gold, silver, silk, lacquer, watches, suiting, bonsai trees and masks and puppets. Lifts that say they are going down go only up. Stairwells are windowless: ground level cannot be found. The plane has now taken off with or without the directors and ladies of Doolittle Wind Quietus. She takes time out in another concrete and stainless-steel lavatory cubicle, and then looks at the watch, whose face has become a whirl of terror. Only now it is merely a compressed circle of pink skin, shiny with sweat.

Her watch, too, has gone. She utters faint little moaning sounds, and then an experimental scream. No one appears to hear or see her, neither strolling shoppers, deafened by Walkmans or by propriety, or by fear of the strange, nor shopkeepers, watchful in their cells.

Nevertheless, screaming helps. She screams again, and then screams and screams into the thick, bustling silence. A man in a brown overall brings a policeman in a reinforced hat, with a gun and a stick.

'Help me,' says Daphne, 'I am an English lady, I have been robbed, I must get home.'

'Papers,' says the policeman.

She looks in the back pocket of her handbag. Her passport, too, has gone. There is nothing. 'Stolen. All stolen,' she says.

'People like you,' says the policeman, 'not allowed in here.'

She sees herself with his eyes, a baglady, dirty, unkempt, with a bag full of somebody's shopping, a tattered battery-hen.

'My husband will come and look for me,' she tells the policeman.

If she waits, if she stays in the Mall, he will, she thinks. He *must*. She sees herself sitting with the flotsam and jetsam beyond the swept no-man's-land, outside.

'I'm not moving,' she says, and sits down heavily. She has to stay in the Mall. The policeman prods her with his little stick.

'Move, please.'

It is more comfortable sitting down.

'I shall stay here for ever if necessary,' she says.

She cannot imagine anyone coming. She cannot imagine getting out of the Good Fortune Mall.

Simon

———◆◆———

Patrick O'Brian

Patrick O'Brian's many books include the Jack Aubrey and Stephen Maturin novels about the British Navy during the Napoleonic Wars, described in *The Times Literary Supplement* as 'a brilliant achievement', several volumes of short stories, a biography of Picasso and distinguished translations of Simone de Beauvoir, André Maurois and Jacques Soustelle. He lives in Collioure, in southern France.

Simon, reading on the hearth-rug, looked up and asked: 'What is a whoremonger?'

'I don't know, my dear,' said his mother, absently, poking the fire; and when she had the logs just so she added: 'but I believe it is pronounced hore, with no w. What is that book?'

'It's an enormous history of England, about Cromwell.' The news of the pronunciation of whore drove history from Simon's mind, for it shed a sudden and brilliant light on odd scraps of conversation he had heard in the kitchen, scraps that children are more likely to pick up than others. 'Maggie is going with Alfred now ... Maggie is going with Mrs Gregory's William ... Maggie is going with George ... Maggie goes with soldiers from the camp.' 'That Maggie,' said Mrs Hamner, the bearded cook, 'is now the village whore.'

The word, formerly connected only with frost and aged heads, instantly took on a meaning more consonant with Mrs Hamner's disapproving tone, since from the context of Cromwell's remark it was clear that whore and harlot were the same creature. Simon knew all about harlots, except for what they actually did, and he was charmed to be so well acquainted with one in the flesh. It was like knowing a phoenix, or Medusa.

'I shall go and tell Joe,' he said to himself, and although the fire, the hearth-rug and the after-tea comfort were wonderfully attractive, he closed the book and hurried out.

Joseph was his elder brother, a heroic figure, already at the university, who spent these evenings of the vacation out with his gun shooting the odd early rabbit along the edge of Barton wood or the pigeons as they came in to roost. Simon sometimes went with him to pick up the dead birds, and he had noticed how cheerfully he would greet Maggie if they met, and she coming home from work: familiar greetings, Christian names, laughter. Joe would be delighted to know that she was the village whore, or harlot.

The question was, where would Joseph be? There were many possibilities, Barton being a fair-sized wood; but in the end he decided on the corner jutting out into Halfpenny Fields, where the path from Wansbury and its glove-factory meandered across the pasture to the village. There might be mushrooms there, and in any case Joe would probably come back that way when it was too dark to shoot.

Simon, big with his news, reached the corner far too early; there were no mushrooms, and although two white scuts fled away into the undergrowth there were no birds coming in yet. Simon lingered for a while, wondering what harlots really did and trying to hoot like an owl through his fists, their thumbs joined tight.

Presently he heard a couple of shots far over on the left-hand side. Joseph must be shooting the pigeons feeding on Carr's broad stretch of kale, unless indeed it was the Carr boys themselves. No. It must be Joseph – the Carrs were at a football match far beyond Wansbury – and he must come back this way. Simon was certainly not going to walk along the wood to meet him and be cursed for putting down all the rabbits, nor would he cut across, with the likelihood of missing him in the thick stuff. He would fool about here, looking for a straight wand that would do for a bow until Joe appeared.

Simon was an enterprising, birds'-nesting little boy, and in this part of the wood he had found a wool-lined crow's nest last spring as well as many of the frail transparent rafts upon which pigeons laid, and of course, the ordinary thrushes' and blackbirds' along the edge. He knew the place quite well. Yet fairly close to the path there was an oak he had never particularly noticed, not a promising tree for nests, but now, with so many leaves already fallen, at a modest height he saw a rounded mass that might well have been a squirrel's dray. With its twisted, nobbly old trunk the oak was easy enough to climb until he could reach the branches, and although the dray was too old and sodden to be of any interest, Simon on coming back to the crown observed with delight that the oak's trunk was hollow. And not only hollow, but provided with a hole at the bottom, through which the evening light showed plainly: one could drop down inside the tree, down on to the deep bed of leaves, push them away and shout out of the hole, terrifying, or at least astonishing, one and all. If only the tree were right on the path rather than some way into the wood the effect would be prodigious, but even so it would still be very great. An eldritch shriek might help, since it would make people look in the right direction.

He lowered himself carefully into the hollow, hung from the edge at arm's length, let go and dropped, dropped much farther than he had expected, into the leaves. They too were far deeper than he had thought they would be, and much wetter. Under the top layer, brown and dry like breakfast-food, came first a porridgy mass and then a vegetable mud, knee-deep. Already his shoes and stockings were hopelessly compromised, and he had scarcely realized the depth of this misfortune before he found that clearing the leaves did not enlarge the hole for more than the handsbreadth of dry on top. That was why the rest was like so much thick and indeed fetid soup, it was stagnant, enclosed. He scooped what could be scooped to one side and, no longer minding his shirt or jersey, tried to thrust his head through the hole. Even forcing it with all his might, there was no hope.

Rubbing his excoriated ears he sat on the dry part and said: 'I must climb up inside with back and feet like mountaineers in a rock-fault.' But the mountaineers he had read of did not have to contend with slippery rotting wood, nor with very short legs. There was one roughly three-cornered space where he could get a hold and gain three or four feet before slipping, but after that it was impossible – the width of the trunk was greater than his outstretched body – and the daylight at the top was of course far out of leaping reach.

When he had fallen half a dozen times he sat for a while, gasping and collecting himself. His bare knees were bleeding; this was nothing unusual with him – they were generally scarred – but it was difficult to see how they could have been barked in a glutinous hollow tree. Not that it signified. As he sat there he found he was trembling, and a new kind of fear – not worry or frustration or dread of reproof, but a cold, deep, unknown fear – began to stir about his heart or stomach.

The sound of a muffled shot calmed it for a while. 'Joe can't be long, and I shall roar out,' he said and he contemplated the dingy wall, reflecting that if only he had not lost his penknife he might have cut hand-holds in the soft wood. Quite suddenly he saw that the wall was no longer clear: daylight was fading fast, the evening cloud gathering.

Another double shot. It seemed nearer – Joe was on his way back and if he could not be made to hear before he passed, there was no help, no help at all.

Simon began to shout, much too soon, 'Ooh-hoo, ooh-hoo, Joe Joe. I'm in the tree. I can't get out. I'm in the tree. Joe, Joe, Joe . . .'

The noise of the shouting inside the tree and its urgency made him begin to lose his head and he leapt at the wall like a frightened, indeed a frantic, trapped animal, eventually falling back exhausted, sitting there and frankly weeping, great racking sobs.

They calmed in time – there was little light now at the top opening none at the bottom – and once again, but with dread-filled and reasonable purpose, he began his shouting. Yet the sound of his utmost efforts was now a coarse whisper, no more, and even when he heard Joseph and Maggie walking along at no great distance, laughing and talking – 'Give over now, do' – he could make nothing better than a high thin pipe and a faint battering on the spongy wood.

'What was that?' asked Joseph.

'It was only an old cat, or an owl. Come on.'

'It might have been Simon, playing a game.'

'Ballocks. Come on, if you want it. I can't be home late again: we'll go to the barn.' Their voices died away. Simon tried two more strangled, almost silent cries and gave up. The anguish of bitterly disappointed hope and underlying terror slowly gave way to a torpid misery; he was cold, too, and soaking wet.

There was one more revival, one more fit of wild-beast leaping at the wall, and then of heart-broken tears, and then a deeply unhappy resignation, huddled for warmth in the least wretched corner.

Overhead it was full night now, stars in the darkest blue. And presently an edge of moon. There was some very small comfort in the moon, though the rising south-wester bellowing through the trees added still more to the pervading threat. Yet, as he looked, the piece of moon was shut out – broad shoulders in the open crown of the tree, and Joseph's anxious voice: 'Simon? Simon?'

'Oh, Joe . . .' said Simon in a recognizable gasp.

'Reach me up an arm, will you, old fellow?'

Shreds and Slivers

Ruth Rendell

I love my love with a ps I because she is psychic; I hate her with a ps because she is psilotic. I feed her on psalliota and psilotaceae; her name is Psammis and she lives in a psalterium.

Forgive me. I am carried away by words sometimes, especially those of Greek etymology that begin with a combination of unlikely consonants. I love my love with a cn because she is cnidarian . . . But, no. Let us return to psalliota. If you want to know what all those other words mean you must look them up in a good dictionary. Psalliota is nothing more nor less than the common mushroom: psalliota campestris, to be precise.

I became interested in fungi only recently. Since being made redundant I have, of course, had time on my hands. Leisure to notice things. I try not to brood. That this year was exceptional for an abundance of fungi first struck me while taking a train to see my wife. I can no longer afford to run a car. From the economy-class window I observed meadows covered with whitish protrusions among the grass. It took me only a little while to realize that these were mushrooms, though I had never seen such a sight before.

Back at home after my day out, I explored my garden. Largely untended (I sometimes mow the lawn) since my wife was stolen from me ten years ago, it has gone back to nature in rather a pleasing way. For instance, shrubs which she planted have transformed themselves into trees. Under them and in mossy corners against the

27

walls, I came upon a variety of fungi: agarics, lepiotas, horns-of-plenty and, of course, the puffball. These names were unfamiliar to me then. Two books and a video started me on what might become a lifelong obsession.

I am not a mushroom-eater myself. My wife was particularly fond of them. But in those days – I won't say when I last saw her for I make a point of seeing her, but when I last spoke to her – the only mushrooms obtainable in the shops were the common kind, and the only differentiation, that between 'large' and 'button'. Things have changed. To the uninitiated these supermarket cartons, wrapped in clingfilm, may appear to contain only 'mixed mushrooms'; I, however, can name them as shitaki, canterelles, boletus and morels, pale slivers resembling slices of blood-drained flesh, lemony fibrous strips, plump glutinous gobbets, chocolate-brown elastic lumps. Well, there is no accounting for tastes.

The day I came upon amanita phalloides in my garden, under the Sessile oak, was the day I saw my wife for the first time for some weeks. You understand that though I think about her every day, go to the town where she lives, keep an eye on her house and spend some time in her local shopping centre, I do not always see her. Needless to say, she never sees me. But on this occasion, invisible among the racks of shellsuits, I spotted her in the distance approaching the vegetable counters. I am not exaggerating when I say my heart quaked. It is always a shock, even after so long.

I watched from my sartorial hideaway. Too far away to see what she bought, I followed her with my eyes from vegetables to pizzas, from pasta to mineral waters and thence to the check-out. That night I ran the video through once again. Yellow and white, with pallid gills and raggedy hat, phalloides blossomed on the screen in all its deadly glory. The Death Cap, as the voice-over called it, adding cheerfully that very small quantities cause intense suffering, then death.

If I were to grow cannabis sativa I would be breaking the law. The police would come, root up and destroy the plants. But it is no offence to grow phalloides, most deadly of all indigenous fungi. With impunity, I might if I wished turn my shady half-acre into a Death Cap plantation. If only I could! But fungi are capricious, inconstant, fungi are fitful and vicissitudinous. Who has not heard of those would-be mushroom farmers who have the kit and precisely obey the instructions only to find their growing barns empty and psalliota flourishing in the fields outside their property?

I have had to be content with what nature has supplied, and for my part can provide only encouragement in the form of shade, moisture and protection. It was October and the young fruit first broke through and the stipe pushed above the ground, its snowy veil bursting to reveal the olive-yellow cap. The flesh, my book says, is white and smells of raw potatoes. How gratifying to discover that this was indeed so and I had not confused phalloides with, for instance, xerula. (I love my love with an x because she is xanthic, I hate her with an x because she is xylophagous.)

Careful not to touch the fruit bodies, using a knife and fork, I sliced into thin strips the cap and stipe of three specimens. They filled a large yogurt pot. With closed eyes, I stood there remembering my wife's ways, her fashion of cooking, her pleasure in eating, her smile. I remembered her slicing raw potatoes and could smell the smell in my mind.

I took the yogurt pot with me next day and went straight from the station to the supermarket. There was no question of my wife's arriving for at least two hours; I have my memories, all too many of them and I know her timetable, the order and regularity of her life. But for a while I waited, pacing, deep in thought, between bedlinen reductions and kitchenware. You must appreciate that until then, apart from the audio-tapes and the carefully chosen articles sent her, and the enlightening letters posted to her relatives, I had taken no positive steps against my wife. The time had come for action. I hesitated no longer.

With a little practice, it takes only seconds to detach the clingfilm from the base of a mixed mushroom carton, slip in a slice or two of phalloides and re-adhere the film. Among the fronds and filaments, the shreds and slivers, my delicate cilia passed unnoticed or passed for wisps of shitaki. I operated on some ten cartons, about half the

29

stock, in this way. The place was not frequented at lunchtime. No one saw me, or if they did, approved the prudence of what they took for close examination prior to purchase. I have noticed how, for example, in these hard times, it is not uncommon for shoppers to taste the grapes before they buy.

I waited long enough to see my wife come in. My heart began to jog. One day, if this does not stop, it will kill itself and me with it. Of course I realized that there was only a fifty per cent chance of my wife consuming one of the fatal batch. But in this game of culinary Russian Roulette, these are very favourable odds. Still, on my next visit with fresh supplies I operated on fifteen cartons. After all, she is not the only one to consider but also her live-in paramour and her extended family who all live nearby and whose sheepish faces and obese forms I often see in the aisles between the sauces and the frozen desserts.

At last, having heard and seen nothing of the consequence of my actions, I was obliged to sacrifice the last of my phalloides, stripping the leafmould under the Sessile oak bare of its potato-scented crop. This time – I was a little late – only fourteen cartons of mixed mushrooms remained and in less than two minutes the contents of the yogurt pot were nestling among the sinuate gills and elliptoid membranes. In fact, I had barely finished when I spotted her entering by way of exotic fruits and, my heart on its treadmill, I slipped away.

Three days later a small paragraph in the newspaper told me that the supermarket had withdrawn all 'mixed mushrooms' due to two unexplained deaths and several cases of severe illness. But the deaths, alas, were not hers nor his nor theirs. When it has blown over and 'mixed mushrooms' are back on the counter, I shall have to begin all over again next year.

At present the ground under the sessile oak is covered with snow. All fungi have succumbed to frost. I shall mark the spot where the spores of phalloides lie deep in the earth, for there must be no trampling or digging. And some mnemonic must be contrived to help me remember the precise location. Oh, I love my love with a mn because she is mnemic, I hate her with a mn because she is mnemonical, her name is Mnemosyne and she is the goddess of remembrance . . .

Forward to Fidelity

Alan Judd

ALAN JUDD is a novelist and also the acclaimed biographer of Ford Madox Ford. His latest novel, *The Devil's Own Work* (Flamingo), won the Guardian Fiction Award. Educated at Oxford, he is married and lives in London.

The Prime Minister watched his colleagues shuffle out of the Cabinet Room. He remained at the centre of the long table, musing. Was it possible to sack everyone? Had it been done? The Cabinet Secretary, his usual authority, looked as moody as a moose on Monday. Better not ask. His own suggestion for a new campaign – Forward to Fidelity – had been received in uncomfortable silence. Either they thought he wasn't serious or they feared he was. He wasn't sure himself; it didn't matter what you did in this job, you got no thanks for it.

Sex and money, money and sex. What did they want, these moralizing journalists? Stoning for adultery, a ban on usury? *Them*? It would virtually depopulate Parliament, of course. Perhaps that was the answer: prohibit adultery for MPs, sack everybody, resign to an almost empty chamber and propose that the journalists move in instead. Give them a week of it.

He went upstairs to the flat for a lunch of scrambled eggs on toast and tea. Afterwards he sat in his armchair beneath the eaves to look once more at the brief for Prime Minister's Questions that day. Now there was this other madness, the latest dictat from the fat cats of Brussels. No Questions for them, no public pillorying and barracking. No toast and tea for lunch, either.

VAT on air the press called it. Ridiculous: it wasn't VAT. NEWT – National Environmental Wealth Tax – was designed to encourage cleaner air but would function so that the cleaner your air, the more of your NEWT went to pay those who were dirtier. It had been nodded through by a majority of governments who had no intention of implementing it. The Greeks had already upped the price of petrol so they would get more from their own taxes and qualify for more from everyone else's. The press had a point.

Not a single voter had been asked, of course. There was national outrage, with the party split, the Opposition doing its weather-vane act and the Lib Dems torn between slavish Europhilia and the scent of Government blood. The usual channels – splendid chap – warned of a possible confidence vote.

The Prime Minister's eyes read the same sentence several times, but his brain pulsed to a different rhythm: since when were these islands governed by dictat? People had stopped asking, more or less, and he certainly was not going to remind them, but the phrase repeated had a rhythm of its own. Part of his brain refused the Whip.

His eyes closed. He was in a noisy panelled room, like one of the Commons bars. The air was thick with smoke. A Eurocrat was slumped unconscious in one corner, his hair streaked grey with the ash from Churchill's cigar and dark red from William Pitt's port. Disraeli said that it served him right, he had no mistress. Gladstone read aloud from a tract. Walpole and Palmerston were dividing India by mobile phone, Melbourne and Lloyd George were arranging to visit some women. You could then, the Prime Minister thought. The Iron Duke and Asquith were discussing sparrowhawks.

No-one addressed the Prime Minister directly, but he felt they were all urging him to something. The urgency increased and their voices became louder. Someone shoved him.

It was his private secretary.

He couldn't afterwards recall reaching the Commons but he knew he entered the chamber with a disabling sense of detachment, as if he were outside himself. He stared at the packed benches as Gladstone took his place between two unsuspecting shire knights. Disraeli dallied with the hair behind the ear of an Opposition woman, flicking it forward each time she patted it back. Walpole strolled in from behind the Speaker's chair and sat on the lap of the

Leader of the Opposition, taking snuff. Lloyd George's voice was everywhere.

The Prime Minister tried to concentrate. There would be supplementaries about ministerial adulteries. He was distracted from the brief by the idea that if MPs were forbidden adultery except with other MPs there would be no party advantage and thus a conspiracy of silence. It would mean more women MPs, of course; hard to feel anything but ambivalent about that.

He was on his feet, speaking. Churchill snored in the chancellor's place. He heard himself say something about VAT and adultery but it didn't come out right. Or did. There was uproar.

Afterwards everyone was unusually quiet and nice, which made him feel he had contracted an unmentionable disease. That was, in fact, what had happened, he realized; it was called failure and in politics people could smell it.

Despite the weather, he took his tea on to the terrace. This would surprise them. He was not alone – he never was – but not many were with him. A wind whipped up river, making it choppy. They were talking about a confidence motion, now very likely.

He stared at the water. What if he jumped in? Sat on the wall and toppled backwards? The Maxwell flip, or flop. In whose interest would it be to save him? By the time they had weighed the pros and cons and waited for the lifebelts and TV cameras he would be out in mid-stream, blissfully unconscious. The Leader of the Opposition, if he were astute enough, would jump immediately because he would win either way; how galling to be saved by him.

But they were so busy talking, they probably would not notice. He put his cup quietly on the wall. Perhaps he could just walk away, disappear. He backed out of the group and made for the gents. No one followed. He took off his glasses and headed next for the public entrance, which he never used. In the corridor he collided unrecognized with the substantial form of the Deputy Chief Whip, after which he adopted the tactic of putting on his glasses for just long enough to take a bearing on the next main point. Very soon he was in the blessed fume-filled freedom of Parliament Square.

He resumed his glasses and walked up Whitehall, threading apologetically through the tourists at the gates of Downing Street.

He felt better than for years. If only people knew how much he wanted to help them.

He took a bus to Piccadilly feeling wonderfully free. The conductor was chatting to a lady passenger. It really was an agreeable job, the Prime Minister thought. He noted the London Transport Jobline number; he would ring and ask how they were getting on.

When he came to pay, there was no money in his pocket. There hadn't been for years; he never went anywhere, there was no opportunity to spend.

'You'd better get off 'ere, then,' said the conductor when they reached Haymarket.

'I shall, of course. It's because I am the Prime Minister, you see.' He smiled. He had read that Stalin used to do this sort of thing on the Moscow Underground.

''Opit.'

Outside Fortnum's he found a lady having trouble with her shopping bags. 'Taxi!' she almost screamed, when he tried to help.

He wandered into the shop, which was gratifyingly busy; something worked, anyway. After a while a man with a security badge asked politely if he could help.

'I'm just looking,' said the Prime Minister. 'I've got no money on me, I'm afraid.'

'Then I'll show you the exit, sir. It's free.'

He walked towards Soho. In Frith Street he had a disagreeable encounter with an aggressive young beggar who would not accept his explanation. In Greek Street he had to avoid a junior minister who stepped furtively out of a doorway. A newspaper headline read: '74PRIME MINISTER: LAST HOURS?' It was starting to rain. He supposed he should get back.

At the Downing Street gates he wiped the rain off his glasses with his tie while explaining to the policeman, a new one.

The policeman's grin was not pleasant. 'And I'm the Iron Lady. On your bike.'

He had better luck with the House police. In the Chief Whip's office they stared as if he had two heads. 'Felt like a walk,' he said. They were certain now that there would be a confidence motion. 'You go in. I'll follow.'

He walked calmly through Members' Lobby, as to his execution. People stared and made way. He paused by the statue of Churchill, just before the chamber entrance. One toe-cap was worn bright where members due to speak touched it for luck. The Prime Minister rested his hand on it.

Walpole sauntered towards him. 'Stay. The wheel comes round. Stay.' The thin lips of Pitt and the Iron Duke parted simultaneously: 'Fight as we fought.' Melbourne shrugged: 'Damn dictats.' Palmerston laughed: 'Enjoy it.' Disraeli winked: 'Woo scorn, flatter.' Gladstone stared hard: 'Talk until their bladders burst.' Lloyd George chuckled: 'Lay it on with shovels.' Churchill growled: 'Buckshot. Both barrels.'

Afterwards, long afterwards, he sat again in the eaves. He had honey in his tea, for his throat. Six hours and thirty-seven minutes; right through the late television news. They would have the devil of a job choosing highlights.

So would he. He remembered being cheered from the House, the Opposition flattened. VAT off air but on everything else, including secondhand goods. Income tax abolished. Adultery criminal for children. The property of Euro-MPs to suffer sequestration; his head had positively swum with merciful intentions at that point. Finally, there had been his call for the House to acknowledge once again no superior body. They had carried him shoulder-high into the lobby but his wave, his long slow wave, had been to his ghostly companions who could rest again now that their own had been restored. Someone had called his performance Bothamesque.

Big Ben struck two, maybe a few more. The Prime Minister stretched, stood and went over to the mantelpiece. He took from his pocket the London Transport Jobline number and hid it beneath the clock. In this game you never knew.

Marriage Lines

————◆————

Penelope Lively

The Dawsons, who were having their marriage counselled, glared at each other across their counsellor. The counsellor known to them as Liz, was a small plump woman who might have been thought attractive had any concessions been made by way of becoming clothes or a flattering haircut. As it was, her manner and appearance spoke of responsibilities heavily borne and an implacable confidence in her own judgement. She treated the Dawsons with maddening patience and impartiality, as though they were children in a nursery school whose behaviour was wayward but inevitable. Her bland attention to their complaints implied that she had heard it all before, that they were in no way unique or especially blighted and that nothing could jolt her from her complacent consideration of their various sources of discord. She drove Ben Dawson to a frenzy. Sometimes the ferocity of his feelings about Liz quite distracted him from his irritation with his wife and the matter in hand.

'And another thing,' Prue Dawson was saying, 'I thought it was settled that when we disagree about how to handle a situation over the children we don't give conflicting instructions but we sit down and talk it over. And now only yesterday you walk in and completely undermine what I've already sorted out. That business with Nicky about the ballet shoes and next Tuesday.'

Liz turned to Ben. 'Do you have a problem with that, Ben?' This was Liz's favourite question. Or comment, or way of moving on, or whatever it was. So far, it had been clocked up five times in this session.

'Yes,' he said sourly. 'Or it wouldn't have been mentioned, would it?'

'Would you like to tell us about this, Ben?' Liz continued.

'No, to be honest. For two reasons – I should find it unspeakably boring, and Prue would get more annoyed than she is already. I daresay you might get something out of it, but I'm not sure what.'

Liz fixed him with her most neutral gaze. 'Thank you for sharing that with us, Ben.'

It occurred to Ben, not for the first time, that he might simply walk out. The only thing that stopped him was that such a move would undoubtedly be interpreted to his disadvantage and held against him. Principally by Liz.

He stared at the floor, which was the only place to look if you were not to catch someone else's eye. The chairs were arranged in a semi-circle, so that Liz sat between her clients. They were chairs of an awkward lowness, forcing the occupant to sit with legs stuck out straight ahead, in a parody of relaxation. The only window was covered by a blind, to exclude reminders of ordinary life in the world beyond. The room was profoundly claustrophobic, which was presumably the intention. Concentrate, it said. Bare your soul. Expose yourself. Go on – wallow in it.

He said: 'Do you mind if we talk about something else now?'

Liz gave Prue the glance of measured impartiality. 'How do you feel about that, Prue?'

'I don't care one way or the other,' said Prue. 'Incidentally,' she added, speaking across Liz to Ben, 'in the end it turned out the wretched ballet shoes were the wrong size. I'll have to get another pair. God knows how, before Tuesday.'

'Are you married, Liz?' said Ben, after a moment. 'Or have you been?'

Liz dealt him a chilly smile. 'That's irrelevant, Ben, isn't it?'

'No, I don't think it is, really. It's a question of credentials. I mean, to advise us you have to have some experience of our situation, don't you?'

'Let's just say I'm in a relationship,' said Liz. The tone of stern professional neutrality once more.

If I hear that dire word again I'll scream, thought Ben. 'Good,' he said. 'Join the club.' He looked at Prue. 'I daresay I could take her to get some shoes tomorrow. I could leave the office early.'

'Oh, right,' said Prue. 'Thanks.'

Liz cleared her throat. She shuffled the papers on her lap. These actions, the Dawsons now knew, meant that she felt the focus of attention had strayed and that she needed to establish control. 'I've noticed that you both mention work quite a bit today. Maybe that's an area we should cover. Ben, could I ask you what you feel about Prue's work situation?'

'What do you mean – what do I *feel* about it? Are you asking if I think she's got a good job, or a suitable job, or are you asking if I think she ought to be working in WC1 rather than WC2, or what, for heaven's sake?'

Liz reflected, eyeing him. At last she said: 'It's interesting that you seem to be getting a bit over-excited, Ben. Do you want to say anything about this?'

'Only that I wish you'd use language with rather more precision.'

Liz turned to Prue. 'What do you feel about Ben's attitude here?'

'Actually I think he's got a point,' said Prue.

Ben shot his wife a look of surprise.

'You think he has a problem with your work situation?' said Liz encouragingly.

'No, I mean I think he's right about language. Sometimes we all have a problem over what it is exactly we're trying to talk about.'

Ben experienced a gust of something suspiciously like affection. 'In point of fact,' he said, 'work is not a prime area of dissension. I entirely approve of Prue's job. I think she's good at it. I try to be supportive.'

'Hmm . . .' said Prue.

'Well, all right. I agree I was a touch unreasonable about the Leeds trip. Next time I'll shut up. But . . .' – he addressed himself to Liz – '. . . by and large and on the whole, work is not something we have rows about. I appreciate that Prue's work is important to her, and that she does it well. I don't resent that. I don't suspect her of sleeping with her colleagues, either.'

Liz's expression of shrewd appraisal meant, he now recognized, that he had said something of deep significance. 'I wonder why you said that, Ben?'

'It was a joke. A rather stupid joke. I was trying to lighten things up a bit.'

'But you said it. There's some sort of sexual tension there, then?'

'Oh, Christ . . .' said Ben wearily.

Prue said: 'Actually there isn't. That's something else we're not in fact quarrelling about. We don't suspect each other of having it off with someone else.'

Liz faintly smiled. She shook her head slightly. 'In fact, Prue, I'm going to suggest that next time you have a full psychosexual session. Doctor Chambers handles that.'

'I thought you were our counsellor?' said Prue.

'Not for psychosexual. That's a separate area.'

'I'm surprised,' said Ben. 'This is interesting. You're suggesting then that the sexual element of marriage is a thing apart? I'd have thought that was a trifle unorthodox.'

'I'm not trained for psychosexual, that's all.'

'You specialize in straight domestic wrangling and child rearing disputes, is that right?'

There was a silence. Liz now wore her expression of personal distaste modulated by infinite professional patience. 'Ben, I have to say that I think you have a serious attitude problem. This is not something to make jokes about.'

'That wasn't a joke,' said Ben. 'It was a conversational style. And I was asking a question.'

Liz turned to Prue. 'Do you have a problem with the way Ben talks, Prue?'

'No,' said Prue. 'Not particularly.' There was a distinct edge of irritation to her voice. 'Possibly it takes a bit of getting used to.'

Liz frowned slightly. 'Has this adjustment been difficult for you?'

'*No*,' said Prue. She glanced rather wildly at Ben, who grimaced. Prue looked at him again and then away, quickly. 'No, that's not the point. Actually it's one of the things I like about Ben.'

'I see.' Liz was now registering muted disapproval.

'There are quite a lot of things I like about Ben,' Prue went on determinedly. 'And in fact I think there are things he likes about me.'

Liz sighed. 'Prue, we're getting off course again, aren't we?'

'Well, I must say I don't quite see . . .' Prue began.

'Compatibility is irrelevant, is it?' said Ben.

Liz turned to him. She was impregnable, he saw. He read in her face absolute complacency and an unswerving rectitude. 'Ben,' she was saying, 'I think we're in trouble again with your basic attitude. I feel that . . .' Language oozed from her, smothering him.

It came to him with sudden clarity that there was something dreadfully awry. He could not imagine how they had arrived in this room, locked into eerie collaboration with this dispiriting woman. He recognized with elation that Prue's discomfort matched his own feverish impatience. He got to his feet. He said: 'Liz, thank you for trying to help us, but speaking for myself I feel there's nothing further I can contribute. I don't know about Prue, but . . .'

Prue also had risen. 'Yes,' she said. 'Me too, in fact. Thank you very much, Liz, but . . .'

They fled. They stepped into the street, still trailing their unfinished excuses. They headed for home, side by side, bolstered by the familiar private apposition of disagreement and collusion which seemed now a protection rather than a constraint.

The Wilderness Club

—◆—

Shena Mackay

When there was such a glut of travel writers that they were piled in bleaching bales on quaysides all over the world, and traders in souks and bazaars couldn't give them away, even with an ounce of rhino horn or a kilo of ugli fruit thrown in, it was hardly surprising that Romney's disappearance went unnoticed.

It was Tusker Laidlaw, at a loss for an anecdote with which to bore the company at Romney's London club, the Wilderness, who remarked that nobody had heard a dicky bird from young Tiny Romney since he had departed for a small archipelago off the coast of West Africa. The members consulted the globe, but, curiously, could not locate the islands. Theirs was a claret and gravy-coloured world, but even when they had rung for old Shell to bring a damp cloth and he had exposed enough blue ocean to make a pair of sailor's trousers, there could be no doubt that the islands had vanished.

''Straordinary thing,' said Laidlaw. 'Reminds me of a tale I heard of the madam of a house of ill-repute in Marsails. Came from Dulwich, of all places, or was it Dunstable . . .'

So exclusive was the Wilderness that its members were obliged under the rules to take turns as Club Bore, and Tusker took his duties seriously. Age had sprinkled salt and pepper on the crumbs of ancient Stilton and twists of biltong in his mane of hair and full beard; he was gaunt and concave in his safari suit, and the upper of his scaly left shoe had disengaged from its sole, exposing a set of

51

pointed yellow teeth. He bored on manfully, one of an endangered species, for where was the glamour of these old hunters now that hoi polloi could gorge on boil-in-the-bag ostrich from the Surrey veldt?

As Tusker bored on, a young woman named Clover Jones wearing a borrowed Paul Smith suit, clenched her lovely jaw as the newspaper's fashion and beauty department stippled stubble on her ivory skin and jelled back her newly-cropped black hair. Clover's brief was to penetrate the Wilderness, whose portals no woman had ever breached. A better journalist than she had bluffed her way into certain male preserves, but this was Clover's big challenge. Gossip columnists had dubbed her 'the Zuleika Dobson *de nos jours*', and she was determined to prove herself as a writer.

A quick snort in the Ladies, a gulp of mineral water, and Clover clamped on her hat, adjusted the Versace sunglasses that could not dim the radiance of her eyes, and strode out to impersonate a long-lost nephew of one Typhoon Tucker, an old India hand. Or was it Typhoo? She ignored the burst of unkind laughter behind her; it was hardly her fault that her father was the paper's star columnist. They'd laugh on the other side of their faces when she was Literary Editor. She just wished she were better briefed to converse with the old buffer. If only she'd taken O-Level Geography, but it was not her fault she'd been asked to leave her boarding school. By the other girls.

Her initial ploy had been to write to Tusker Laidlaw, posing as a would-be biographer, but he had smelled a rat, as the remaindered copies of his memoirs suggested that no publisher would touch him with a bargepole. A researcher had spent days in the cuttings library before coming up with any Wildernessers at all for Clover. Waiting for a taxi, she concentrated her mind: brinjal, she remembered, bhaji, Bhageera, that's Indian for panther, Shere Hite, no, Khan, tiger; Kaa, a snake; Baloo a bear, and King Louis, he's the king of the swingers, a Jungle VIP . . .

And as Tusker still bored on, 'young' Tiny Romney was lolling in the back of a taxi stuck in traffic, in a cacophony of car hooters and police sirens.

'I do not believe it!' the taxi driver kept repeating. 'One minute bleeding Marble Arch is there, the next it's gone! One minute it's standing there minding its own business, the next – Wham! Gone! I don't believe it!'

'When you've seen as much of the world as I have, my friend,' said Romney wearily, suppressing a belch, 'you'll believe anything.'

Sharp, heavy pains racked him as masonry shifted inside him. He was heading for the ugliest place he could imagine, his club. There was nowhere else for him to go. The driver stared at his passenger. Big when he had boarded, now in his striped djellaba he seemed to fill the cab. Rivers of sweat gushed from his huge forehead, splashed his dark glasses and coursed down his marble-white cheeks. Grinding noises came from the vast stomach. Suppose he was a pregnant woman in disguise, taking advantage of our NHS, about to give birth? To a baby the size of an elephant. With Muggins acting as midwife.

'Not in my cab, you don't,' he started to say, but the traffic began to move and he was forced to drive on. A look in the mirror showed no movement from chummy who even seemed to have shrunk a little.

There were those who said that Romney was as camp as a row of tents, others who retorted that he *was* a row of tents, or at least a marquee, while some swore that no woman was safe in his company. None of them was entirely right. Romney was an omnivore.

Clover Jones had once written a feature on 'Men Who Love Too Much' (it had to be spiked: all her interviewees fell in love with her), but had not encountered a single example of the rare syndrome from which Romney suffered. Documented case histories were few; in England there was the man with an orchestra inside him, and a woman who had ingested Hampstead Garden Suburb in blossom time. Her story ended in tragedy after a trip to the bulb fields of Holland, and the post-mortem revealed advanced botanical hyper-aesthesia and an abnormally receptive nervous system. The pathologist was able to return a missing giant water lily to Kew.

Romney's agony abated as Marble Arch diminished and settled under his heart. He cursed himself. He had fled England because he wanted to preserve it, and within an hour of his return he had eaten part of its heritage. It was not even his favourite monument. He had risked removing his shades for a second, and with the nostalgic recognition had come the dreaded intake of breath, the burning salt-breaker of tears, the racing pulse. Then the uncontrollable suction, and the edifice embedded in his innards.

London, on an evening on the verge of spring, was the most dangerous place for Romney, but what could he do? He had fallen in love with the lush islands of his exile, and, bloated with them, he had floated back to the mainland. What had he to look forward to? He dared not visit the opera or ballet or any art gallery, and as for human contact – he shuddered at the thought of the near miss before Marble Arch had left a crater in the road. He had glimpsed, darkly, a lighted upper window, a paper lampshade printed with the globe, bunk beds, a jumbled pinboard, two children's heads. Just in time, a parental hand had pulled down the blind.

Like Clover's, his academic career had been cut short, when early signs of the disease were manifest. As a small chorister he had sobbed so loudly at the other boys' pure trebles that he had to be removed from the chapel, and he was stretchered off the field at the inter-house match although he had only been a spectator. His last school report had read: 'Romney, alas, is entirely lacking in the gaiety and innocence and heartlessness which we look for in our boys.'

Now he knew himself condemned to live out his life in the twilight of the Wilderness Club, to take his turn as the Bore, to watch Tusker Laidlaw spooning quince jelly on to his suppertime bone. He would cultivate the mushrooms and ferns of the dank tiled bathrooms, and while away the aching hours in the library, devouring its mildewed books. And when that all became too much to bear, there were the assegais to fall back on.

Clover paid off her cab, turning down the driver's offer to take her to Madame Jojo's later. God, it wasn't fair! Even dressed as a bloke! She remembered seeking refuge from her beauty's impact in a convent retreat. On her way home to inform her parents of her new-found Vocation, she had been rudely awoken from a reverie of wimples by the sight of Reverend Mother and Sister Anthony pelting after the bus.

Now a bitter wind blew away her courage and flimsy pretext. Sick with fear, she hovered near the club's entrance. Then she saw her chance. A huge striped figure was mounting the steps. As the heavy door opened, Clover hurled herself forward, to catch hold of its skirts and be pulled inside.

She tripped and crashed on to hard mosaic, hitting her head on the corner of a glass case. Lying in the brownish gloom, she was aware of spears and snarling heads on the walls and woozily recalled the rumour that to be blackballed at the Wilderness was to be shot, and as the mummified creature in the glass case swam into focus Clover wondered if she were indeed the first woman to cross this threshold. Then the great striped person was lifting her tender!y, propping her up. Simultaneously, automatically, they raised a hand to remove their dark glasses.

A Winter Admiral

Michael Moorcock

M ICHAEL MOORCOCK was born in London in 1939. He has been a professional writer and editor since 1956. Besides some award-winning novels, his most recent work includes *Blood: A Southern Fantasy* and *Lunching With The Antichrist* (a collection of short stories). He is currently based in America where he is working on the final novel of his Pyat/Holocaust sequence, *The Vengeance of Rome*.

After lunch she woke up, thinking the rustling from the pantry must be a foraging mouse brought out of hibernation by the unusual warmth. She smiled. She never minded a mouse or two for company and she had secured anything she would not want them to touch.

No, she really didn't mind the mice at all. Their forebears had been in these parts longer than hers and had quite as much right to the territory. More of them, after all, had bled and died for home and hearth. They had earned their tranquillity. Her London cats were perfectly happy to enjoy a life of peaceful coexistence.

'We're a family.' She yawned and stretched. 'We probably smell pretty much the same by now.' She took up the brass poker and opened the fire door of the stove. 'One big happy family, us and the mice and the spiders.'

After a few moments the noise from the pantry stopped. She was surprised it did not resume. She poked down the burning logs, added two more from her little pile, closed the door and adjusted the vents. That would keep in nicely.

As she leaned back in her chair she heard the sound again. She got up slowly to lift the latch and peer in. Through the outside pantry window, sunlight laced the bars of dust and brightened her shelves. She looked on the floor for droppings. Amongst her cat-litter bags, her indoor gardening tools, her electrical bits and pieces, there was nothing eaten and no sign of a mouse.

Today it was even warmer in the pantry. She checked a couple of jars of pickles. It didn't do for them to heat up. They seemed all right. This particular pantry had mostly canned things. She only ever needed to shop once a week.

She closed the door again. She was vaguely ill at ease. She hated anything odd going on in her house. Sometimes she lost perspective. The best way to get rid of the feeling was to take a walk. Since the sun was so bright today, she would put on her coat and stroll up the lane for a bit.

It was one of those pleasant February days which deceives you into believing spring has arrived. A cruel promise, really, she thought. This weather would be gone soon enough. Make the best of it, she said to herself. She would leave the radio playing, put a light on in case it grew dark before she was back, and promise herself Charlie Chester, a cup of tea and a scone when she got home. She lifted the heavy iron kettle, another part of her inheritance, and put it on the hob. She set her big, brown teapot on the brass trivet.

The scent of lavender struck her as she opened her coat cupboard. She had just re-lined the shelves and drawers. Lavender reminded her of her first childhood home.

'We're a long way from Mitcham now,' she told the cats as she took her tweed overcoat off the hanger. Her Aunt Becky had lived here until her last months in the nursing home. Becky had inherited Crow Cottage from the famous Great Aunt Begg. As far as Marjorie Begg could tell, the place had been inhabited by generations of retired single ladies, almost in trust, for centuries.

Mrs Begg would leave Crow Cottage to her own niece, Clare, who looked after Jessie, her half-sister. A chronic invalid, Jessie must soon die, she was so full of rancour.

A story in a Cotswold book said this had once been known as Crone's Cottage. She was amused by the idea of ending her days as the local crone. She would have to learn to cackle. The crone was a recognised figure in any English rural community, after all. She wondered if it were merely coincidence that made Rab, the village idiot, her handyman. He worshipped her. She would do anything for him. He was like a bewildered child since his wife had thrown him out: she could make more in benefits than he made in wages. He had seemed reconciled to the injustice: 'I was never much of an earner.' That apologetic grin was his response to most disappointment. It probably hadn't been fitting for a village idiot to be married, any more than a crone. Yet who had washed and embroidered the idiot's smocks in the old days?

She had heard Rab had lost his digs and was living wild in Wilson's abandoned farm buildings on the other side of the wood.

Before she opened her front door she thought she heard the rustling again. The sound was familiar, but not mice. Some folded Cellophane unravelling as the cupboard warmed up? The cottage had never been cosier.

She closed the door behind her, walking up the stone path under her brown tangle of honeysuckle and through the gate to the rough farm lane. Between the tall, woven hedges she kept out of the shade as much as she could. She relished the air, the winter scents, the busy finches, sparrows, tits and yellowhammers. A chattering robin objected to her passing and a couple of wrens fussed at her. She clicked her tongue, imitating their angry little voices. The broad meadows lay across the brow of the hills like shawls, their dark-brown furrows laced with melting frost, bright as crystal. Birds flocked everywhere to celebrate this unexpected ease in the winter's grey.

Her favourites were the crows and magpies. Such old, alien birds. So wise. Closer to the dinosaurs and inheriting an unfathomable memory. Was that why people took against them? She had learned early that intelligence was no better admired in a bird than in a woman.

The thought of her father made her shudder, even out here on this wide, unthreatening Cotswold hillside and she felt suddenly lost, helpless, the cottage no longer her home. Even the steeple on the village church, rising beyond the elms, seemed completely inaccessible. She hated the fear more than she hated the man who had infected her with it – as thoroughly as if he had infected her with a disease. She blamed herself. What good was hatred? He had died wretchedly, of exposure in Hammersmith, between his pub and his flat, a few hundred yards away.

Crow Cottage, with its slender evergreens and lattice of willow boughs, was as safe and welcoming as always when she turned back into her lane. As the sun fell it was growing colder, but she paused for a moment. The cottage, with its thatch and its chimney, its walls and its hedges, was a picture. She loved it. It welcomed her, even now, with so little colour in the garden.

She returned slowly, enjoying the day, and stepped back over her hearth, into her dream of security, her stove and her cats and her rattling kettle. She was in good time for 'Sing Something Simple' and would be eating her scones by the time Charlie Chester came on. She had never felt the need for a television here, though she had been a slave to it in Streatham. Jack had liked his sport.

He had been doing his pools when he died.

When she came back to the flat that night, Jack was in the hall, stretched out with his head on his arm. She knew he was dead, but she gave him what she hoped was the kiss of life, repeatedly blowing her warm breath through his cold lips until she got up to 'phone for the ambulance. She kept kissing him, kept pouring her breath into him, but was weeping almost uncontrollably when they arrived.

He wouldn't have known anything, love, they consoled her.

No consolation at all to Jack! He had hated not knowing things.

She had never anticipated the anguish that came with the loss of him, which had lasted until she moved to Crow Cottage. She had written to Clare. By some miracle, the cottage had cured her of her painful grief and brought unexpected reconciliation.

It was almost dark.

Against the sprawling black branches of the old elms, the starlings curled in ranks towards the horizon, while out of sight in the tall wood the crows began to call bird to bird, family to family. The setting sun had given the few clouds a powdering of terracotta and the air was suddenly a Mediterranean blue behind them.

Everything was so vivid and hurrying so fast, as if to greet the end of the world.

She went to draw the back curtains and saw the sunset over the flooded fields, fifteen miles away, spreading its bloody light into the water. She almost gasped at the sudden beauty of it.

Then she heard the rustling again. Before the light failed altogether, she was determined to discover the cause. It would be awful to start getting fancies after dark.

As she unlatched the pantry door something rose from the floor and settled against the window. She shivered, but did not retreat.

She looked carefully. Then, to her surprise: 'Oh, it's a butterfly!'

The butterfly began to beat again upon the window. She reached to cup it in her hands, to calm it. 'Poor thing.'

It was a newborn red admiral, its orange, red and black markings vibrant as summer. 'Poor thing.' It had no others of its kind.

For a few seconds the butterfly continued to flutter, and then was still. She widened her hands to look in. She watched its perfect, questing antennae, its extraordinary legs, she could almost smell it. A small miracle, she thought, to make a glorious day complete.

An unexpected sadness filled her as she stared at the butterfly. She carried it to the door, pushed the latch with her cupped hands, and walked into the twilight. When she reached the gate she opened her hands again, gently, to relish the vivacious delicacy of the creature. Mrs Begg sighed, and with a sudden, graceful movement lifted her opened palms to let the admiral taste the air.

In two or three wingbeats the butterfly was up, a spot of busy, brilliant colour straining towards the east and the cold horizon.

As it gained height, it veered, its wings courageous against the freshening wind.

Shielding her eyes, Mrs Begg watched the admiral turn and fly over the thatch, to be absorbed in the setting sun.

It was far too cold now to be standing there. She went inside and shut the door. The cats still slept in front of the stove. With the pot-holder she picked up the kettle, pouring lively water over the tea. Then she went to close her pantry door.

'I really couldn't bear it,' she said. 'I couldn't bear to watch it die.'

Beautiful Things

Maggie Gee

MAGGIE GEE is the author of seven novels, *Dying in Other Words*, *The Burning Book* and *Light Years* (all in Flamingo paperback), *Grace* and *Where Are the Snows* (both in Abacus), *Lost Children* (Flamingo) and (forthcoming) *The Keeper of the Gate*. She lives in London with her husband and daughter.

They never said thank you for the presents. Which were beautiful, weren't they? Beautiful things. Expensive. Every time Jane stared at her still white face in the mirror, unhappy, now, unadorned, the face of her family, she thought of her sister's kids and the presents.

She had stopped herself ringing many times. 'It's different for her,' Jane told herself. 'Working. Two kids. She's just busy.'

—All the same, she needed some word, some return.

What had she given them? Books, children's classics in handsome gift editions, things that the kids would grow into one day, a new world, she had thought when she bought them, something to take her nephews away from the telly that flickered against the daylight from morning till night. She had bundled her purse out of her bag as fast as she could to show she had money, comforting thick new glossy wads of money the equal of anyone else's, proving that she was a person, someone with a right to touch the tooled leather of the books, not someone abandoned, a widow, half what she was.

Yet she did feel so reduced. They had drawn her, the shops, since she had been widowed, shining in the distance, offering a welcome to the lonely, though on the way home she ached. Big stores like vast overheated lagoons where she could sail on the effortless escalators up to Furniture and Fittings, looking at new cream velvety carpets now there was no danger from Kingsley's dropped ash, picking up china figurines of neat miniature people to live with her in the silence, beautiful things to take home. It was always a long way home.

Sometimes at night since her husband had died Jane felt that her life was a minuscule capsule of light and safety surrounded by thousands of miles of cold gleaming streets and unfriendly pavements and sudden terrifying movements of hungry living things which would never know or care for her. Then again, sometimes the safety of the hot lit house was too much and she longed for fresh air, longed for someone, anyone, to phone or write or dance in the street or dive in through the window and claim a kiss as easily as Kingsley once kissed her, coming home: 'Mmm . . . is it chicken? I can smell garlic . . . Thanks, my love.'

But to widows, nothing happens. No reason for a chicken to sizzle in the pan, no plantain frying.

Christmas was a time of false hope. Tearing open her cards, which said 'Thinking of you', 'Take care of yourself' (because *they* didn't care), 'Come and see us!' (but never a time or place), 'Hope you're managing OK' (as if she had a business), 'Best love' – but if they loved her best, why did no one ever visit?

She'd spent Christmas Day with Kingsley's family – who welcomed her, sadly – going to the Pentecostal Church with them, though it wasn't her church and hadn't been Kingsley's for over a decade. Missing Kingsley so much, she had come home too soon, driving back to her empty house with the lights left on against thieves and the battlements of beautiful, silent things she had bought with the life insurance and the university pension which Kingsley had only told her to expect when he was almost dead of lung cancer.

New Year tasted bitter. The weeks crawled by. *They never said thank you* . . . Forget it, let go. She drove herself out of the house, out into the back garden where she hardly ever went these days, wrenching back the bolts, chains, stupidly frustrating armoury of locks and unfindable keys that the police recommended for women alone. Strong as death, the back door, but she was stronger.

Her garden was dank and sparse with early February, one of a double row between mean streets that she'd never thought of as mean when she lived here with Kingsley. Then, every room in the house had been scattered with books and papers, his writing, their food, which he loved, his ashtrays, grey, overflowing: temporary things not permanent things, shed feathers and fur of two beings living over and under and inside each other, for they were very happy, still very much lovers when she first began to notice his cough wasn't going away and he was too thin. They used to dance, laugh, fly . . .

Now the house was different, immaculate. Nearly every week since the money had arrived she had bought something new that Kingsley might have liked, to make it a little more perfect: a cushion, a bowl, a bookcase, two chairs, a vase. And felt more afraid. For it must be dangerous to have such beautiful things. Which the world would try to take from her, as Kingsley was taken away . . .

Hardly any light in the garden. Why weren't there any snow-drops this year? Staring down, Jane noticed a bulb, upturned, naked, white and shiny, lying on the black soil, a green curved funnel of leaf sailing stoutly off to one side. Uprooted by something, but not dead yet. Then she saw another. What . . . ?

Right beside her, noiseless, at her feet, glistening, stalled in the middle of a zigzag motion, quivering minutely, watching her with bright black button eyes, alive: a grey squirrel. Now one step nearer, front paws pressed flat on the ground, head cocked, *asking* . . .

She bent to press the bulbs back in, slowly so as not to alarm him, but he fled up the apple tree and over the fence in a series of graceful, weightless leaps, *come back* . . . He was gone.

And the uprooted bulbs might die . . . everything got lost, taken, stolen.

A little rush of lonely indignation sent her straight inside to the phone. She would ring Sheilah now, *why not? I sent them such beautiful things, and they never bothered to say thank you* . . . Dialling her sister's number with rigid fingers.

'Hallo?' Her sister's familiar flat voice.

'Did you get the presents all right?'

'Yes.'

'Did you like them?'

A pause. 'You shouldn't have, Jane. Such *beautiful things*.'

A real note of complaint. As if they didn't deserve them, Jane thought. Perhaps she's right. 'So they did arrive then,' she said, with cool unkindness. *Six weeks since Christmas, and not a bloody word*.

'Of course they arrived. You're saying the kids should have written, aren't you?'

The doorbell exploded, violently loud, two feet from where Jane stood gripping the phone in the hall, and her heart jerked and leaped.

'It's the *door*—'

'I'm not deaf—'

The bell stopped, then another great blare of sound, then another. '*Wait!*' she yelled at the door, then to Sheilah, 'Hang on for a moment,' happy to bang the receiver down on its side on the hall table.

The man stood on the doorstep, too close to the door so she almost fell over him, a small man, grinning, twitching, flinging open his hands in welcome, tight silver-grey curls as he bobbed his head, blinked his dark eyes. Unfamiliar, surely. But seemed to know her. 'We-ell,' he said, 'where's my man, my friend?'

'Who . . . ?'

'Your husband, my friend. I need a little bit of help,' conspiratorially, bowing and touching his forehead, then off on his story before she could take a deep breath and tell him that Kingsley was dead. 'I live jus' down the road, you know, three, four doors away. We got the old-fashioned toilet, you know, and the cistern it's gone and come right off the wall, the water gone through the ceiling and wreckin' the carpets, you never see such a mess, and I think of my friend and I think he's going to lend me ten pounds so I can go to the plumber's shop and get me a ballcock, give it you straight back.'

'Yes,' she said dumbly, 'of course, I could lend you . . .' Then stopped. Because she knew all her neighbours, didn't she? Didn't forget faces. I don't know you, she thought, and you never knew Kingsley, did you? You're a con man, a brilliant con man . . .

But was he? For there was a plumber's shop on the corner, though there was a betting-shop too . . . and how could he know she had a

70

husband? *Nonsense*. He guessed . . . but if he's really a neighbour, and the water's pouring through his ceiling . . .

'He's dead, my husband,' she said. 'Didn't you know he was dead? If you were his friend . . .'

'That's terrible, terrible,' he said, but impatiently, contorting his frame more and more, bending forward and back again, rocking, the low wintry sun springing over his crest of frosted grey hair, 'so he's dead, he's dead, he's gone . . . I need jus' ten pounds, for a few hours, that's all, you get it back when the wife comes home, no trouble. Right?'

Then she said: 'I'll come with you to the plumber's, that's best.' Because she would not be made a fool of, stolen from, left with nothing, unthanked, abandoned.

'No, no, that's all right.' He was dipping and diving, hopping from foot to foot in her doorway, ready to run, dance, lie, fly, win horse-races, interrupt phone-calls, dive through the door and take all her money and never never thank her – she suddenly saw he might save her.

The voice in the phone began to squeak, repetitive, petty, a small pallid whine. *No*. Jane ignored it. Sifting through the ten-pound notes in her bag, thin pigeon-coloured things, just one from so many, of course she could afford it. 'Take it.' He grasped it in an instant, was turning away . . .

She knew if she jumped on his shoulders he'd run down the road with her like an athlete, nip into the betting shop, treble their money by shuffling it up into storm clouds of racing pigeons, straight out through the back and away into the beckoning streets beyond, away down the great noisy arteries and veins of blue roads and alleys and pathways forking and budding and forking again as the weather grows warmer and sky begins to leak between the buildings, pours around the sides of the tower-blocks, pale blue, brighter blue, sun like a slow flash of lightning washing through walls and opening windows and now they are riding a widening river of light away into spring . . .

And the doors of the house are left open for squirrels to enter, so the beautiful things will be stolen, one after another, pale porcelain figures perched in the apple-trees a little while longer before they crash down, her carpets pecked at for birds' nests, her mirror a multi-coloured jigsaw of bluebells, daffodils, tulips.

And the phone moans on at blue air, which blows through, and lets go, and forgets.

Humphrey's Mother

Penelope Mortimer

PENELOPE MORTIMER was born in Wales; she stayed for six weeks. Her childhood was spent in Oxfordshire, Thornton Heath and Derbyshire, and later she lived mostly in London. Her novels include *The Pumpkin Eater*, *The Home*, *Long Distance* and *The Handyman*, and she has written two volumes of autobiography, *About Time* (Whitbread Prize 1979) and *About Time Too* (1994). André Deutsch is reissuing her *Life of Queen Elizabeth the Queen Mother* in paperback in the autumn of 1995.

In May 1927 the girl who was to be Humphrey's mother – new shingle, dimpled knees – was taken to a ball in nearby Cambridge. Her escort was a gentleman farmer called Jimmy Campbell. Humphrey's mother was taken from Jimmy in an 'Excuse Me' by a small, fair boy who told her he was reading Law and that his name was Tristram Coots. He charlestoned with neat abandon, but never stopped staring at her with pale blue eyes. There was something lewd, almost brutal in this stare that made her blood jump. She danced clumsily and ran out of chatter. When he casually suggested a breath of air she hung back, patting her shingle, glancing busily about, uncertain whether she wanted to be rescued. He took her hand and yanked her on to the terrace as though pulling a cork.

'Oh!' Humphrey's mother squealed, holding her wrenched arm, pouting. He was blond and dapper, like an innocent choirboy now she could no longer see the stare. 'Very well,' she said, softening, 'I forgive you.'

The night was warm. Starched shirt fronts and scraps of chiffon glimmered on the lawn, there was scuffling in the shrubbery, champagne spilled on pine needles, punts gently creaked under the willows. 'Ah, the lilac!' Humphrey's mother murmured and inhaled lilac, straining the seams of her taffeta. Tristram put his arm round her waist. They strolled towards the deeper shadows. She told him about her pony, Cracker and her labrador, Patch. He led her by the hand under low branches, further and further into the dark.

She couldn't stop giggling.

'Where are we going? I can't see a thing! *Tristram* . . . !'

'I want to show you something.'

'What? Where? *Tristram* . . . !'

They stumbled out into a clearing, a few tree stumps, sawdust and splinters. Tristram sat down and began undoing his tie.

She was in stitches, doubled up, breathless. 'Well, what do you want to show me?'

He patted the ground beside him.

'Oh, all right then! But *really* . . . !' She plumped down, endured a final seizure, tidied herself. Tristram took off his dinner jacket, folded it and put it on a tree stump.

'I do like your braces,' she said admiringly.

The next moment she was being raped. Tristram was strong as a young bull, equally purposeful and clumsy. He tore through taffeta, crêpe de Chine, suspender belt, ramming his way into her virginity with snorts and groans and every appearance of pain. It was this that stopped her initial struggles and screams. She knew from her mother that sex had nothing to do with pleasure, but Tristram actually seemed to be suffering. 'There there . . .' she murmured, stroking his bucking head, 'hush . . . there there . . .' He pounded on. She was very uncomfortable and hoped it wouldn't last long. He collapsed on her with a final, agonized whimper.

'Are you all right?' she asked, anxious.

A muffled groan.

'If you don't mind . . . You're awfully heavy . . .'

He rolled away and lay still. She pulled at her damp camiknickers, tried to straighten her stockings.

Moving his head with difficulty he recognized her.

'Oh God, we didn't use anything.'

'Didn't we?'

'You know what I mean.'

'Oh. Oh yes. Of course.'

'You won't get in pod, will you?'

'Oh no. Absolutely.'

Tristram became a frequent visitor to the house, much approved of by her parents, adept at passing the scones. There were occasional scuffles in the old schoolroom, once – recalled with particular joy – in the stables. By October, Humphrey's mother realized with astonishment that she was pregnant. Tristram unenthusiastically suggested marriage. Although the Woolsack was his eventual aim, the most he could hope for in the immediate future was the occasional brief, supplemented by pocket money from his father. It would be hard on her, but he supposed there was no alternative. Humphrey's mother, much matured in the past four months, said she would think about it. She gave him a loving kiss, saddled Cracker and rode over to Jimmy Campbell's.

Humphrey's mother and Jimmy were married in the village church on All Saints' Day 1927. The young bride was plump and radiant, the bridegroom appeared proud. Tristram was the first to throw confetti, showering them with gratitude. Humphrey was born full term in March 1928. If Jimmy Campbell was puzzled, he didn't say so. Humphrey's mother, after a few hours of panic and despair, regained her giggle and her dimples.

Two years later, in a moment of irritation at the way her husband slurped his game soup, she said: 'About Humphrey, dear. He's not yours, you know.'

'Never thought he was,' Jimmy said.

'You mean – you knew?'

Jimmy slurped his soup. 'Needs something. More salt. Drop of sherry. Something. Have a word with Cook, will you?' That was her marriage.

Humphrey grew into the spitting image of Tristram Coots – slight but substantial, with cropped fair hair and sky-blue eyes. His nature seemed to be Jimmy Campbell's. If there was a resemblance to his mother no one noticed it, since no one except Jimmy knew what Humphrey's mother's nature was, and by then Jimmy had forgotten.

* * *

In the summer following his eighteenth birthday Humphrey left school for National Service. On his last night at home he was summoned to Jimmy's study: stuffed fish, stuffed vixen, ageing leather, all dearly familiar.

'Ah, my boy. Want a word with you. Have a cigar.'

'Thanks, Dad.'

'Everything all right?'

'Fine.'

'Good. Good.' A pause while Jimmy brushed invisible crumbs off the seat of his armchair, plumped the cushion. At last he sat down, forcefully blew his nose, mopped his moustache. 'Wanted a word with you.'

'Yes, Dad.'

'Given this a bit of thought. Can't say I like it. Not long since you were a tiddler, y'know.'

Humphrey waited.

'Great opportunity for you, the Army. Have a cigar. Ah, you've got one. Well now. Fact is.' He stopped dead.

'Yes, Dad?'

'Your mother – your mother and myself. Damned awkward really.'

So that was it. 'Oh,' Humphrey mumbled. 'I'm sorry.'

'Kept quiet, you understand. Never discussed it. No reason to.'

'Quite.'

'There you were. Did our best. Fact is.' He stopped, stared blankly at Humphrey.

'Go on, Dad.'

'That's the whole point, my boy! That's it!' Jimmy swiped the arm of his chair triumphantly. 'Not mine. You.'

Humphrey returned the stare.

'Couldn't have any more. Something wrong. Don't know what. Womanish. There you are.'

'For God's sake, Dad, what are you talking about?'

'Damn it, don't I make myself clear? Five months gone when I married her!'

Jimmy's raucous breathing, the measured tick of the clock, someone clacking across the tiled hallway, a door shutting. Humphrey stared.

'You . . . aren't my father?'

'Began to think so, over the years.' An almost inaudible mutter: 'Fond of you, y'know . . .' Then abruptly jovial: 'Let's have a snifter, eh?' He bustled away to the drinks table. 'Confounded girl never cleans the glasses properly.' Silence while Jimmy buffed and polished.

After a long pause Humphrey cleared his throat. 'Who is . . . was he?' he asked.

Jimmy was holding up the glasses one by one, squinting through them: 'Eh? Oh. Chap called Coots.'

'Is he . . . alive?'

'Haven't the foggiest.' Jimmy busied himself, paused, added gruffly: 'You're going into the Army. Got a right to know these things. Blood and so on. Can be tricky.'

'I see,' Humphrey said, not seeing. He dropped his head in his hands, fingers dug into scalp, aware of the glug of pouring, two sharp hisses of the soda syphon, chink of ice cubes. Something important had happened; nothing had happened. Everything should have changed; everything was the same. He wanted to know more; he didn't want to know anything. He ducked automatically as Jimmy ruffled his hair.

'Dam' sight easier to keep quiet, I can tell you.'

'Yes, Dad.'

'Well—' The armchair creaked. A long, relieved sigh. 'Leave it at that, shall we? No need to make a song and dance about it.'

'No. I suppose not.'

Jimmy chuckled hopefully. 'What the blazes does it matter who rogered your mother? You've been a Campbell all your life.'

'I know . . .' Humphrey's face crumpled. He hid it behind his hands.

'Pshaw! Thought you had more spunk in you!' Breathing heavily, moustache and eyebrows quivering, Jimmy hauled himself up, took a few strides across the room, wheeled round. 'Bloody insult! Thought of that, have you?'

'Insult?' Humphrey asked incredulously.

'First-class education – best I could afford anyway. Did all I could, damn it. Son and heir. Means a lot to me.'

'I know that, Dad! Good Lord, I don't—'

'Going to think Coots is your father now, are you? Never clapped eyes on you? Never paid a penny?'

'Of course not! I didn't mean . . . I'm sorry . . . Please, Dad . . .'

Jimmy made a sound of some sort. It might have been derisory. He blew his nose for a long time, then turned, stuffing his handkerchief deep into his pocket.

'Don't want you to do anything you don't think's right, y'know.'

'No, of course. I know you don't.'

'Bit of a teaser. Common sense, that's what it all comes down to. Best let sleeping dogs lie, eh?'

'If you think so.'

'Why stir up trouble? Damned awkward for your mother. Not fair, old chap. Not cricket, as we used to say.'

'You mean – just go on as we were?'

'Why not? Doesn't make a blind bit of difference.'

'I suppose it doesn't.'

'Good. Let's leave it at that, shall we?'

With one leg in his pyjamas Humphrey sat on his bed trying to imagine the future, but all he could imagine was the past: riding on Jimmy's shoulders to the sheep-dip, sitting on his knee driving the harvester, learning – with some repugnance – how to milk a cow, being shown different countries on the globe, asking why so many were coloured pink, why there was so much sea. With one leg in his pyjamas Humphrey sat on his bed and wept.

'By the way,' Jimmy grunted as he heaved in beside his wife, 'thought he ought to know. Told the boy about Coots.'

'Coots?' Humphrey's mother asked. 'Do we know him, dear?'

On being reminded, she said vaguely: 'Ah yes. A very odd young man,' and gave the ghost of a giggle.

The Ghost
of the Rainforest

Barry Unsworth

BARRY UNSWORTH was born and brought up in Durham. In 1973, his fourth novel, *Mooncranker's Gift*, won the Heinemann Fiction Prize. *Pascali's Island* was shortlisted for the Booker Prize in 1980 and made into a successful film. *Sacred Hunger*, his tenth novel, was joint winner of the Booker Prize in 1992. Barry Unsworth is a Fellow of the Royal Society of Literature and lives in Italy.

What got into Clare Barraclough nobody knew. She was always so self-possessed and watchful. Then, in the course of a single evening, at a reception in Singapore, she wrecked her husband's career, that edifice she had done so much to protect. Such a pity, such a nice man. Rather clumsy, rather vague . . .

They were a little late in arriving. Bernard went off at once in search of the men's room. He needed it immediately and he needed to know where it was because he knew he would need it again. With the years his bladder had weakened. Clare took a glass of vodka from a passing tray and crossed the room to the huge plate-glass windows. This was floor number sixty, the top one, and the whole wall on this side was made of glass.

She stood with her back to it, looking at the other people gathered there. Many of the faces she knew. London, Los Angeles, Toronto, Rome, Paris . . . Now Singapore. Over years of conferences she had seen lines of fatigue, bitterness, arrogance, resignation, settle on these faces. There were not many happy ones, and this was odd, in a way, because the International Association for the Creation of Work was an organization dedicated to the relief of poverty, and doing good is supposed to make people happy. What do they see when they look at our faces, she wondered, Bernard's and mine? And where is Bernard?

'Bernard is taking a risk, leaving you all on your own.' It was one of the American representatives, a man with the face of an impertinent baby, a gift of ready laughter and a phenomenal memory for names. 'Will I do as a stopgap?' he said, and made a comic leer.

Clare smiled at him with practised warmth. Even this man, whom she disliked, whose dislike she sensed, had to be kept well-disposed, if possible. He might still be intending to give his support to Bernard in the voting for the new president, due to take place the following day, though she felt fairly sure he had committed himself to the French candidate, no doubt for some favour promised in return. At this thought she felt the tension gather deep within her, like a physical pain. She took a drink from her glass and was surprised to find there wasn't much left: normally one drink would see her through an affair like this. 'Oh, he is around somewhere,' she said. She narrowed her eyes at him and kept the smile going. 'It's all a matter of trust,' she said. 'You know, Roger, trust.' But of course he didn't.

'It's Ronald,' he said, 'not Roger. Well, you wouldn't easily miss him in a crowd.'

'Ronald, of course,' she said, but he was moving away; perhaps he was offended, perhaps he had seen someone more rewarding to talk to. Bad either way. On an immediate social reflex, she began to disengage in the opposite direction, as if she too had spotted someone. 'Slip of the tongue,' she said, but he probably didn't hear this. She encountered a waiter and took another glass.

Still no sign of Bernard. That wretched Ronald had been right: he was not someone you would fail to see in a crowd. He was a big, shambling, gentle man, with a mane of greying hair. He was clumsy – there was generally a space created round him. He looked like a caricature professor of some abstruse subject; and a professor is what he would probably have been, had he not given up his academic career when it was barely started. His aims were very simple in those days. He had wanted to be useful, to work for humanity. She had encouraged him, she had shared his idealism. Thirty-odd years later, here they were. IACW. The initials didn't even make a pronounceable sound ... Clare, whose second glass was well down by now, felt a sort of vague sorrow, followed by a rush of angry love. He must get the post, he deserved it so. He was

Vice-President already, he was the natural choice. And it was the last chance: he would be retiring in four years. It would make such a difference. *He must get it . . .*

But where was he? He should be here, they should be moving about among the crowd, saying the things that needed to be said to the people they needed saying to. Bernard had no sense of direction, he easily lost his way even in places he was familiar with. She saw him wandering with tormented bladder, lost among corridors, striving to understand the wavering cadences of Malay cleaning-women . . . She caught the eye of the retiring president, a solemn silver-haired Swede, who raised his glass to her across the room. Clare smiled and returned the gesture, discovering in the process that her glass was empty again; she was sipping air. Was Brotherus making some signal to her, congratulations discreetly disguised? Perhaps he knew something. But the Swedes went in for this business of maintaining eye contact and raising glasses to people. They did it in their own homes, at their own dinner tables.

All the same, there would be people in this room with a good idea of the way things were likely to go next day. Could it really be true that their happiness, their sense of worth, hers and Bernard's, could depend on a gaggle of career philanthropists? At the thought came the beginnings of an anger long unfamiliar, long overlaid, an anger of her youth when the sense of injustice was vivid.

From the night outside came the sudden low rumble of thunder. Clare turned to glance through the plate glass. Darkness had descended on Singapore from one moment to the next, like the drawing of a curtain – almost, it seemed, while they rode up in the lift. Below lay the heart of the city, lit in its pride, monument to a culture purely financial, a vast complex of steel and glass and stressed concrete, with no visible past – its past lay below the pavements and roads and the basements of banks and business houses and shopping centres: the hacked and suffocated rainforest which the rains still came daily in search of and the hot vaporous air that hung about the city still sought to nourish.

Glimmers of lightning showed to the south, over the harbour.

There was no sound of rain, but the glass was suddenly flecked with drops. She turned back to the room, which had its own, separate, air conditioned climate, cool and constant. She moved forward with the idea of making her way to the bar for another drink. But she found herself appealed to by a man called Cooper who worked in the legal department. 'Isn't that right, Clare?' he said, rather loudly. He was attempting to explain something to a faintly smiling Chinese woman. 'Looked at one way,' he said, 'public bodies are like any other businesses, like multinationals. They split off, they diversify. The Association was once part of the Organization for Industrial Development. Isn't that right, Clare? Same with the workforce. You find three types, just as you do in any other big company. There is the majority, who beaver away as clerks or security guards or what have you and look forward to their pension. There are those who go in to make a career, as they might go into the Civil Service for example. And there are the public men, who are given senior posts in recognition of services rendered. Isn't that right, Clare?'

'No, it bloody well isn't,' she said briskly, and felt a welcome quickening of her rage. This was directed almost entirely at Bernard now. All the same, she was not ready to let him be included in Cooper's categories. 'There are people like my husband,' she said 'who spend their whole lives in the service of a cause—'

At that moment she saw him. She saw him enter, hover briefly, then move with his gait of a peaceful, purposeful bear off to the side towards the barrier of luxuriant tropical house-plants in their tall pots. It seemed that he intended to pass through them, a difficult proceeding and rather pointless. Then, screened by the thick-bladed foliage, he paused, lingered. She was puzzled for a moment, only for a moment. Then with dreadful suddenness she understood: Bernard had not succeeded in his search and now, being unable to wait longer, was availing himself of the cover afforded by the shrubs. Like a child, because his own view was blocked by the leaves, he thought others could not see him.

Like a child ... But she could see him. And if she, then others too. And they would talk. The story would get around that Bernard had exhibited himself. Panic descended on her, she could hardly breathe. He had ruined everything.

It seemed an eternity that Bernard remained motionless there, relieving himself among the greenery. Then she saw him emerge and pad discreetly away. No one seemed to have noticed anything, there was no change in the appearance of things. Bernard looked at her over the heads of the crowd and she looked back. Reproach was on her face. And on to Bernard's face, immediately, came the knowledge that she had seen him.

It was this, the look on his face that changed everything. Beyond the indifferent throng stood her love and he was ashamed because he thought he had failed her. It was wrong that he should think so, wrong that his face should wear that look. It came to her that she had been wickedly selfish to push him so. He had never wanted any of this. It made not a scrap of difference whether anyone else had seen him or not. It was not thus that they should enter upon the evening of their lives together.

Clare smiled. What she had dreaded had happened and it was not a disaster at all. That painful knot of anxiety dissolved as if it had never been. Bernard would not be left alone; she would be with him in disgrace too. She took some dancing steps forward, towards him. As she did so, she pointed her forefingers upward and as she passed through the crowd, with precise and delicate movements like those of a Chinese dancer, she tipped over glasses and plates held in precarious balance by her fellow guests. Drinks splashed about, anchovies and mayonnaise slithered over shirt-fronts and the bosoms of dresses. Expostulations followed in her wake.

When she reached Bernard, she was still dancing. He looked stunned. She took his hand and wordlessly drew him out of the room and into the lift. Outside it was raining still, a warm, steady downpour. Across the street was a small, triangular park, where some of the last remnants of the rainforest still held out. They stood there, close together in the drumming rain. She felt completely happy.

After a moment Bernard spoke. 'What the hell are we standing here for, in the rain?' he said. 'You crazy bitch. Do you realize that you have ruined my whole career?'

Dressing Up

Angela Huth

A NGELA HUTH has written several novels including *Sun Child*, *Invitation to the Married Life* and
her latest, *Land Girls*. Her third collection of short
stories will be published shortly. She has also
written plays for radio, TV and the stage, makes
occasional documentaries, and is a frequent broad-
caster and critic. Married to a don, Angela Huth
lives in Oxford and has two daughters.

'Please just one more chance,' cooed Prunella in her most persuasive voice. 'Just lunch and the afternoon.'

There was a long silence while her daughter, on the other end of the line, weighed up the pros and cons of her mother's request.

It was two months now since the unfortunate incident and how beastly Audrey had been about it. A very minor mishap: no ill-effects on the children. They had had fun as they always did on visits to their grandmother. It wasn't Prunella's fault Audrey had been held up in traffic, so arrived late to collect them on that particular day. By six, Prunella was exhausted, in need of something. She must have had two gins and tonics before Audrey had arrived: perhaps she had drunk them faster than usual, having started late. What with one thing and another, on the way down the path to Audrey's car she had stumbled, cut her knee, felt dizzy. There had been quite a palaver, Audrey pulling her up, grumbling away, telling the children to buzz off and find a plaster. 'You're irresponsible, Mother,' she had hissed when the children, all concern for their grandmother, had run off. 'How do you expect me to feel about leaving them with someone who *drinks*? I shan't let them come again.'

Prunella hadn't felt like arguing. She had sat on a kitchen chair, one stocking an ignominious roll beneath her knee, watching Audrey savagely dab the bloody patch. The children hugged her

91

goodbye, said they hoped they would see her soon. But since then her punishment had been put into practice. Banned from seeing the two people she loved most on earth, these days.

The silly feud had gone on long enough. Prunella knew she must swallow pride and anger, apologize, make promises not to touch a drop before the children arrived or while they were there: promise anything.

'One more chance, then,' said Audrey at last, in her tight little voice. 'You know the conditions.'

'I've missed them so much. They must wonder why they haven't been for so long.'

'They haven't said anything.'

Prunella knew Audrey was lying. She was able to detect her daughter's lies on the telephone every bit as distinctly as Audrey could detect her own small indulgence of alcohol.

The morning of the children's visit, the hours passed so fast in busy preparation that Prunella did not stop for coffee, let alone fortification. Happiness made it so easy.

The bell rang on the dot of twelve. Audrey was always punctual, and superior with it. She gave a hurried smile, trying to disguise the twitching of her nostrils, the mean detection of drink on her mother's breath. Hoping to catch me out, the bitch, thought Prunella. But it didn't matter. With George and Anna wriggling under each arm she felt bold, strong.

'Do I pass the breath test?'

'Don't be stupid, Mother. I'll be back at five.'

Once Audrey had gone, the children burst from their straitjackets of polite demeanour – always worn in the shadow of their mother – hugged their grandmother and rushed to the kitchen.

This was the room in which Prunella spent most of her time, and it blazed with signals of her life. Old photographs and theatre posters covered the walls. A pair of satin shoes from *Cavalcade* stood in third position by the stove. Necklaces from *The Boyfriend* twinkled in the fruit bowl. The children, accustomed to the Formica sterility of their kitchen at home, had loved the room since their earliest childhood.

Dressing Up

As usual, they ate hungrily of their grandmother's food, promised not to tell about the chocolate pudding. They encouraged familiar stories about Prunella's past, which had been a very glamorous time. A dancer, a singer, a bit of both, friend of famous actors. She was a star, their grandmother. They could tell that, even today, with her bright red hair (they didn't believe their mother, who said it was a wig), gipsy earrings and scarlet nails. Beneath her apron, she wore velvet dresses of crimson or purple or sapphire that flashed a patchwork of light. She smelt of antique powder and inspired strange excitement.

'How best shall we pass the afternoon, little ones?'

'Dressing up,' they said.

Of all the old-fashioned activities Prunella devised for them, dressing up was the favourite. She pointed to a huge box waiting under the window. (It had taken three whiskies to give strength, last night, to drag it downstairs.)

'How did you manage this by yourself, Gran?'

'Easily!'

'You're brilliant, Gran,' said Anna.

Dishes cleared, Prunella sat at the table giving advice and encouragement as the children ruffled through the pantomime clothes. She panted a little, felt light-headed. Well, the children's visits were dizzy times, stirring up the old quietness till the kitchen became a place she could hardly recognize.

What she wanted was a drink.

The children were ready at last. George was a small laughing cavalier, ostrich feather from his hat swooping right under his chin. Anna was a shepherdess in laced bodice and yellow skirt.

'Wonderful!' Prunella clapped her hands. 'You look real professionals.' This, they knew, was her highest compliment. She had been the most professional professional in her time. 'On with the show.'

'Not without you.'

'What, me?'

This moment of mock surprise was a small charade enjoyed at every visit. Prunella would feign reluctance, then find herself persuaded.

'Well,' she would say, as she did now, 'if that's what you want . . .' She stood up. Knees shaky. Fended off a gust of scarves and jackets they threw at her.

'Just a moment, darlings. Gran needs a . . . to keep her going. Music, George. Put us in the mood.' She opened the fridge, took out the bottle of white wine, drank a quick tumbler.

George, child of the technological age, always had trouble working the maplewood box his grandmother called the radiogram. But eventually he coaxed the old table to spin the 78 record, 'Bye Bye Blackbird'. They had known all the words for years.

Suddenly fortified, Prunella swiped at a second glass of wine, picked up her skirts.

'Now off we go. Follow the silly old bat.'

'You're not a silly old bat, Gran.'

The children knew the rules: copy every movement precisely. This afternoon Prunella was full of invention. They skipped around the table, waving their arms as if carrying invisible boughs. They grabbed apples from the bowl and threw them high. They climbed a chair up on to the table, creaking the old pine top as they twirled between bowls of hyacinths, and leapt down the other side.

'Oh happy chorus lines, darlings!' Prunella downed a third quick glass. 'Up we go again!'

This time, the table-top her stage, she did a few steps of the cancan. Amazed by their grandmother's high kicks, the children gave up trying to copy, entranced.

'Can still kick a leg, can't I? Let's find a cancan record.'

Jumping ambitiously back down on to a chair, Prunella missed her footing. There was a crack, a thud, a dignified whimper, all muffled by the music. She flung one fat arm dramatically behind her.

'Gran? – Quick, George.'

George slithered off the table.

'Are you doing your dying scene, Gran?'

Anna joined him on the floor. She prodded a vast velvet hip, its lights twinkling less brightly in the shadow of the table. She could see, so close, that the silvery skin of Prunella's eyelids looked like wrinkled blue worms lying side by side. When her eyes were open, you didn't notice this. Anna wished they would open now. The record slurred to an end. *Blackbird, bye bye* . . . Then, beastly silence.

'Think she's dead?' asked George.

'Suppose I'd better feel her heart.' Anna was top in biology at school. She ran a reluctant finger over the left velvet breast.

'She's a funny colour,' observed George.

'I'll ring for an ambulance.' Anna had recently been made a prefect for her coolness in a crisis.

'Better not say she's dead,' said George, 'or they won't hurry.'

One of the ambulancemen, on his knees, locked his mouth to Prunella's.

'Kiss of life,' Anna explained.

'Couldn't fancy that.' George giggled.

'What about you two?' The ambulanceman sat back on his heels, with his own mouth made silly with lipstick.

'Our mother will be here any minute,' said Anna.

'Good. Because we'd best get a move on.' He was helping the second man attach a drip to Prunella's arm, stiff in its last defiant flourish. As they struggled to move her on to the stretcher, George disliked the sight of his grandmother's knee, that only moments before had been so impressive in its high kicks. Anna hated seeing the shock of red hair had tipped sideways, proof of her mother's theory.

'Poor old Gran,' she said.

'If she's not dead, then it's her best-ever Juliet dying.' Tears of admiration ran down George's cheek.

Audrey, hurrying punctually down the path, found her way impeded by the stretcher-bearers. In the second she paused, she saw the multi-coloured mound of her mother, clown-white face bruised with blue eyelids, blobs of salmon-pink rouge ironic on the old cheeks. She screamed.

From the front door the children watched her vivid journey.

'Cool it, Mum. Gran had a fall.' Anna herself felt a strange calm.

'You idiots!' Hearing the slam of the ambulance doors, Audrey flinched.

'Quick! We must follow. What *happened*?' She ripped off George's hat, threw it nastily to the ground. He had no time to answer before she ran indoors to the kitchen, saw the empty bottle, the upturned chair. Again, the children watched her from the door.

'Christ! I don't believe it. Never *ever* again,' she shouted.

Anna hitched up her skirt with pitiless hands.

'No use threatening us,' she said. 'Gran may be dead.'

'On the other hand,' said George, 'it may just be one of her dying scenes.'

He sensed the sweetness of his grandmother's revenge. With an appropriately solemn look, he replaced his feathered hat, tilting it in just the way she had assured him, light years ago, was correct for a laughing cavalier.

Hotel des Voyageurs

———◆———

William Boyd

WILLIAM BOYD has published six novels, including *Brazzaville Beach*, which won the James Tait Black Memorial Prize, and *The Blue Afternoon*, which won the 1993 Sunday Express Book of the Year Award. Eight of his screenplays have been filmed, including recently *A Good Man in Africa*, based on his novel, which won the 1981 Whitbread Literary Award for the Best First Novel and a 1982 Somerset Maugham Award. His most recent book is a collection of short stories, *The Destiny of Nathalie X*.

Monday, 26 July 1928

Paris. Boat train from London strangely quiet, I had a whole compartment to myself. Fine drizzle at the Gare du Nord. After breakfast I spent two hours trying to telephone Louise in London. I finally got through and a man's voice answered. 'Who's calling?' he said, very abruptly. 'Tell Louise it's Logan Mountstewart,' I said, equally brusquely. Longish silence. Then the man said Louise was in Hampshire. I kept telling him that Louise was never in Hampshire during the week. Eventually I realized it was Robbie. He refused to admit it so I called him every foul name I could think of and hung up.

Lonely bitter evening, drank too much. A protracted street prowl through the Marais. The thought of Louise with Robbie made me want to vomit. Robbie: *faux bonhomme* and fascist shit.

Tuesday

More rain. I cabled Douglas and Sylvia in Bayonne and told them I was driving down. I then hired the biggest car I could find in Paris, a vast American thing called a Packard, a great beast of a vehicle, with huge bulbous headlamps. I set off after lunch in a thunderstorm resolved to drive through the night. The South, the South, at last. That's where I will find my peace. Intense disgust at the banality of my English life. How I detest London and all my friends. Except Sholto, perhaps. And Hermione. And Sophie.

Wednesday

Crossed the Loire and everything changed. Blue skies, a mineral flinty sun hammering down. *Beau ciel, vrai ciel, regarde moi qui change*. Opened every window in the Packard and drove in a warm buffeting breeze.

Lunch in Angoulême. Ham and Moselle. I had a sudden urge to take Douglas and Sylvia some sweet Monbazillac as a present. Drove on to Libourne and then up the river to St Foy. I turned off the main road, trying to remember the little château we had visited before, in '26, near a place called Pomport.

I must have missed a sign because I found myself in a part of the countryside I did not recognize, in a narrow valley with dark woods at its rim. Blonde windcombed wheat fields stirred silently on either side, the road no longer metalled. And that was when the clanking started in the Packard's engine.

I stopped and raised the bonnet. A hot oily smell, a wisp of something. Smoke? Steam? I stood there in the gathered, broiling heat of the afternoon wondering what to do.

A goatish farmer in a pony and trap understood my request for a 'garage' and directed me up a dusty lane. There was a village, he said. St Barthelmy.

St Barthelmy: one street of ancient shuttered houses, with pocked honey-coloured walls. A church with a hideous new spire, quite out of proportion. I found the garage by a bridge over the torpid stream that wound round the village. The *garagiste*, a genial young man in horn-rimmed spectacles, looked at the Packard in frank amazement and said he would have to send to Bergerac for the part he needed. How long would that take, I asked. He shrugged. A day, two days, who knows? And besides, he said, pointing to a glossy limousine up on blocks, he had to finish Monsieur le Comte's car first. There was a hotel I could stay in, he said, at the other end of the village. The Hotel des Voyageurs.

Thursday

Dinner in the hotel last night. Stringy roast chicken and a rough red wine. I was alone in the dining room, served by an ancient wheezing man, when the hotel's other guest arrived. A woman. She was tall and slim, her dark brown hair cut in a fashionable bob. She wore a dress of cobalt blue crêpe de Chine, with a short skirt gathered at the hips. She barely glanced at me and treated the old waiter with brutal abruptness. She was French, or else completely bilingual, and everything about her was redolent of wealth and prestige. At first glance her face seemed not pretty, a little hard, with a slightly hooked nose, but as I covertly gazed at her across the dining room, studying her features as she picked at her meal, her face's shadowed planes and angles, the slight pout of the upper lip, the perfect plucked arcs of her eyebrows began to assume a fascinating worldly beauty. She ordered a coffee and smoked a cigarette, never once looking in my direction. I was about to invite her to join me for a *digestif* when she stood up and left the room. As she passed my table she looked at me for the first time, squarely, with a casual candid curiosity.

Slept well. For the first time since leaving London did not dream of Louise.

Friday

Encountered the woman in the hotel's small garden. I was sitting at a tin table beneath a chestnut tree, spreading fig jam on a croissant, when I heard her call.

'Thierry?'

I turned, and her face fell. She apologized for interrupting me, she said she thought I was someone else, the linen jacket I was wearing had made her think I was her husband. He had one very similar, the same hair colour too. I introduced myself. She said she was La Comtesse de Benoit-Voulon.

'Your husband is staying here?' I asked. She was tall, her eyes were almost on the same level as mine. I could not help noticing the way the taupe silk singlet she wore clung to her breasts. Her eyes were very pale brown, they seemed to look at me with unusual curiosity.

She told me her husband was visiting his mother. The arc of an

101

eyebrow lifted. 'The old lady and I . . .' she paused diplomatically. 'We do not enjoy each other's company so, so I prefer to wait in the hotel. And besides our car is being repaired.'

'So is mine,' I said, with a silly laugh, which I instantly regretted. 'Quite a coincidence.'

'Yes,' she said thoughtfully, frowning. That curious glance again. 'It is, isn't it?'

To fill my empty day I walked to the next village, called Argenson, and lunched on a tough steak and a delicious tangy *vin rouge en carafe*. On the way back I was given a lift in a lorry piled high with sappy pine logs. My nose prickled with resin all the way back to St Barthelmy.

The hotel was quiet, no one was in the lobby. My key was missing from its hook behind the desk so I assumed the maid was still cleaning the room. Upstairs, the door was very slightly ajar, the room beyond dark and shuttered against the sun. I stepped inside. La Comtesse de Benoit-Voulon was lifting a book from my open suitcase.

'Mr Mountstewart,' she said, the guilt and surprise absent from her face within a second. 'I'm so glad you decided to come back early.'

Friday
I must make sure I have this right. Must make sure I forget nothing.

We made love in the cool afternoon darkness of my room. There was a strange relaxed confidence about it all, as if it had been prefigured in some way, in the unhurried, tolerant manner our bodies moved to accommodate each other. And afterwards we chatted, like old friends. Her name, she said, was Giselle. They were going to Hyères, they had a house there. They always spent August in Hyères, she and her husband.

Then she turned to face me and said: 'Logan? . . . Have we ever met before?'

I laughed. 'I think I would have remembered.'

'Perhaps you know Thierry? Perhaps I've seen you with Thierry.'

'Definitely not.'

102

She cradled my face in her hands and stared fiercely at me. She said in a quiet voice: 'He didn't send you, did he? If he did you must tell me now.' Then she laughed herself, when she saw my baffled look, heard my baffled protestations. 'Forget it,' she said. 'I always think he's playing tricks on me. He's like that, Thierry, with his games.'

I slept that afternoon, and when I woke she had gone. Downstairs the old waiter had set only one table for dinner. I asked where the lady was and he said she had paid her bill and left the hotel.

At the garage the limousine had gone. The young *garagiste* proudly brandished the spare part for my Packard and said it would be ready for tomorrow. I pointed at the empty blocks where the Count's car had been.

'Did he come for his car?'

'Two hours ago.'

'With his wife?'

'Who?'

'Was there a woman with him, a lady?'

'Oh yes.' The *garagiste* smiled at me and offered me one of his yellow cigarettes, which I accepted. 'Every year he spends two days with his mother, on his way south. Every year there's a different one.'

'Different wife?'

He looked at me knowingly. He drew heavily on his cigarette, his eyes wistfully distant. 'They're from Paris these girls. Amazing.' He shook his head in frustrated admiration. Once a year St Barthelmy had a visit from one of these astonishing women, he said, these radiant visitors. They stayed in the Hotel des Voyageurs ... One day, one day he was going to go to Paris and see them for himself.

Saturday

At the Café Riche et des Sports in Bergerac, I finish my article on Sainte-Beuve. I pour a cognac into my coffee and compose a telegram to Douglas cancelling my visit. *O qu'ils sont pittoresques les trains manqués!* That will not be my fate. I unfold my road map and plot a route to Hyères.

103

Grace

——◆——

Jane Gardam

Clockie Gosport had this great diamond in the back of his neck. Under the skin. At the top of the spine. In among all the wires that keep the show on the road. Just on the bone they break when they hang you. Clockie Gosport.

He was never a one to mention the diamond. Never. Very quiet and modest. A thoughtful man, born over Teesport in a street right on to the pavement, no back door or yard or running water or electric. And clean? Every part of it including the old man, Old Gosport, Clockie's father, who was made to strip in the passage every night home from the Works and bath in the tin behind the screen.

She was a silent woman, Ma Gosport. She held the world together, packing in the lodgers head to tail in the upstairs double, the family all crammed about. She took in both day- and night-shift men and every hour God gave she was washing and possing and mangling and hanging out bits of sheets. She hung them out, courtesy of Mrs Middleditch and the hook in her wall across the way. All was hygiene.

And this story went around. 'Clockie Gosport got a diamond in his neck.'

'Is it true you got a diamond in yer neck, Clockie?' (He was Clockie because way back someone had said: 'Like a watch. Watches has bits of diamond in them.')

Clockie always smiled. 'Now how could I have a diamond in me neck? They'd have me head off.'

107

That was as a grown man. At school he'd said nothing, just stared. He had these poppy eyes. The other kids said it was the diamond pushing them forwards. 'Gis yer diamond, Clockie. Come on yer booger, gis yer diamond.' They would grab at him and Ma Gosport or the school teacher would wade in and cuff them all about.

Nobody cuffed Clockie though. It was tradition. When Clockie had been five or six he'd been cuffed about at home for screaming and it was found to be the meningitis. There'd been silence all down Dunedin Street that night and folks coming and sitting quiet on the step and Old Gosport weeping. And Ma Gosport had been slapping and bashing the sheets in the back and then getting into her things for the walk to the Infirmary. Mrs Armitage and Mrs Middleditch had gone with her, the one excited, the other grim. They'd gone in order to support Ma Gosport back after the news, and Ma Gosport had stuck out her chin and never spoke once on the road, the three of them walking abreast in their hats and coats. She gave the women presents later, Mrs Middleditch a jet brooch of her grandmother's and Mrs Armitage a steak pie.

For Clockie had recovered and, before she left the Infirmary, the doctor had called Mrs Gosport in – 'No, just the mother please' – and had put his arm round her.

'Mrs Gosport, your boy will get better and he's a lucky lad. We're very interested, though, in the foreign body lodged in the neck.'

'It's a diamond,' said Ma Gosport. The doctor brooded.

'What exactly do you *mean* by a diamond, Mrs Gosport?'

'I don't know. It just happens sometimes in the family. There comes a bairn with the diamond. It means luck.'

'Have . . .' the doctor covered his face with his hands and swirled them about, 'has anybody ever seen it?'

'No. Well, it's under the skin, isn't it?'

'We ought to examine it, you know. It is most fascinating.'

So she let them, but it was long ago before the war when X-rays were feeble and what with air raids coming and hospitals so busy Clockie's diamond went out of folks' minds.

Clockie was a poor scholar and slow talking. He never read. He grew very good-looking. Beautiful really. He began work at the new chemical plant after the War, sweeping a road a mile long. He brushed with men to either side of him, a thin grey line, and every now and then a machine came along that gobbled up the dirt. Then the men stopped, drew on a fag, slung it away, lined up again, swept on. At the end of the mile they knocked off for a can of tea and walked back and started again. It didn't worry Clockie. It was regular work and you could listen. It was surprising what you heard.

''Ere Clockie,' they said on wet days, 'how 'bout releasing this diamond and we all get off to Paris.'

They'd glance at the back of his neck now and then, but it was always covered by the sweat-rag his mother gave him boiled each morning. They'd not have thought of touching it.

When he got a girl though, she wanted to touch it, of course she did. She was Betty Liverton, dumpy little thing, all charm.

'Welsh,' said his mother. 'Not to be trusted.' Betty had her hands round his neck second time out.

Clockie wasn't sweeping any more. He'd graduated first to the suction machine and found affinity with all forms of mechanical life. Now he was the feller with the screwdriver round the ethylene plant and everybody shouting for him.

He'd moved up to the mechanics' canteen where Betty Liverton washed the mugs. Short little legs, lovely chest, freckles, soft eyes – she watched him with his curly hair. Big feller, Clockie.

Then down Ormesby Lane, by the bit of wood and stream that's not overlooked, they lay down beside the kingcups and put their hands on each other and she screamed.

'What ist?' He was undoing her dress.

'Stop it. Dear Lord, it's true!'

'What's true?' His blue pop-eyes were shining. He wasn't laying off for long.

'It's true. In the back of yer neck. The diamond.'

He pushed her down. (And him thought slow!)

'Get off. I want to see. It's right on the surface, I could bite it out.'

'Does it bother you then?' He took both her wrists in one

hand and held them in the grass above her head. She was amazed.

'It doesn't bother me. I just never could believe it.'

She forgot the diamond. All she could think of that night in her bed as she played back her deflowering beside Ormesby Beck was that it couldn't have been his first time.

'Was it yer first time?' she asked when they were married.

'It come natural,' said Clockie.

She became the envy of the street with her sleepy honeymoon looks.

They got a couple of rooms up the road and Ma Gosport made the best of it, taking in another lodger and then another when Old Gosport went at last, spotless to his coffin. She never liked Betty Liverton.

Clockie stayed tranquil, so tranquil that it was a puzzle to some that after the first days of marriage were over and Betty grown brisk there were so quickly two girls and a boy, all the image of their father. It was only image though. There was not his temperament, not the peace of him. They grew up to be rubbish.

'Well, their mother's rubbish, isn't she?' said Ma Gosport. 'She got tired of him. There wasn't a thought between them.'

Clockie grew quieter still after the kids were flown and Betty went off with Alan Middleditch. 'That's Wales for you,' said Ma Gosport just before she died.

And Betty drank port-and-lemons down the golf course and was always well away by eight o'clock, talking of her husband who thought he had a diamond in his neck.

Clockie used to walk the beaches of the estuary in time, among the sharp sand-grasses and the grey flowers. He met folks there. Once he met a daft fairground girl, white-headed. He was an old man now and they lay quiet in the sand dunes. The girl lay beside him like a pearly fish. She said: 'You've got this thing in the back of your neck. It'll be a diamond.'

'Have you heard tell of this, then?'

'Oh aye,' she said, 'long since. There's them with the diamond.'

'Where you from, girl? Which country?'

But she didn't seem to know.

He fettled for himself at home till his hip went and he had it done and a date fixed for the other one, but by then he was failing. He was no great age, but old for a man of his history always living in the reek of the Works. The road he'd swept was a bit of a motorway now, the chimneys all plumed with gases. In hospital he grew poorly and they sent for his children and a son came he'd not seen for years bringing a little one with him called Meg, golden-haired. Before they left, Clockie put out a calloused old hand and touched her hair. He put the hand under the hair and at the back of the neck he felt the diamond. They looked at one another.

The doctors had wanted him to have the foreign body removed on the occasion of the first operation and they were still on about it now. 'It can't be doing you any good, Grandad. Is it First War shrapnel? You're a lucky old devil.'

'I wasn't born First War,' said Clockie. 'It's said to be a diamond.'

Well, they were full of it. Clockie lay thinking of Meg.

''Ere,' he said late one night, 'Nurse. Tell them OK. I'll have it done. They can take out the diamond when I'm under the knife for the hip. They tell me it's but a matter of lifting it off. Now then, if it does turn out to be a diamond, it's to be for Meg. She'll not need it, she's got her own. But you're to tell her I said.'

The surgeons laughed their heads off. One said he'd once had a patient with a tin of Harpic stuck up his bum. They put off the hip for a week until the big man could come down from Newcastle.

'Let's have another look at the little lass,' said Clockie and when she was brought he sent her father out and said: 'Meg, you and I are old friends. What's this behind the curtains?'

And she said: 'It's a diamond.'

'That's right,' said Clockie, 'you'll be grand. You'll always be grand, girl. You and me, Meg, we know the ropes of living and dying. We're safe, girl.'

The next day they did the hip successfully and nipped out the diamond from the back of the neck and they killed him of course.

The thing rattled into the kidney dish, a vast great lump of glass. They all went mad. One doctor who was South African said he'd

111

seen many an uncut diamond but never one as fine as this. The great man said: 'You know, this could be a diamond.'

Then Clockie began to die and it was all hands to the pump and in the midst of the red alerts going out, and Clockie going out, a soft young nurse (she was an Armitage) cleared away the kidney-dish and washed the diamond down the sluice. It was a wide-lipped sluice without a grille and so the diamond was taken straight down into the Middlesbrough sewers and then far away out into the North Sea where it is likely to be washing around for ever.

When she was told of her grandfather's death, Meg put her face in the back of his chair to savour the nice salt smell of him. She put her thumb in her mouth and the other hand she wound round to the back of her neck to make sure of the diamond.

Headless

---◆---

Brian Aldiss

BRIAN ALDISS has just completed the versification of all the poems of Makhtumkuli, the Central Asian poet. His own poems, *At the Caligula Hotel*, were published by Sinclair-Stevenson earlier this year. He is busy writing *The Twinkling of an Eye*, a compendium of life. He lives in Oxford.

A vast crowd was gathering to see Flammerion behead himself. The TV people and Flammerion had rehearsed almost everything so that the event would go without a hitch. It was estimated that some 1.8 billion people would be watching: the largest TV audience since the nuking of North Korea.

Some people preferred to watch the event live. Seats in the stadium, highly priced, were booked months in advance.

Among the privileged were Alan Ibrox Kumar and his wife, Dorothea Kumar, the Yakaphrenia Lady. They discussed it as they flew in to Düsseldorf.

'Why is he giving all the proceeds to Children of Turkmenistan, for heaven's sake?' Alan demanded.

'The terrible earthquake . . . Surely you remember?'

'I remember, yes, yes. But Flammerion's European, isn't he?'

For answer, she said: 'Get me another gin, will you?' She had yet to reveal to him she was divorcing him directly after the beheading.

The Swedish Royal family had reserved two seats in a back row. They felt that Sweden should be represented at what was increasingly regarded – by the media at any rate – as an important event. The Swedish Government remained furious that their offer of a prominent site in Stockholm had been turned down by Flammerion's agent.

Fortunately, six Swedes, two of them women, had since

volunteered to behead themselves, either in Stockholm or preferably Uppsala. They had named the charities they preferred.

Dr Eva Berger had booked a seat in the stadium on the day the box office opened. She had counselled Flammerion, advising against his drastic action on health grounds. When she realized she was unable to deflect him from his purpose, she begged him that at least a percentage of the proceeds go towards the Institute of Psychoanalysts. Flammerion had replied: 'I am offering you my psychiatric example. What else do you want? Don't be greedy.'

Later, Dr Berger had sold her seat for nineteen times the amount she had paid for it. She felt her integrity had paid off.

Dr Berger's feckless nephew, Leigh, happened to be a cleaner in the Düsseldorf stadium. 'Thank God I'm not on duty tonight,' he said. 'There'll be one hell of a mess. Blood everywhere.'

'That's what the public pay for,' said his boss. 'Blood has a whole vast symbolism behind it. It's not just a red liquid, son. You've heard of bad blood, and princes of the blood, and blood boiling, or things done in cold blood, haven't you? We've got a whole mythology on our hands, no less, tonight. And I need you to do an extra shift.'

Leigh looked hangdog and asked what they would do with the head when Flammerion had finished with it.

His boss told him it would be auctioned at Sotheby's in London.

Among those who were making money from the event was Cynthia Saladin. She had sold her story to the media worldwide. Most people on the globe were conversant with what Cynthia and Flammerion had done in bed. Cynthia had tried her best to entertain, and was now married to a Japanese businessman. Her book, *Did Circumcision Start Flammy Going Funny?*, had been rushed into print, and was available everywhere.

Flammerion was passably good-looking. Commentators remarked on the numbers of ugly men who had bought seats in the stadium. Among their numbers were Monty Wilding, the British film director whose face had been likened to a wrinkled plastic bag. Monty was boasting that his exploitation-flick, *Trouble Ahead*, was already at the editing stage.

The Green Party protested against the movie, and about the self-execution, claiming that it was worse than a blood-sport and would undoubtedly start a trend. British sportsmen, too, were up in arms. The beheading clashed with the evening of the Cup Final replay. F. A. IN HEAD-OFF COLLISION ran the headline in the *Sun*.

There were others in Britain equally incensed by what was taking place on the Continent. Among them were those who remained totally ignorant of the whereabouts of Turkmenistan.

As so often in times of trouble, people turned towards their solicitors, the Archbishop of Canterbury and Nick Ross for consolation – not necessarily in that order.

The Archbishop delivered a fine sermon on the subject, reminding the congregation that Jesus had given His life that we might live, and that that 'we' included the common people of England as well as the Tory party. Now here was another young man, Borgo Flammerion, prepared to give up his life for the suffering children of Central Asia – if that indeed was where Turkmenistan was situated.

It was true, the Archbishop continued, that Christ had not permitted Himself to be crucified before the television cameras, but that was merely an unfortunate accident of timing. The few witnesses of the Crucifixion whose words had come down to us were notoriously unreliable. Indeed, it was possible (as much must be readily admitted) that the whole thing was a cock-and-bull story. Had Christ postponed the event by a millennium or two, photography would have provided a reliable testament to His self-sacrifice, and then perhaps everyone in Britain would believe in Him, instead of just a lousy nine per cent.

Meanwhile, the Archbishop concluded, we should all pray for Flammerion, that the deed he contemplated be achieved without pain.

Visibly put out by this address, the British Prime Minister made an acid retort in the House of Commons on the following day. She said, amid general laughter, that at least *she* was not losing her head. She added that the Archbishop of Canterbury should ignore what went on in Europe and look to her own parish. Why, a murder had taken place in Canterbury just the previous month. Whatever might or might not be happening in Düsseldorf, one thing was certain: Great Britain was pulling out of recession.

This much-applauded speech was delivered only hours before Flammerion performed in public.

A s the stadium began to fill, bands played solemn music and old Beatles hits. Coachloads of French people of all sexes arrived. The French took particular interest in 'L'Evénement Flammerion', claiming the performer to be of French descent, although born in St Petersburg of a Russian mother. This statement had irritated elements of the American press, who pointed out that there was a St Petersburg in Florida, too.

A belated move was afoot to have Flammerion extradited to Florida to be legally executed for Intended Suicide, now a capital offence.

The French, undeterred, filled the press with long articles of analysis, under such headings as FLAMMY: EST-IL PÉDALE? T-shirts, depicting the hero with head and penis missing, were selling well.

The country which gained most from the event was Germany. Already a soap was running on TV called *Kopf Kaputt*, about an amusing Bavarian family, all of whom were busy buying chain-saws with which to behead each other. Some viewers read a political message into *Kopf Kaputt*.

Both the Red Cross and the Green Crescent paraded round the stadium. They had already benefited enormously from the publicity. The Green Crescent ambulances were followed by lorries on which lay young Turkmen victims of the earthquake in blood-stained bandages. They were cheered to the echo. All told, a festival air prevailed.

Behind the scenes, matters were almost as noisy. Gangs of well-wishers and autograph hunters queued for a sight of their hero. In another bunch stood professional men and women who hoped, even at this late hour, to dissuade Flammerion from his fatal act. Any number of objections to the act were raised. Among these objections were the moral repulsiveness of the act itself, its effect on children, the fact that Cynthia still loved her man, the fear of a riot should Flammerion's blade miss its mark, and the question whether the act was possible as Flammerion proposed it. Among the agitated objectors were cutlers, eager to offer a sharper blade.

None of these people, no priest, no sensation-seeker, no surgeon offering to replace the head immediately it was severed, was allowed into Flammerion's guarded quarters.

Borgo Flammerion sat in an office chair, reading a copy of the *Russian Poultry Dealer's Monthly*. As a teenager, he had lived on a poultry farm. Earning promotion, he had worked for a while in the slaughterhouse before emigrating to Holland, where he had robbed a patisserie.

He was dressed in a gold lamé blouson jacket, sable tights, and lace-up boots. His head was shaven: he had taken advice on this.

On the table before him lay a brand new cleaver, especially sharpened by a man from Geneva, a representative of the Swiss company which had manufactured the instrument. Flammerion glanced at this cleaver every so often, as he read about a startling new method of egg-retrieval. Figures on his digital watch writhed towards the hour of eight.

Behind him stood a nun, Sister Madonna, his sole companion in these last days. She was chosen because she had once made a mistaken pilgrimage to Ashkhabad, capital of Turkmenistan, believing she was travelling to Allahabad in India.

At a signal from the Sister, Flammerion closed his periodical. Rising, he took up the cleaver. He walked up the stairs with firm tread, to emerge into the dazzle of floodlights.

An American TV announcer dressed in a blood-red gown said sweetly: 'If your immediate viewing plans do not include decapitation this evening, may we advise you to look away for a few minutes.'

When the applause died, Flammerion took up a position between the chalk marks.

He bowed without smiling. When he whirled the cleaver to his right side, the blade glittered in the lights. The crowd fell silent as death.

Flammerion brought the blade up sharply, so that it sliced from throat to nape-of-neck. His head fell cleanly away from his body.

He remained standing for a moment, letting the cleaver drop from his grasp.

The stadium audience was slow to applaud. But all had gone exceptionally well, considering that Flammerion had had no proper rehearsal.

Twenty Years

———————⟡———————

Doris Lessing

DORIS LESSING was born in Persia in 1919. Her first novel, *The Grass is Singing*, was published in 1949. Since then, she has published novels, stories and plays. She has been awarded many prizes and has been shortlisted for the Booker Prize three times. In August 1991, she received the honorary title of Distinguished Fellow in Literature in the School of English and American Studies conferred by the University of East Anglia.

A large room – no, more of a small hall ... decorated with too much plaster pressed into shapes reminiscent of moulded puddings touched with gold ... far too many people standing upright each holding a glass while fitting 'bite-sized' canapés into their mouths and making conversation ... what is this? A cocktail party, and no one here had not said earlier: 'Oh God, I'll have to drop in for at least half an hour.' Now they glanced about over their interlocutors' heads, to see who else was there who should be spoken to or at least noticed. They tried not to look at their watches for they were off to restaurants or – much too late – to homes in suburbs or even other towns. An office party, and it was to celebrate half a century's existence of a firm, an occasion important enough to merit this illustrious hotel.

There were a couple of chairs in a corner, and in these people sank for a few moments to rest their feet and gather their forces.

One woman had settled there for rather longer, perhaps fifteen minutes, and she was staring in at the crowd. Not easy to keep one person in view, heads kept intervening, shoulders; and sometimes for a whole minute or two the person she seemed to be concentrating on was hidden from her. But she sat on, sure of her intention.

She was different from most of them there, not only because she was older. She was fifty? A young sixty? She wore – well, she was elegant enough, and fresh, for she had not spent all day working in an office.

The man she intermittently kept in view was middle-aged, handsome in a well-worn way, and was probably something in a design department. His clothes insisted on individuality – dark green jacket, a black silk polo-neck.

The crowd was thinning a bit, people slipping away, hoping to be unnoticed. Now she could see him and she looked steadily at him, and with a frown. Had he noticed her? He had glanced at her once, twice, but went on talking to the man in front of him, and again looked past him, in her direction. His thoughtful look was not unlike hers, but it had in it something of affront or even grievance. He turned himself about deliberately so he stood four-square to her, and their eyes met, and while they looked long at each other neither tried to conceal it. She remained where she was, not frowning now, but not smiling either. After a few moments when he might easily – it seemed – simply walk away, he took some large strides through a by now sparse crowd and stood over her.

'Well,' said he, 'this is certainly not where I'd expect to see you.'

'I don't see why not?'

Again, he might easily have taken off, but he sat down in the other chair. A waitress was circulating with wine, garnet and yellow, and she took a white wine, he a red.

'Twenty years?' she enquired finely, but with something like a grimace.

'I suppose it can't be far off twenty years.'

The way they were looking at each other now denied the twenty years.

Yet they were wary, he more than her. On guard. Noting this, she smiled. Deliberately.

'What are you expecting? Surely not that I am going to throw my wine in your face?' And she laughed.

'*You* throw . . .' He was genuinely astonished. And accusing.

'I've often enough wanted to – well, something of the kind. Much worse, if you must know . . . like killing you, for instance.'

But now, as if for the benefit of an imaginary spectator, he demonstrated male reaction to female irrationality, with a dropped jaw, raised brows, an, as it were, detached quizzicality.

'*You* kill *me*,' he merely let drop, with a cold smile.

'Well, it did wear off, but there's quite a residue of . . . I don't think time does soften all that much, not really.'

And now his face lost its deliberate theatricality. He was serious. He examined her. Then he drank half his wine, shook his head in a way that might have meant, sour wine this! – put the glass back on a passing tray.

'Anyone would think,' said he, 'that there was something you have to forgive me.'

At this it was her turn to direct at him a derisive laugh that matched his earlier theatricality.

There was something here that didn't fit, and both could see it, and were prepared to show they could see it.

'I waited for you all day,' he said at last, deliberate. 'I was sitting in the garden of that bloody hotel all day. And then I came back after dinner and stayed till midnight. Waiting. It was raining.'

She shifted her legs about, seemed to reject what he said, might have got up and walked away, on an impulse that definitely was as much from the past as from present discordance. She sighed . . . 'And I waited for you. I didn't go away at all. I stayed until midnight. Then I took a room in the hotel and woke up at five in the morning. I waited. In the garden, where we said. It was not raining.'

He laughed, short and angry.

She laughed: the same.

'You haven't changed,' said she, irritable.

'You are suggesting I didn't wait all day and half the night for you?'

'As it happens yes, that is what I am suggesting.'

'Oh for God's *sake*,' he exploded, and she smiled, lips compressed, in a way he recognized, for in a crescendo of anger he said, 'You certainly haven't changed. You never gave me credit for anything.'

'Just as well then that we didn't manage to make the same place, the same time.'

And now their eyes blazed up with regret, and a far from dead emotion.

'Oh *no*,' she began, and gathered herself to get up and go. He put out a hand to hold her. She subsided, looking at the large but fine

125

hand that gripped her bare forearm. She shut her eyes, holding her breath.

'My God,' he said, softly.

'Yes,' she said.

Then his hand fell lingeringly off her arm, and both sighed.

'I heard you were married,' she remarked.

'And of course you were.'

'Why of course?'

He let that pass. 'We have both been married,' he summed up, lips tight and amused – life's like that.

'I *am* married.'

'I suppose I am, really,' he confessed.

'How like you,' she accused, with bitterness.

'Oh no, not like that, you're wrong, as it happens it is she who . . . but never mind.'

'No, never mind,' she said.

'Children?'

'Two,' she said. 'The girl is sixteen. The boy, fifteen.'

'Grown up,' he said. 'And I have three. Three girls. A houseful of women.'

'Just your style,' she said, but quite amiably. She laughed. Not unamiably.

'So what did happen that day?' he enquired, achieving an amused detachment.

'That far off day.'

'Not so far off, evidently,' he said, and again their eyes blazed up at each other.

By now they were almost alone in the room, and the last guests, looking back, noticed these two, locked in their intensity.

One woman actually laughed and shrugged, worldly and envious, indicating the couple to her companion. A man. He grimaced.

'I waited for you,' he insisted.

'Really?'

'Yes, really. Why should you doubt it?'

She thought seriously about this. Then: 'I doubt it because – I waited so long. And because – well, it seemed all of a pattern with . . .'

'Really? It really did? And what had I ever done to make you think
... I adored you,' he accused her. Fierce. Intimate, his face near
hers. 'You knew that.'

'Then why ...?'

'*I was there*,' he said.

She shut her eyes. She sat, eyes closed, and there were tears on
her lashes.

He groaned, seeing them.

She opened her eyes. 'Then it was the wrong day. We got the day
wrong.'

'Certainly not the wrong hotel,' he said. 'No.'

'I can't go past that hotel now without feeling sick.'

'No. In fact I don't go near it.'

'The Green Swan?'

'The Green Swan.'

'Then why didn't you telephone me?' he asked.

'Because – it was the last straw,' she said. 'Why didn't you ring
me?'

'But I did. I rang twice. Then I thought, to hell with her.'

'You did ring me?' she said derisively, but with what seemed like
hope that it was true.

'Yes, I did.'

She snarled prettily. 'Well, water under bridges.' She got up, and
now he didn't stop her. Perhaps she had expected him to. He
watched her stand there hesitating. He looked at her bare brown
forearm, as if he still had it in his grasp. Then he stood up.

'I don't think I feel that,' he said. A proposition.

She shook her head slightly, teeth gripping her lower lip.

She walked towards the exit: walked clumsily – blind.

He followed just behind her. 'Darling,' he said, in a low voice.

She shook her head and walked on, fast.

'You bloody fool,' he heard her say, softly, wildly, accusing. 'You
poor bloody fool.'

And he said, 'You mean, you don't believe I was there? Ah, poor
darling, poor darling.'

But she had gone. He was now the last guest in the room, ignored
by the waitresses who were tidying up. They were all aware of him,

though, and he realized they knew something had happened, had been watching them. We must have been putting on quite a show, she and I, he thought.

Quickly he walked out of the big room, through corridors, and then out of a side door of the hotel into a street that was dark, lights blurred because of rain. He stood on the pavement, his back to the hotel. There was no one in the street. Then a young woman came through the rain towards him, under a black umbrella, which hid her face. As he had done then, all those years ago, he stared: Is it she? Has she come at last? But she went on past him, and he turned his attention to the end of the street where she had come from. He stared as he had done then, through grey shrouds of rain. No one came, no one. And he went on standing there in the shabby street, while bitterness filled his throat and it seemed to him the twenty years still to be lived through were empty years, and because she had not come that day her absence had shadowed his life, forbidding him all love, all joy. He could not face what he still had to live through, and it was her fault . . .

Then, suddenly, he thought, I bet she isn't standing somewhere in the rain grieving for me. She hasn't given me a thought. When did she ever care a damn about me – not really . . . here I am standing here like a dolt thinking about her and she . . .

A clean and cold bitterness jolted him like electricity, and he walked briskly away to his own life full of the energy of decision.

Legacy

❖•◆•❖

Frank Ronan

FRANK RONAN's first novel, *The Men Who Loved Evelyn Cotton*, won the 1989 Irish Times/Aer Lingus Irish Literature Prize and was followed by *A Picnic in Eden* and *The Better Angel*. He edited *In My Garden*, a collection of Christopher Lloyd's *Country Life* articles. His most recent novel is *Dixie Chicken*. He is working on a novel and has just completed a collection of stories, *Handsome Men Are Slightly Sunburnt*.

The money came through on Friday, seven months after it was expected. Reasons had been given all along, and, towards the end, reasons had regressed until, in Virgil's ears, they were spoken with the thin sound of excuses. But you cannot expect a solicitor to acquit himself by declaring his own incompetence, and he had tied himself to Virgil's cause by promises made from one week to another; by spinning a thread of hope so ingenious that you could not help but feel he was a clever man, and it was only afterwards that Virgil came to the just conclusion that, had the solicitor used in the cause of the legacy one-tenth of the energy he had expended in dissimulation, the matter could have been cleared up by early summer.

God, Virgil told himself, not for the first time, moves in mysterious ways. He told himself this small and hackneyed truth, this get-out clause of put-upon believers, as though it had the profundity of an original revelation. The phrase was one of his greatest comforts, repeated often during his favourite pastime of marking remarkable lines in the Bible with multi-coloured highlighting pens. God's mysteriousness had provided him with the time to reconsider his attitude to money: pursuing this money had led him, for the first time in his life, into real poverty.

The plan, to begin with, had been simple: half the money was destined for worthy charities such as the sending of Bibles in Serbo-Croat to needy Bosnian refugees, and the other half to the establishment of himself as a missionary in the jungles of Brazil. Indeed, his first act on hearing the news of his father's death had been to buy himself a set of tapes which would teach him Portuguese in seven weeks. There was no reference to redemption in the language course, and that had troubled him for an hour or two, until he came to his senses and chided himself for his lack of faith. The words were not important. His faith would shine through and do the work for him.

He was not badly worried by losing his job in the middle of June. The money, his solicitor told him, was imminent, and the redundancy would give him extra time for study and prayer before he flew to Rio. If anything, he was relieved that he would no longer have to defend his profession to the other young turks at his church. There were some among them who considered paste-and-cutting for a tabloid newspaper to be a morally out-rageous occupation. These whited sepulchres did tend to be those who served God on social security, but Virgil had never pointed that out to them, knowing something of the practice of true humility and charity.

The bank had tired of his overdraft and promises some time in September; his landlord had been threatening eviction from October on and, throughout November, baked beans and pasta had been his locusts and honey, and the lack of heating in the flat made it a desert for him. Every morning he thanked God for the humbling experience (no doubt designed by God so that Virgil would have some understanding of the exigencies of his future flock) before crossing the road to the phone box to see if the money was through yet. The days took on a meditative rhythm, as he coloured in the few blank passages of his Bible, in the gaps between the Australian soaps. The evenings were not a problem. There was usually an evangelical meeting somewhere in South London and the long walks there and back were good for the soul.

The day before the money came through, the offices of the organization which sent Bibles to Bosnia were raided by the fraud squad and a personal friend of Virgil's was arrested. Virgil took this as a sign from God, said a prayer for the blackened soul of his friend, and hoped that he himself wasn't mentioned in the organization's records. He was shocked by his own naïvety and decided to do something about it. A man who saw goodness in everything would not last long in Brazil. He decided to spend his first evening of wealth in the West End, observing sinners in action.

Soho seemed a likely place to start. He pinned his money into his pocket with safety pins and took the Northern Line to Leicester Square. It was still the afternoon, but already he felt out of place walking down Old Compton Street in his waxed jacket and corduroys. He decided that his first investment should be in clothing which blended him into the crowd a little more. He found a respectable-looking shop, the window of which was not festooned with leather brassières and, heady at the prospect of spending money for the first time since June, entered.

By practising the shop assistant's art, the assistant made him feel about six inches tall within three minutes. He couldn't find the price tags on the clothes and was too embarrassed to ask, knowing also that with the amount of money he had in his pocket a few pounds either way wouldn't make any difference. He chose some black things with DOLCE E GABANA written across the front of them in large white letters, such as he had seen the other young men in the street wearing. Black suited him, he told himself. It was rather priestly, in fact, and wouldn't go to waste. It was a shock to him that, once he was wearing the new outfit, with his old clothes bagged on the counter, the amount of money asked by the assistant was as much as he had in his pocket. But there was no turning back without a loss of face, and he paid and left the shop, muttering the Lord's Prayer to himself to stem the feeling of inexplicable elation as he searched for a cash machine.

Finding a den of sin was not as easy as he had expected. The bars he went into were full of clean good-looking young men who seemed to have nothing but goodwill to express to each other. Indeed, some of them were openly embracing in much the way that he and his friends embraced at church meetings. And some of them wore large silver crosses around their necks. Unused to drink, by eight o'clock Virgil had begun to speculate whether the people he was encountering were not very much like him. He fell into conversation with a lad of his own age in a bar called Crews, who said that he was a model and who, within ten minutes, had told Virgil that he liked him very much, and Virgil felt confident enough to talk about the legacy, which was an opening for the young man to say how broke he was, and Virgil said that that was fine. He had enough money for both of them, if the other would consent to show him round.

Mark, which was the name of his new friend, put the seal on Virgil's confidence when he replied to this request by saying that they were all going to heaven. It wasn't until much later, when they were actually in the place, that Virgil realized Heaven was a nightclub, but by then he was too drunk and full of goodwill to care.

He was smiling and looking round him at the thick crowd of whooping, grinning men, embracing and dancing together. There was no sign of any sin that he recognized. There were, admittedly, a few girls in suspiciously erotic clothing, but since the men seemed to be taking no notice of them, the atmosphere was not spoiled by their presence. Mark seemed to know half the people there, and introduced him freely. Virgil said something about being part of a new community, but he was slurring, and the music was loud, and his remark went unnoticed. Then Mark urgently asked him for thirty quid and disappeared through the crowd once it was in his hand. When he returned he handed Virgil what looked like an aspirin, and took one himself.

'I was beginning to have a bit of a headache,' Virgil said. 'Thanks.'

He wondered about asking what the thirty quid had been for, but Mark had started to dance and it seemed a churlish and mean question. He felt the music come at him, not through his ears, but across the floor and up his legs, and the next thing he knew he was holding on to Mark, feeling an incredible welling of affection for all the world. Mark asked him if the White Dove had come up yet, and that was when he knew he was full of the Spirit.

'I love London,' he said. 'I never knew all this was going on, under my nose. God moves, God moves. God moves something – you know what I mean.'

Mark agreed and said it was a good one, and told him to take deep breaths.

A week later, when he caught the plane to Rio, Mark came with him. He still had vague missionary intentions, but Copacobana seemed more comfortable than the jungle, so they stayed there. There was Mark's soul to be saved first of all, and money to burn.

Not Shown

Penelope Fitzgerald

PENELOPE FITZGERALD was born in Lincoln in 1916 and brought up in Sussex and London. Four of her novels have been listed for the Booker Prize, which she won in 1978 for *Offshore*. Her latest one, due out in 1995, is *The Blue Flower*. She finds novels hard to write, but short stories much harder.

Lady P lived at Tailfirst, which was not shown to the public. Fothergill was the resident administrator, or dogsbody, at Tailfirst Farm, which was shown 1 April to end October, Mon, Wed, Sat; no coach-parties, no backpackers, guide dogs by arrangement, WC, small shop. It was the old Home Farm, sympathetically rebuilt in red brick between 1892 and 1894 by Philip Webb (a good example of his later manner), the small herb and lavender garden possibly suggested by Gertrude Jekyll. The National Trust had steadfastly refused to take it over; still, they can make mistakes, like the rest of us.

'Now Fothergill, as to the room stewards,' said Lady P, returning with frighteningly renewed energies from the Maldives.

'The ladies . . .'

'The Trust calls them room stewards . . .'

'Two of them, of course, are your own recommendations – Mrs Feare, who was at the Old Pottery Shop until it closed, and Mrs Twine, who was dinner lady at the village school.'

'Until *that* closed. Faithful souls both.'

'I'm sure they are, and that is my great difficulty.'

'Don't confuse yourself with detail. I don't see any difficulty. You must treasure Twine and Feare, and dispense with Mrs Horrabin.'

'I should very much like to do that,' said Fothergill.

Lady P looked at him sharply. 'I'm told in the village that you only engaged her last Wednesday. Now, in any group of employees, and perhaps particularly with low-paid employees, a dominating figure creates discord.'

'Do you know Mrs Horrabin well, Lady P?' asked Fothergill.

'Of course not. I've been obliged to meet her, I think twice, on my Recreation Committee. She comes from the industrial estate at Battisford, as you ought to know.'

'I do know it.'

'You don't look well, you know, Fothergill. When you came into the room I thought, the man doesn't look well. Are you still worrying about anything?'

He collected himself for a moment. 'In what way am I to get rid of Mrs Horrabin?'

'I'm sure you don't want me to tell you how to do your job,' said Lady P.

'I do want you to tell me.'

Fothergill lived in one of the attics (not shown) at the Farm, on a salary so small that it was difficult to see how he had survived for the past year. Undoubtedly there was something not quite right about him, or by the time he was fifty-six – if that was his real age – he would be married (perhaps he had been), and he would certainly by now have found some better employment. Lady P, who found it better in every way not to leave such things to her husband, had drafted the advertisement, which was specifically aimed at applicants with something not quite right about them, who would come cheap: 'Rent-free accommodation, remote, peaceful situation, ample free time, suit writer.' Fothergill wasn't a writer, but then he soon discovered there wasn't much free time either.

'I do want you to tell me,' he repeated.

He had known very little about architecture when he came, nothing about tile hanging, weather boarding, lead box-guttering or late Victorian electrical fittings, and he had never heard of Philip Webb. He learned these things between maintaining the garden, the very old Land Rover and the still older petrol mower. But the home-made fudge and home-made damson cordial were manufactured and supplied by a Pakistani-owned firm in Sheffield, no trouble there and, to his surprise, Mrs Feare and Mrs Twine had agreed to come. 'You're a novelty for them,' said the man who came to clean out the cess-pit. It was gratifying to Fothergill to be described as a novelty.

So far there had been worryingly few visitors, but he disposed carefully of his small force. Mrs Twine couldn't stand for too long, and was best off in the dining-room where there was a solid table to lean against; on the other hand, she was sharper than Mrs Feare, who let people linger in the conservatory and nick the tomatoes.

Mrs Feare was more at home in the shop with the fudge and postcards, and her ten-year-old-old son biked up after school to work out the day's VAT on his calculator. Mrs Twine also fancied herself in the shop, but had no son to offer. Fothergill hurried about between the garden, the white-painted drawing-room and the cash-desk. Each day solved itself, by closing time, without complaints. A remote, peaceful situation.

Mrs Horrabin had driven up to the front door of the Farm at 9 a.m. last Tuesday. To avoid shouting out of the bedroom window he had come downstairs, unbarred, unlocked and opened. 'The house is not shown today, madam. Can I help you at all?'

'We'll see,' said Mrs Horrabin.

Hugely, beigely, she got out of her Sunny, and with a broad white smile told him her name.

'I've decided to take over here.'

'I'm afraid there are no vacancies.'

'Shirley Twine won't be coming back after the end of this week.'

'She said nothing . . .'

'She'll take a hint.'

'Mrs Feare . . .'

'I'll give her a hint as well. They won't either of them break their heart over it, they can get another little job easily enough.' She stared at him boldly and unpeaceably. 'Some can, some can't.'

Although from long habit Fothergill pretended not to understand her, he was in no way surprised. He was pretty sure he had never met Mrs Horrabin before, but that didn't mean that through one of life's thousand unhappy coincidences she might not know something unacceptable about him. He had lived in so many places, and so often left them in a hurry.

'Didn't you once work as a credit manager in Basingstoke?' she asked now. 'An uncle of mine lives there.'

She belonged to the tribe of torturers. Why pretend that they don't exist?

'You have it in mind,' he said, 'to take away my last chance.'

Mrs Horrabin ignored this. 'I know what's wrong with this place. You've got these two old boilers standing in the corners of the rooms and they make people afraid to come in at all. In any case they don't particularly want to look at what's on show, they want to have a good poke around. They want to see the bedrooms and the john.'

In default of a decent piece of rope Fothergill had placed a handwritten card, PRIVATE, on the front stairs. Mrs Horrabin actually trod on it – visitors wearing stiletto heels not admitted – on her way up. In rage and disgust he followed her into the never-used, pomegranate-papered front bedroom where, marching in, she dragged down the blinds.

'It isn't necessary to restrict the light in here,' he said, clinging to his professional status, 'there are no watercolours.'

'I like them down. Just for half an hour or so.'

She sat down on the double bed, whose box-springs reverberated, and took off her jacket. She was wearing a very low-necked blouse, with machine embroidery. 'I don't believe you know what to do next,' she said.

Fothergill cried, 'It's only twenty past nine in the morning.' It was not quite what he had meant to say. He went on, 'You're making a grotesque mistake.'

'Well, perhaps I am, we'll have to see,' said Mrs Horrabin. 'At least, though, you've got your own teeth. You can't go wrong about that, you can always catch the gleam of dentures. Anyway, the choice isn't so wide round here.'

But from her great beige bag, which she had never so far left hold of, a loud monotonous chirp began, like a demented pipit.

'That'll be Mr Horrabin outside in your drive.' She opened the bag and took out her Ownphone. 'Tweety calling Bub . . .'

'Your husband knows you are here?'

'He always knows where I am. He isn't against my enjoying myself, he stretches a point there, but he likes to feel included.'

'Included in what way?'

'He's an area salesman for alternative medicines . . . He wants me at home, it seems, so I'm letting you off for this morning . . . But I'll be back tomorrow. We'll be able to manage quite well between us.'

He shouted, 'You have robbed me of Mrs Feare and Mrs Twine, you have taken away my peace of mind, and what's worse I find you completely unattractive.' Or perhaps he had never said the words aloud, since Mrs Horrabin was standing self-approvingly in front of the cheval glass, with the calm smile of the powerful, smoothing down the shoulders of her jacket.

While Fothergill allowed himself to think backwards into the trap of his mind, Lady P had been talking on, passing to many other topics, and now gracefully returned. He mustn't blame himself too much, she said, for the disappointing figures. Apart from the fact that they didn't do teas, the great drawback was that nothing interesting had ever happened at Tailfirst Farm. Not a murder, she didn't mean that, although it would certainly create interest, but perhaps some sad and unexpected accident . . . She laughed a little, to show that a joke was intended, but saw that Fothergill had been quite prepared to agree with her. He hasn't much spirit, she thought. Probably he never thinks much about anything except keeping his job.

The Beetle

A. L. Barker

A. L. BARKER left school when she was sixteen and joined the BBC after the Second World War. Her début collection of short stories, *Innocents*, won the first Somerset Maugham Prize in 1947, and her novel, *John Brown's Body*, was shortlisted for the Booker Prize in 1969. She is the author of eleven novels and eight collections of short stories.

He had become a voyeur. What else could you call it, the way he spied on people, watched the casual motion of their thighs, the roll of their hips, watched the probing steps of old women and the staggering babies – before you know it, their mothers said, they'd be running all over the place – he watched and envied the very dogs and cats – oh cats, synchronized and svelte!

When it struck he was signing a cheque, not a big one, not shocking, just the same old cheque he signed every week for the petty cash account. The world suddenly went liquid, like the bottom of a murky pond. He lay sprawled across his desk until his secretary came to find out why he wasn't answering the phone.

'What's the matter with me?' he asked the first available doctor.

'You've had a stroke.'

He wasn't a stroke subject: didn't smoke, drank in moderation, at forty years old weighed just 154 pounds, no cholesterol problem, was acknowledged the demon bowler for his club's First XI and could run a man out before the crack of his ball had ceased echoing round the field.

'You have high blood pressure, Mr Mallory.'

'Just get it down in time for my cricket club's jubilee match next month. They're counting on me.'

'I'm afraid that's totally unrealistic. The human organism does not scruple to present the most undesirable and ignoble aspects of things as they really are.' The doctor's smile was wintry. 'You suffered a leak into a parietal cavity and some brain cells have been destroyed, with consequent partial paralysis. Badly damaged cells cannot recover, others less affected may take over their functions, and this process could continue for a long time.'

'How long?'

'Months, years.'

Mallory was not accustomed to being regarded with pity. 'What are you trying to tell me?'

'It is too early to say what degree of motive power will be restored, but an active man like yourself learns new ways of dealing with his disability. I should warn you that total recovery is rare. However, there are always exceptions. One should never give up hope.'

Having reduced the odds, the doctor's smile warmed slightly.

Mallory, nursing a dead arm and a petrified leg, rejected the optimism and cheery quips of well-intentioned friends.

Team-mates, coming to visit, slapped him gingerly on the shoulder. 'Don't worry, old boy, when those gorgeous physiotherapists get their hands on you you'll be up and doing again in no time.'

Mallory said: 'I don't need – physiotherapists, I need a Frankenstein.'

Chrissie, bless her (he did, for where would he be without her?) rose to the occasion, in fact she frothed to it. Eagerness was her failing. It tended to conceal her virtues: generosity, compassion, fidelity, a pure and open heart. Mallory, who was on a short fuse, fighting to retrieve some measure of independence, felt humiliated every time she rushed to take over the minimal tasks he used to do for himself.

Grimly fumbling with the buttons of his shirt, he found anarchy in his hands: his left consistently undoing what his right had just done up. He sweated – with rage was it, or weakness? – and cursed aloud at the squalor and pettiness.

Chrissie came running. 'Darling, let me . . .'

He held her off. 'When I want help I'll ask for it.'

'You don't have to ask me . . .'

'Yours or anyone's.'

The Beetle

The superstition that if you prepare for the worst it won't happen also served to shield Mallory's infinitely precious, intensely vulnerable conviction that he *would* walk and run again. Why else should he dream, vividly and often, that he was springing across the field, rubbers squeaking on damp grass, progressing from A to B without effort or need of it, simply by the God-given right to put one foot before the other?

The conviction was real enough to get him out of his chair and try. He stood for a moment, gripping the table which was set for lunch. His leg suddenly gave like a dry twig and down he went, landing on his back. Savage, he snatched at the tablecloth. Chrissie found him under a welter of knives and forks and fell to her knees crying, 'Geoff – darling, what are you doing?'

'Can't you see what I'm doing? I'm relaying the table. Now stop asking damn fool questions and help me up.'

She took him to Sainsbury's for a change of scene. Wheeling him in his chair he wondered if she might be evincing the sort of pride she had never actually been able to claim.

The cheese aisle of Sainsbury's resounded to the screams of children denied chocolate and crisps.

'Why do brutish infants abound in plague proportions in supermarkets?'

'I wish you wouldn't say such things!'

He clapped his hands over his ears. 'Just get the bloody cheese and let's get out of here!'

Sitting in the garden on a warm sunny evening you'd think he'd be relaxed and happy. Beside him, Chrissie was weeding, grubbing among the deadnettles and ground elder. She hadn't been able to find her gardening gloves and the thought of her nails filling with earth disgusted him. A fringe of long grass stood up round the beds; the first thing he used to do was trim the edges so that it looked a finished job by the time he had mowed the lawn.

Chrissie kneeled, something he couldn't do, sat on her heels, and he was filled with an almost murderous envy. She turned to him.

'Geoff?'

149

'Just admiring the view from the rear,' he said bitterly.

She rose from her knees. She had something in her hands and brought it to him. 'Look.' It was a big beetle with feelers that twitched inquiringly. 'Isn't it wonderful? Such shining armour!'

'It's ugly!'

'Darling . . .'

'Take it away. You know I can't bear bugs! Oh God . . .' His hand went to his ribcage where his heart was supposed to be.

Moving to comfort him, she dropped the beetle. Mallory closed his eyes. There was a definite knocking in his chest. A heart murmur?

'Oh my darling . . .'

'Has it gone?'

'It's on its back, it's lost a leg.'

'Kill it! Cripples are better off dead.'

'Geoff – please. I don't know what to do when you talk like that.'

There were tears on her cheeks. The hand she put out to him wavered and fell to her side.

He sighed. 'I'm OK. See to the beetle.'

It had righted itself and was regrouping its legs. There weren't enough of them to maintain its heavy body. It fell sideways. Like me, he thought, reaching for his stick.

'Geoff!'

He positioned the ferrule end alongside the creature and waited. There was more than a bug's worth of intelligence under that carapace. Using the stick as a brace the beetle tried to pull itself upright. After several attempts it succeeded, stood on its available legs, feelers working with questing fury.

Chrissie cried: 'Darling, it's going to be all right!'

Flaps on either side of the beetle's body lifted to reveal a pair of wings. It launched itself, flew with a whirring sound into the darkness of the shrubbery.

'It's going to be all right.' He reached for her hand. 'I think it was a cockchafer.'

Rather an unpropitious name, he thought, but did not say so.

Crying in a Bucket

Christopher Hope

The Blitzerlik family had camped for the night somewhere between Lutherburg and Zwingli. The wine was going around the fire in a plastic sack, five litres of rough white they call a 'five-man-can'; an udder of intoxication. Their campfire was a solitary light on the dusty road that arrows between somewhere and nowhere in the immense darkness of the desert.

Although it was only about seven in the evening, the temperature was already below freezing, and falling. Even in autumn, Karoo nights can kill. The moon had barely risen and the stars were yet to show their blazing fury. The Southern Cross hung in the sky with a heavy, established look; important but a little silly, like a Boer among his minions.

The nomads of the Karoo, in the far Northern Cape, do not drink to forget. In order to forget you must have something to remember. They drink to dream. So when the father of the family, Old Adam Blitzerlik, tossed something in a dangerous arc through the flames, I knew as it landed beside me, with the smell of scorched string, that he was at the crossover point where one dream ends and another waits to begin.

I had their message on election day, over at the Hunters Arms in Lutherburg. The hotel was unusually packed. A dozen cops drawn from distant stations crowded the dining room in hourly relays and munched through huge T-bone steaks, before buckling on their weapons and setting off to guard the polling booths, and to patrol the town for bombs.

The hotel bar was thick with election officials, foreign monitors and even the United Nations, in the persons of Jean-Paul from Geneva and Matthias from Vienna. They usually wore their baseball caps when we got news of gun-play among the white right-wingers boycotting the election. When we had bomb threats they pulled on their loose blue waistcoats and walked up and down in front of the hotel.

Clara, the owner of the Hunters Arms, was proud of the UN presence. 'Those guys phone Geneva,' she said. 'I feel I'm back in the world.'

To celebrate she went out and bought a pair of blue bell-bottomed trousers, a gold blouse and a hair-piece that she wore on top of her thinning blonde curls in a towering beehive. She put in a formal request to Jean-Paul and Matthias to declare the Hunters Arms a UN safe haven. The UN had promised to consider its position.

The message from the Blitzerliks came to Clara in the way of messages in those parts. Someone turned up in the backyard of the Hunters Arms, stared at the sky, offered the usual compliments regarding her health, expressed the hope that hunting would be good in the springbuck season, and then abruptly told her that the Blitzerlik family had something 'to give the Englishman'.

Clara rolled her eyes and laughed in her wild barking way when she told me the message. The Blitzerlik family, being travellers, had so few possessions that everything they owned was strapped to the back of their cart, pulled by two emaciated donkeys. A tin kettle, a black three-legged pot and a 'roaster', an iron grill for cooking over the fire. The Blitzerliks were not in the giving business, said Clara. They were the sort of people you gave things to. And when you did, they boozed it away. She had watched the nomads in their carts straggle into town to vote for the first time in their lives and it made her heart bleed: 'What must they *think*? For crying in a bucket!'

Around the campfire sat Old Adam Blitzerlik, no more than thirty, too young to warrant his venerable status. His wife, Mina, looked about fifteen and she fed the fire with handfuls of wiry ashbush. Ma and Pa Blitzerlik, Adam's parents, drew heavily on their pipes, their tiny wrinkled walnut faces wrapped in heavy woollen scarves. Old Adam rolled a cigarette from a scrap of newspaper and struck a match to the bitter, black tobacco. The winebag went round again, accompanied by a single cup. Each measure judged precisely. Half a cup, left to right around the circle, to be taken at a gulp, and passed on. Stringing a necklace of cheap dreams.

Now Grandfather Blitzerlik invited me to examine the gift. Mina fed the flames with candebush and it flared as brightly as if she had doused it with paraffin. The parcel was wrapped in thick brown paper, butcher's paper, I guessed, often re-used, tied with coarse string, which showed what at first I thought was sealing wax on the knots. I realized later this was dried blood. The paper was ripped in places where Old Adam had helped himself to cigarette paper. Through the holes I glimpsed the red and black bindings of two notebooks. The cheap and serviceable notebooks you will find at any stationers in England.

Grandfather Blitzerlik, after shaking his pipe to clear the stem and spitting into the fire, began to speak in his melodious Afrikaans. I was from England, and so I would understand his story. It did not strike him as odd that he was speaking Afrikaans to an Englishman. The English were magical beings, capable of anything. Long ago had they not come to the Karoo, at the behest of their Queen, 'the old auntie with diamonds in her hair'? And did not her soldiers, in their red dresses, 'kick the Boer to Kingdom Come'?

Well, then, some years ago a white farmer had found a baby in the ruins of a camp. The sole survivor of a wandering family which had slept too close to its fire one night. The farmer, an Englishman from the Zwingli district, had taken the boy home and raised him. The boy grew up to read and speak English, the only person in a hundred miles to possess these talents. He called him Witbooi.

It happened at that time that the travelling people were suffering badly – 'crying' – at the hands of the farmers. So they had come up with a plan. Money had been collected among the nomads, from sheepshearers and jackal hunters and fence builders. And they had sent this young man, Witbooi, to England, to ask the Queen to send the red dresses back to kick the Boer to Kingdom Come! Was it not a very good plan?

A good plan, I said. And what had happened to their messenger?

Here opinions differed. Old Adam reported the rumour that the English Queen had liked this Witbooi so much she had begged him to stay in England. She had given him a farm and a thousand sheep.

Mina contradicted him flatly. Witbooi, she said, was dead; killed by savages while on his travels in England.

It did not matter what had happened, said Grandfather Blitzerlik. Perhaps, as an Englishman, I had not heard of the voting? A new world was at hand where they themselves would kick the Boer to Kingdom Come.

Best of all, said the young wife Mina, in the new world there would be free telephones. Therefore it had been decided that I should take the notebooks that Witbooi had written on his journey through England. Should I meet him I could return the notebooks to him. Or to the Queen, if I preferred.

I said I did not understand about the phones.

Old Adam gave me a pitying look. He pointed to the stars now blazing beaches of light in the black oceans above our heads. People would talk to each other, without wires, through the help of the stars. And there were more stars in the Karoo than anywhere in the world. He hoped the star phones reached England soon.

When I returned to the Hunters Arms, Clara took one look at my parcel and begged me to leave it outside in the backyard until the 'ceremony' was over. I stood the parcel on the kitchen step and she advised gloves before I opened it.

I told her about the phones. 'For crying in a bucket,' Clara said, 'don't they know that Lutherburg is on a party line – one line between thirty farms?'

Her beehive had listed to the left; a little like the Leaning Tower of Pisa. 'Who are they going to call on these star phones?' she demanded. 'Each other?'

We all went into the bar. Although the UN had declined to declare the Hunters Arms a safe haven, after negotiation it had been decided that Jean-Paul would take up a position in the window wearing his cap and his blue waistcoat. This way, any mad right-wing farmer who thought of shooting up the place would know that the UN had taken the hotel under its auspices.

The ceremony began. The official election monitors, members of Peace Committees and various foreign observers assembled in the street and while what Clara called 'our official UN party' watched through the windows, they began transferring the ballot boxes into wheelbarrows to be transported to the post office where they were to be locked up overnight before being taken to the counting station. A small setback occurred when it was discovered that the official sealing wax had vanished. Clara saved the day by giving the monitors – who had begun blaming each other – a bottle of her nail varnish. The ballot boxes were sealed with bright orange Namaqualand Blush, and the procession of barrows rolled rustily down the street and everyone clapped. Clara said it made her proud to be a South African.

When I looked for my parcel it had disappeared. Instead I found a policeman with an enormous belly, held in check by his gunbelt, on guard outside the kitchen door. I asked if he had seen my books. He demanded to know if I had left an unattended parcel on the hotel premises. Notebooks, I said. There was blood on the paper, he retorted. I was very lucky it had not been destroyed in a controlled explosion.

There was enough starlight for me to peer through the barred windows of the post office. The ballot boxes were lined up like soldiers. Beside them, a sort of lesser relation – but sealed in blood, not nail varnish – was the parcel. Waiting for morning.

Ta for the Memories

Deborah Moggach

DEBORAH MOGGACH was born in 1948, one of four girls in a family of writers. She has written ten novels, including *Porky*, *The Stand-In* and *The Ex-Wives*, and has adapted several for television. She has also written screenplays and two books of short stories. Her most recent book is *Changing Babies*, a book of short stories, and she has a new novel due out in the autumn of 1995. She lives in London with her two children.

Edith knew nothing about pop music. For a start, she called it pop music. Apparently you were supposed to call it something else nowadays. Then there was the sight of people at pop concerts, swinging their heads round and round as if they were trying to get a crick out of their neck. Didn't they know how silly they looked? And the noise! Edith had a bicycle and a cat, both virtually silent. The only noise she made was singing in her local choir. Haydn's *Creation* was next on the agenda.

So the name Kenny Loathsome meant nothing to her. The girls in the office moaned. 'You lucky sausage!' said Muriel in Rights. 'You'll meet him! You'll touch him! Don't wash!'

The last book Edith edited had been *Signs and Symbols in Pre-Hellenic Pottery*. That was more her thing. The publishing firm where she worked was a family business, the last of the musty old outfits in Bloomsbury. They were attempting to drag themselves into the nineties – ill-advisedly, Edith thought – by putting some glitz into their list and had signed up this Kenny Loathsome to write his autobiography.

Muriel pointed a trembling finger at her magazine. 'That's him.'

Actually, Edith did vaguely recognize him. She had videotaped a programme about Schopenhauer and got *Top of the Pops* by mistake. With horrified fascination she had watched Kenny Loathsome snarling into a microphone – a tadpole-shaped man with disgusting hair. If she went on TV she would wash her hair first. He was the lead singer, apparently, in a group called The Nipple Faktory. Obviously spelling wasn't one of their strong points.

'He's had sex with nine hundred women,' breathed Muriel.

· 'One thousand two hundred,' said Oonagh from Reception.

'Hope they kept their eyes closed,' said Edith, 'and held their noses.'

So that was how she found herself flying to the Côte d'Azur, to the hideaway of a famous pop star. He called it a hideaway, apparently, but you could see it for miles. It was the colour of pink blancmange and was festooned with satellite dishes. A servant-type person ushered her into Kenny Loathsome's den, a dark room lined with antique guns. He sat slumped in a leather chair watching Arsenal play Sheffield Wednesday. For half an hour this was the only information she could prise out of him. When the match was over he bellowed, either with joy or rage, and drained his tumbler of Southern Comfort. She introduced herself.

'I've come to help you write your autobiography.'

'Yeah, darling. Trouble is, I can't remember nothing.'

It was the drugs that had done it. During dinner – caviare, hamburgers and champagne – he itemized the substances he had ingested over the past twenty-five years. He said he had been a walking chemist's lab: 'Acid, speed, coke, methadone, quaaludes, diazepam.'

'My head's reeling,' she said.

'Not as much as mine was, darling.'

'What was the point of taking an upper if you were just about to take a downer?'

He said they had totally nuked his brain and the past was all a blur. The next afternoon, when he emerged blinking into the sunshine, she saw that under the hair his face was ravaged by the years of abuse. Not unattractively, actually. She had always been drawn to older men, but in the past they had been the professorial type. Back in her room she removed her glasses and put in her contact lenses.

They got down to work – well, she did. She took out her tape recorder and prodded him with questions – his childhood in Accrington, his spell as a delivery driver for a firm of wholesale butchers. 'Why are you called Loathsome?' she asked.

'Dunno.'

'Did your Mum call you that and you didn't know what it meant?'

He paused and nodded. 'Except I didn't have a Mum. It was me foster parents.'

'Poor Kenny.' She thought of her sunlit childhood in Oxfordshire, labradors and sisters and Marmite sandwiches. No wonder he didn't want to remember.

He sat there, his face furrowed with concentration. 'Think!' she ordered. 'Martial said "To be able to enjoy one's past life is to live twice."'

'Martial? What team does he play for?'

'You must remember something. What sort of delivery van did you drive?' she asked. 'Who were your friends at school?'

He spoke stumblingly. After her second glass of Rémy Martin she said recklessly: 'If you can't remember, make it up!' She was an *editor*. What was happening to her?

He kept depraved, nocturnal hours, getting up at noon and staying up till late. At three in the morning, yawning, she switched off the tape recorder. 'Could you ever sing at all? Did you have any talent whatsoever?'

He shook his head.

'Funny, isn't it,' she said. 'You can't sing and you're a millionaire. I've got a beautiful voice and I'm broke.'

He laughed his gravelly laugh, choking in his cigarette smoke. 'And who's the happiest little camper?'

A week went by and he didn't make a pass at her. What was wrong? She put up her hair but he didn't seem to notice; her eyes stung from her blithering contact lenses. She wasn't sure she wanted him to try, but her pride was at stake. What was she going to tell them back in the office? He seemed to live in a state of amiable, alcoholic stupefaction. While she transcribed her tapes, he watched satellite game shows or spent hours on the phone to his business manager. He was suing his band over some recording deal (note that she now said 'band' not 'group'). He tussled with faxes about alimony suits and palimony suits. All the worry had given him a peptic ulcer. No, nothing happened. The most exciting event in her bedroom was when she dropped a contact lens and, blindly searching for it, knocked against the panic button and summoned a vanload of gendarmes from Nice.

The only things he really loved were his vintage cars. He took her into his triple garage where they slumbered under dustsheets. 'Feel that bodywork!' he said, stroking the sleek flank of an Alvis or something. 'She's, like, responsive, know what I mean? She don't want nothing from me – like, me house in Berkshire and half me assets. That's why I love her, see?' He sighed. 'Dynamite when she's warmed up. 'Cept I've lost me driving licence.'

'You could always get a bike,' said Edith briskly. She was beginning to suspect that his legendary conquests were as much a fabrication as the past they had been cobbling together in the gloom of his den.

In two weeks they were finished. As she waited for her taxi he ruffled her hair. 'Take care, darling,' he said. 'See you around.' Around where? Nowhere *she* went.

She arrived back in London looking radiant. That fortnight had changed her in a way nobody could guess. At the rehearsal that night her voice soared. Next day she met a breathless reception in the office.

'Your tan! You look great without your glasses! Go on, tell us. What happened? Did you . . . ?'

Edith smiled mysteriously. She dumped her transcripts on her desk. She looked at the heap of paper. She had given him a past, she had created it for him. He was grateful to her and in a curious way she was grateful to him. So why couldn't he create a past for her? For didn't Alexander Smith say: 'A man's real possession is his memory. In nothing else is he rich, in nothing else is he poor' (*Dreamthorp*, 1863).

'Oh, it was extraordinary all right.' She sipped her Nescafé, gazing at the pairs of round eyes. She was Scheherazade, she was all-powerful. 'He was even better than all the stories.'

'How? What did he do? Did he, you know . . . ?'

She nodded, she sipped, she took her time. 'We stayed up all night. We didn't get up till lunchtime.'

'What did he do?'

'He stroked my flanks, his eyes full of desire. He murmured, "How responsive you are . . . when you're warmed up, you're dynamite!"'

They sighed, like a breeze through pine trees.

'We went up to my room. Our lovemaking was so intense that we rolled off the bed and I hit his panic button. Half the Nice gendarmerie arrived. As George Dennison Prentice said—'

'Who?'

'In his *Prenticiana*: "Memory is not so brilliant as hope, but it is more beautiful, and a thousand times as true".'

She wasn't sure about this, but they didn't seem to notice.

Soon after that, the firm was bought by a multinational media conglomerate which owned six satellite TV stations and Edith was made redundant. Her tan had long since faded. She went to work for a professor of Middle English who was writing a book called *Courtly Love: Legend and Myth*. Which had she created – legend or myth? Did she actually know, or care? She only knew she was grateful to Kenny Loathsome and he would never know why. For he had made her happy with her two rooms in Peckham High Street, and besides, it was simpler to be loved by her cat.

The next September his book was published. She heard he was doing a signing in Harrods, so she went there and queued. It was all women, nudging and giggling. When she finally got to his table he didn't recognize her. She knew he wouldn't. His head was bent down as he wrote, laboriously. She noticed, for the first time, that he was thinning on top.

'What shall I write, love?' he asked, without looking up.

She smiled, and pointed to the empty page. 'Just write "Ta for the memories."'

165

Back to My Place?

Max Davidson

MAX DAVIDSON has studied the Parliamentary menagerie from two vantage points. He was an official of the House of Commons for fifteen years, during which time he published novels such as *Suddenly in Rome* and *Beef Wellington Blue*. After a spell as a TV critic, he is now the *Daily Telegraph*'s Parliamentary sketch-writer.

Hale knew, before he had been in the House three minutes, that they meant to get him. The policemen at the main gate avoided his eye and even the attendant in the Members' cloakroom forsook his usual banter and buried himself in his newspaper. They knew, he thought. They *knew*.

In the lobby, a journalist hurried towards him, notebook in hand. 'Can I have a word, Mr Hale?' He made a gesture of dismissal and, quickening his step, strode past the door leading to the tea room and down the stairs to the bar. Reg poured him a whisky in silence; from a man normally bursting with tips for the 2.45 at Market Rasen, it was the most eloquent sign yet.

He downed his drink and, breaking with habit, downed a second. Two Labour members sat in the corner, watching him curiously. One of them he knew – they had served on a committee together and got drunk in a café in Strasbourg, arguing about jazz – but the other he couldn't place. Barry something? From one of those safe seats in Sheffield? How little he really knew this place. People sneered that it was a gentleman's club but, even after ten years, it could be the loneliest place in London.

'Cheers, Paul!' called the man he knew, raising his pint glass in greeting. The warmth seemed genuine, unmuddied by sympathy. He smiled back, forcing himself to be genial, and made a joke about the previous day's debate in the House, when the Chancellor had made such a fool of himself. The other two laughed. Did they know?

Were they just being kind? Perhaps the gossip had passed them by. Perhaps they didn't read *that* paper. It wasn't renowned for its left-wing editorials. Could he possibly be safe?

Big Ben struck twelve and the bar began to fill up. The Clerk Assistant dropped in for his customary pink gin, and three girls from the library, absurdly youthful with their short skirts and high, carrying laughs, sat down by the window. He had a third Scotch, then a fourth, and shook himself like a dog. Were these singles or doubles? You never knew with Reg. Then Roger from the Whips' Office put his head round the door and his heart missed a beat.

This wasn't where Roger did his drinking: it was too public, too plebeian. He was looking for someone – him, presumably. The Chief must have issued his summons: it was only a matter of time now. He took refuge behind a pillar and waited tensely as Roger's narrow, darting eyes quartered the room.

Then, miracle! He missed him, the little bastard missed him! As Roger disappeared and the door closed behind him, Hale was seized with a wild, despairing hope. A smile split his face and he took another deep gulp of Scotch. In two hours, the House would be sitting and, two hours after that, who knows, some new story might have broken to put his little peccadillo in perspective. There might be a row at Prime Minister's questions, or the IRA . . .

'Paul, the Chief wants to see you,' said Roger, looming with brutal suddenness over his left shoulder. He must have used the bar's other entrance, the one leading to the terrace. 'Now, please, Paul.'

The Chief Whip was standing by the window, looking down into the courtyard. He was wearing one of his country suits and his broad farmer's bottom dominated the room. He turned and gestured to Hale to take a seat.

'I'm sorry about this, Paul.' Did he mean it? It was so hard to tell with this man. 'The Press are bastards.' He certainly meant that. He was on the right of the Party and gave the impression that, if he had his way, all newspaper articles would be vetted by Central Office.

'The paper got it wrong. I was only—'

'No need for explanations, Paul. I don't know who she was and I don't care. All that matters, as far as I'm concerned, is that she wasn't Mrs Hale and that we've got a by-election next week. Bad timing. *Bloody* bad timing,' he repeated, making a show of clenching his fist. Handing out bollockings wasn't his style: it was an open secret that he was only marking time in the Whips' Office until the next reshuffle.

'It was a one-night stand,' Hale persisted. 'In France. Two years ago. The only reason the picture appeared at all—'

'Yes, yes, yes.' A small bead of perspiration appeared on the Chief's forehead. His own mistress – another open secret – had just completed her first three years in post. A smooth, ultra-discreet liaison whose fail-safe mechanics were the stuff of a spy novel. 'Nobody's blaming you, Paul. Could have happened to anyone. Rub of the green. You'll be back within two years. At the outside.'

'Back?'

'The PM wants you out, Paul.' The Chief's face hardened, then twisted into a little tic of sympathy. He glanced at his watch. 'By five o'clock please, Paul. If you would be so good.'

'But—'

'No buts, Paul. The Party won't wear it. You've got to go. There's no alternative.'

'Listen, damn you! *Listen!*' Hale lurched to his feet, shaking with fury, with resentment, with the memory of past slights. The whisky was beginning to talk in him. 'I know there's a by-election. I know I've been stupid. I know I've got my name in the papers. But so what? Well? So bloody what? It's not a hanging offence – or it wasn't a hanging offence until some idiot moved the goalposts. It's not even as if I'm a Minister. I'm the PPS to the most insignificant Minister in the most insignificant department in the whole bloody Government – which, as you very well know, means getting paid sweet f.a. for sucking up to the right people and trooping through the division lobbies at three o'clock in the morning to support EC regulations nobody else believes in. When I think—'

The Chief rose without ceremony and looked at his watch.

'Five o'clock please, Paul.' He wagged an admonitory finger. 'Or we'll crucify you.' His father had been a rector in Saffron Walden. He was fond of biblical metaphors.

Hale sat in his place behind the Environment Secretary, listening to the Prime Minister. 'I refer my honourable friend to the answer I gave earlier ... With respect to my right honourable friend ... The right honourable gentleman should know better than that ... In 1979 ...' The Chamber was packed and the exchanges between the Prime Minister and the Leader of the Opposition were being greeted with noisy roars; yet it seemed to Hale, still fighting the effects of the whisky, as if every eye was trained on him, as if everybody was concerned with just one question. Would he go or stay? Only he could resolve it.

'Point of order, Madam Speaker!' he shouted suddenly, staggering to his feet. The Prime Minister was fielding a question about prisons and the House was momentarily quiet. There was an embarrassed pause. 'Sit down, Paul!' shouted a voice behind him. 'He's drunk!' called someone from the other side.

The Speaker frowned and got to her feet. 'I'll take the honourable gentleman's point of order after Prime Minister's questions.'

More shouts of 'Sit down!' from both sides of the House. The Prime Minister sat down, stood up, sat down again. The Chief Whip whispered something to his deputy. A woman in the Press gallery laughed.

'But Madam Speaker!' roared Hale. 'Madam Speaker!' His voice was hoarse and he was starting to sway from side to side. 'This is urgent. It can't wait. Really it can't. I have an important personal statement to make. I won't, ah, I won't ... *detain* the House.'

He paused for breath and leaned on the bench in front for support. Someone behind him was pulling at his coat tails and there were still those cries of 'Sit down!' from the other side. But the baying seemed to be dying down and the mood of the House was changing.

'I've been very foolish,' he resumed, cursing the whisky, cursing the Chief Whip, making one last effort to stand up straight. 'I know what I did was wrong. We've all done it, haven't we? We're all fallible. We're all – human. But when I think of my lovely wife and my lovely children . . .' And now the whole House was still, people were craning to listen and there was one of those perfect Parliamentary silences. 'What I would say, and say from the bottom of my heart and with all the, ah, all the, ah . . . *emphasis* at my disposal . . .'

As he passed out, the murmurs were of sympathy, not outrage; and the four backbenchers who carried him unconscious from the Chamber, while a Labour member rose to present a ten-minute rule bill on fox-hunting, might have been Valkyrie bearing a dead warrior from the battlefield to his final resting place.

Happy Hour

Rose Tremain

ROSE TREMAIN is the author of six novels: *Sadler's Birthday*, *Letter to Sister Benedicta*, *The Cupboard*, *The Swimming Pool Season*, *Restoration* (Sunday Express Book of the Year Award 1989, Booker Prize shortlist) and *Sacred Country* (winner of the 1993 James Tait Black Memorial Prize and the 1994 Prix Femina Etranger). She has also written three volumes of short stories, including *The Colonel's Daughter*, which won the Dylan Thomas Short Story Award in 1984. She has written numerous plays for television and radio. Rose Tremain lives in Norfolk and London with the biographer Richard Holmes.

The Mystery

He had seen it in his mind. His mind had made a private film of it, which he could describe, shot by shot, to his work pal, Sol. 'OK,' he'd say, 'listen up, Solly. The year is now, right, 1946, and I'm me, Frank, and the place is here, New York City, and I'm at the waterfront early.

'It's near dawn and there's some fog or mist in the air and it's cold and I can see my breath. I pan out over the water. It's like the world ends there in the mist, you know? Like they used to believe, that the world had an edge. And then I hear it, that old ghostly siren, that boom-boom of a vast liner and so I know she's there and coming closer.

'The scene fills up. There's a crowd all round me, stamping in the cold, shouting, kids waving flags, throwing stuff. There's a band playing. And I'm jigging up and down. I've got the ring in my pocket and I hold onto it like it's the fuckin' crown jewels. And I'm so happy, Sol. And then the passengers start to walk down off the ship and I know that in the next minute I'm going to see her . . .'

Sol was a sceptic. He was also undereducated and forgot that the word had a 'c' in it, so he said to Frank: 'I'm a septic. I don't believe things is ever the way you picture them.'

'Maybe not for *you*,' replied Frank, 'but I'm not talking about you, Sol. I'm talking about me and the arrival from England of my

177

fiancée, Marie. You don't have no fiancée, Sol, sad but true. But I got Marie and this scene is all on film, buddy. Every second of it. Right here.' And Frank tapped his head.

It was winter when she embarked, so cold in New York, it reminded Frank of being holed up in Bastogne in December, 1944. He said to Sol: 'All the important days of my life – good and bad – take place in low temperatures.' He kept Marie's ship's cable in his pocket and warmed his hands on it. 'My life on its way to you stop,' it read. 'Yours forever stop Marie stop.'

He had the ring safe and looked at it every night of the ten nights of her journey. He had his hair cut and his suit cleaned and his best shoes shined. He helped his mother prepare the small room where Marie would stay until the wedding. He put a picture of himself by her narrow bed.

And then he got up on a grey morning of freezing mist and made his way through a labyrinth of unfamiliar streets to the quayside. There, he waited. The scene that unfolded was exactly like the one he had described to Sol, frame by frame. He heard the boom-boom of the siren and saw the liner slide towards him out of the milky light. A US Navy band played and the crowd shouted and sang and Frank jigged up and down hollering: 'Marie! Marie!'

One by one, the passengers disembarked, smiling and waving. They were swept into the arms of the crowd and led away into the tall, beautiful city. The band played on and on and then suddenly stopped and the day and the place fell silent. Marie had not arrived. All the passengers were gone and Marie was not among them. This was the mystery.

The Hypotheses

When Frank remembered this day, he remembered it dark. 'The sky just never seemed to lighten, not even for an hour,' he'd say.

When the evening came on, he was sitting at his mother's kitchen table and in the corner of the room stood an object at which Frank and his mother kept staring. It was Marie's trunk.

It had been delivered at four o'clock. The address on the label was written in Marie's round hand-writing and Frank's first thought when he saw it was that Marie must be inside. He put his arms around the trunk and called to her.

'Don't, Frank,' said his mother. 'Don't be macabre, dear.' But he got out his army knife and picked at the locks until they gave. Inside the trunk was a collection of items Frank had never seen during his brief moments with Marie in the cold room above the pub where she'd worked. He took out a badminton racquet, walking stick, a lacquered tea caddy, a manicure set, a leatherbound copy of *Pickwick Papers*, a D-Day Special Issue of *Picture Post*, a box of nylons he recognized as his own gift, a candelabra made of silver plate, an Indian rug, a snapshot of Marie aged eighteen or nineteen taken with her parents just before they were killed in the Blitz, and a jewel case containing a ruby brooch.

Frank and his mother gaped. 'You know that's a beautiful brooch,' said the mother.

'Sure,' said Frank, 'but where are her clothes?'

'With her on the ship. She's maybe been detained.'

'Detained why?'

'Don't ask me, Frank. Maybe she committed a felony?'

'A felony? Like *what*? Marie, a felony?'

'I said don't ask me. Maybe she cheated at cards.'

'Marie don't play cards.'

'Or maybe you didn't wait long enough?'

'I asked some guys in uniform: "Are all the passengers gone?" And they told me yes, so I thought I must have missed her and I came back here.'

'Maybe she was sick, Frank, and couldn't be moved off the boat, or unless—'

'What?'

'She died at sea.'

Frank called Sol then. He said: 'We saw this in the war, Sol, you remember? The British don't like to talk about death.'

'Frank,' said Sol, 'if she'd died you would have gotten a cable.'

'Not necessarily. I'm not Next of Kin yet.'

'Did you call England?' asked Sol.

'I called the pub. They said "Marie's on her way to America" – as if I didn't know.'

'Well then,' said Sol.

'Well what?'

'Take it easy.'

'I can't take it easy. Where *is* she, Sol?'

'Like they said, "on her way".'

Later, in the pitch dark, trying to sleep, Frank thought, there'd be something worse than her dying. The worst would be if she'd been there all along and seen me from way up on the deck, seen me jigging up and down like a moron and thought, there he is, the jerk, and he works in a lousy asbestos factory and suddenly I don't love him. He remembered a conversation he'd had with Marie two nights before he embarked for Normandy. They sat in the middle of a village green, with the dew falling, drinking rum from a bottle and she said: 'When the war's over, Frank, you must do something with your life that makes people happy. People get happiness from such small things; so you just have to choose a small thing and do that.'

'Like what?' he asked.

'Oh,' she said, 'I don't know, Frank. Use your imagination.'

And so he thought, that's it, that's what happened. She saw me and she decided asbestos isn't part of human happiness and so she changed her mind. Now, the crew are hiding her till the boat turns around and sails back to England. The snooty Captain's enjoying the story. He's putting his hand round Marie's shoulders.

A Version of the Truth

It came so many years later, Frank thought he'd no longer be interested to hear it. He was dying from all his millions of breaths of asbestos dust, so nothing from the past counted for much. But then, he was surprised somehow.

He was sitting in the cocktail bar of a London hotel. A pianist was playing. Frank looked not at Marie sitting beside him, but up at all the crystal chandeliers scintillating with modern light.

'I somehow imagined England dark,' he said, 'like it was in the war. I had a film of England in my mind – dark sky, dark rooms – and it didn't change. But then I never had the knack of imagining things right, did I? Did I, Marie?'

Happy Hour

Marie had ordered an Hawaiian cocktail, at which she stared very closely, as if, under the paper parasol, there might be something alive in it. Still looking at the cocktail, she said: 'I've explained it to you, Frank.'

'OK. But I still don't really get it. Why the hell didn't you just get on the boat?'

'I sent you a proxy – everything of value that I had. A brooch. Some candlesticks. Everything. Because you saved us all really, you Americans, and we owed you a debt of gratitude.'

'I didn't want any lousy candlesticks. I wanted you.'

'I know. But I loved England more. Even just that village green where we sat before you left. I loved that place more than you and me on it. You know?'

'Well, I know now. But you could have written. You could have answered my letters.'

'I thought there was no need, really. I thought that at heart you understood. I hope you gave the ruby brooch to your wife, Frank, did you?'

'No,' said Frank, 'to my mother. She died with it on.'

At this moment, they looked up and smiled and each saw the remembered beauty of the other.

The pianist started talking softly then, not seeming to care whether anyone heard him or not. 'Ladies and gentlemen,' he said, 'welcome to Happy Hour. Sit back. Enjoy a little time. And send me, if it moves you that way, your lifelong requests . . .'

Poor Toni

———◆———

Allan Massie

A LLAN MASSIE was born in Singapore in 1938. He has written twelve novels, including *The Last Peacock*, winner of the Frederick Niven Award in 1981, *A Question of Loyalties*, winner of the Saltire Society/Scotsman Book of the Year, and the widely acclaimed Roman trilogy, *Augustus*, *Tiberius* and *Caesar*. His most recent novel is *The Ragged Lion*. He also writes non-fiction and for newspapers. He is a Fellow of the Royal Society of Literature and lives in the Scottish Borders.

In the fall of the afternoon, when the lights came on in the piazza, Gaetano arrived, and they would play bridge. They did this principally to please Toni's mother, who didn't like being in Rome, but couldn't summon the will-power to return to Venezuela. Or perhaps it was money she lacked, Dallas couldn't be sure. One day it seemed one thing, the next the other. It was that sort of life they were leading.

Toni's mother was Lily-Ann. She would have liked, Toni said, to be addressed as 'Miss Lily-Ann', because she had been a Southern Belle, and still saw herself that way. She had been spoiled as a girl, Toni said, and had never recovered. 'It made her a lousy mother.' As for Toni, she had been a star of Venezuelan television when she was sixteen, some years back. She had very nice legs, but usually hid them in trousers, and it was some time after he met her that Dallas realized how nice they were. That was one night when Gaetano was playing the piano in the bar where he worked, and Dallas and Toni got drunk and went to bed together. 'It's all right if Gaetano doesn't know,' she said; but Dallas wasn't sure. He thought it might complicate matters.

Lily-Ann complained a lot in the mornings, as well as in the afternoon when they played bridge. Gaetano was the best player, but she wouldn't admit that. She disapproved of Dallas too, and quarrelled with Toni because she had lost her modelling job, and they didn't know where money was coming from. In theory there

185

was a monthly cheque from Toni's ex-husband in Munich, but the theory wasn't always translated into practice. When that happened Dallas lent Toni money. Calling it a loan made things more comfortable. It was because of the loans that Lily-Ann tolerated Dallas. Once he suggested he lend her money to buy her air ticket, but it was one of the days she lacked willpower. 'There's nothing for me in Venezuela,' she said. Dallas thought there was nothing for her in Rome either; but he was wrong there. There was Toni, poor Toni, and Lily-Ann intended to keep a tight hold.

After bridge they went out to eat, leaving Lily-Ann in the apartment because she didn't like Italian food any more than she liked Italy or Italians. Then they went on to Gaetano's bar. He played a gentle sub-jazz with neat improvisations on popular tunes. Toni sometimes let herself be picked up by men who would buy her whisky rather than Stock, the Italian brandy they usually drank.

She would make them buy whisky for Gaetano and Dallas too. Most times she declined to go off with them, but sometimes she did so.

One night when this happened Dallas got into conversation with a pretty American boy called Erik. He had soft blond hair and a creamy voice, and he complained that men were always trying to pick him up. Dallas said, politely, that he could see why. 'I don't like it because I'm not that way,' Erik said, moving his face very close to Dallas.

'Well, that's fine,' Dallas said. 'It doesn't worry me. Nothing does. Have a drink.'

Later, when they had had a few drinks, Erik crossed over to the piano, and laid his hand on Gaetano's shoulder and asked him if he could play 'La Vie en Rose'.

'It's my favourite song,' he said, 'my very favourite. It says everything.'

'You're an old-fashioned boy,' Dallas said, and drank some brandy. 'The Stock solution to all our problems,' he said, reciting the old line, but then called the barman and said he would switch to grappa.

Erik said he was a drama student and sang and danced too.

'Just a chorus-boy at heart,' Dallas said.

After that, Erik was often in the bar, and always asked Gaetano to play 'La Vie en Rose', and would sing it with him. He sang it almost well enough. Toni said he was a bloody little tart, and Dallas smiled. Then one night, when Toni had gone off with an admirer, Gaetano and Erik departed together, and Dallas was left alone with his grappa and the barman. When he went back to his hotel there was a big moon over Monteverde and the air was fresh and good. They were beginning to assemble the market stalls in Campo dei Fiori.

Gaetano picked a quarrel with Toni on account of her departure with the man who had bought her whisky, who was a big Dane called Oskar. So he stopped coming to the apartment to play bridge, and Toni refused to go to his bar. Dallas had said nothing about Gaetano and Erik, though that was why Gaetano had picked the quarrel, and when he still went to the bar himself, Erik was always there, purring like a kitten.

Lily-Ann was displeased about the lack of a fourth for bridge.

'What about Oskar?' Dallas said to Toni, but her reply was brief and obscene. So that was over too, and they recruited an Englishman who wore an Inverness cape and used to arouse the derision of the boys who hung around the piazza and would wolf-whistle as he passed. He pretended not to hear them. 'I've always only been able to make love to people of my own class,' he confided to Dallas. His bridge was poor, but he talked a lot about 'my friend the Cardinal' – though Dallas always wanted to say: 'I thought we had more than one of them here in Rome' – and he called Lily-Ann 'Miss Lily-Ann', which together in her view made up for the quality of his bridge.

Dallas now slept more often with Toni, except on nights when she went to Rosati's in the Piazza del Popolo, which was full of people who hoped to see film-stars or get into movies themselves. Sometimes she said Charles Bronson was there, but of course if she went off with anyone, it was somebody less famous.

That didn't happen too often though, because most of the people at Rosati's were already attached, and because the strain of living with Lily-Ann was having its effect on Toni's looks. Rosati's was expensive, and the requests for a loan from Dallas were becoming more frequent. He continued to oblige because it was easier than saying no. In exchange she suggested he move into the apartment. He managed to say no to that.

'My paper has the hotel number,' he said, 'and you don't have a telephone.'

'You could always arrange to pick up messages,' she said; but he let that rest. Altogether he was getting too involved. So he went round to Gaetano's bar to see how things stood.

'No, *caro*,' Gaetano said.

'Why not? You know Erik is a little bitch.'

'Certainly,' Gaetano said. 'But, you see, the little bitch is in my system and, to tell you the truth, *caro*, though he is indeed a little bitch, I was glad to have the excuse to leave her. You too, my friend, are now looking for an excuse, isn't that true?'

'Do I need one?'

'Certainly,' Gaetano said, 'or you will feel bad. You could have had Erik. He would rather have gone with you at first than with me, but not now.'

'It's an excuse I'm not sorry to have passed on,' Dallas said, and tapped Gaetano on the head, and came away.

He crossed the river and walked through the town he loved as he had loved no other, and up past the Jesuit church and its piazza where the wind always blows waiting for its companion the Devil to emerge from the church, which he never does, and past the Palazzo Venezia where Mussolini used to keep his study light burning to persuade the ever-sceptical Romans that he never ceased from work, and then along the narrow Piazza dei Santi Apostoli and past the Trevi Fountain, till he reached a little bar, by the offices of *Il Messagero*, which opened at four in the morning. It was a bar where he had more than once got into a fight and he rather wanted to do so now, but there were no takers that morning, and he drank grappa and Peroni chasers till the sky was blue. Then he had breakfast at the English tea-rooms in Piazza di Spagna, ham and poached eggs and Indian tea; and then, checking the time in London, called the news editor of one of the papers for which he wrote and told him the news from Berlin sounded interesting: so why didn't he go there and write something?

'Why not?' said the news editor. 'Time you did some work, you lazy sod.'

He turned back to the American Express and fixed himself a rail ticket. That was fine then. He went to the Greco for a coffee and started to feel guilty; so went back to Amex and inquired about flights to Venezuela.

'Give me two open tickets,' he said. 'Make one of them one-way.'

He handed over his plastic, and this time they checked that the card hadn't been reported stolen, though it was the same girl who had supplied the rail ticket. She looked at him oddly as she completed the transaction, and he asked for an envelope, and went down the street to the central post office, and dispatched the tickets with a note to Toni. Then he collected a bag from his hotel and took a taxi to Stazione Termini.

Only when he was in the train did he wonder, with his experience of the Italian post, whether the tickets would ever find their way across the river to her apartment off Santa Maria in Trastevere; and, if so, whether she and Lily-Ann would use them or cash them in, so that she, poor Toni, could go on trying her luck at Rosati's. If she did, he hoped she would strike gold. He liked her and had nothing against her, except what she had almost come to the point of demanding from him.

Parker 51

———◆———

Lesley Glaister

LESLEY GLAISTER was born in 1956 and was brought up in Suffolk. She was educated at Felixstowe, Stockwell College of Education, the Open University and the University of Sheffield. Her novels include *Honour Thy Father* (1990, winner of the Somerset Maugham and Betty Trask Awards), *Trick or Treat* (1991), *Digging to Australia* (1992), *Limestone and Clay* (1993, winner of Yorkshire Author of the Year) and *Partial Eclipse* (1994). She lives in Sheffield with her three sons and teaches creative writing at Sheffield Hallam University.

She didn't write much, only birthday and Christmas cards, only the odd letter. But she did have a certain way with words – a relationship you might almost say. She liked to play with them, listen to them, taste them in her mouth. She thought of herself as a flibbertigibbet, for instance, and she liked the flutteryness of this word, as if, when she said it, a fledgling was flapping on her tongue. She loved her own name, Rose, because it made her tongue curl like a fat pink petal, secret in her mouth. She was alive to words, noticed the connections.

One night she stood on a bridge with Nat – a name she didn't like, too slight and swattable – they stood hand in hand, as lovers do, gazing at the moon reflected on the water's surface.

'See how it glitters,' she said. 'It glistens, it glimmers, it glisters . . . all the gl's, Nat! It glints, it gleams, it glows; it's all glossy, glamorous . . .'

'Hey, Honey.' Nat laughed and stopped her mouth with a kiss. 'You swallowed a dictionary?'

She was excited. It worked for other sounds too: shine, shimmer, shiver, sheen; swift, sweep, swish, swoop, swoosh. She began to collect words, lists of words that were related through sound and meaning. At the same time she fell, or teetered on the edge of falling, in love with her GI. Nat Racket. It was 1946. They had only weeks before he was to return home to Philadelphia.

'Come with me, Baby,' he said. 'Come home with me and meet my folks. They'll love you. Marry me, Baby.'

'I don't know,' she said which was the only thing she could honestly say because she didn't. She liked Nat enough to marry him. She liked his hard skinny body, the way he kissed her and the other things they did. She liked his chewy American voice. She liked the idea of America, of becoming American, having kids and a backyard, walking to the store on sidewalks to buy popsicles. The drawback was the name. If she married Nat she would, for the rest of her life, be called Rose Racket, and all her children would be little Rackets.

'Let's wait,' she said. 'We can write . . . *think* I'll marry you. Give me time.'

When at these words Nat pulled from his pocket a long package, she thought he was about to give her time in the shape of a gold bracelet watch she had admired at the NAAFI. But no, when she opened the package, her fingers trembling with the paper and ribbon, when she opened the black leatherette box, there was revealed no watch, but a fountain pen. It was dark maroon red and shiny. She felt for one swoop of her heart, disappointment.

'A Parker 51,' he said. 'Finest pen money can buy. Write me with it.'

And she did. At first she wrote to him every day, sucking the blue-black ink into the pen's belly and watching the words flow from the gold nib. Sometimes she wrote so fast that she seemed to be scorching the white sheets of paper with hot black words. Sometimes she sent him one of her word-lists; flip, flick, tickle lick, twiddle, fiddle, prickle, nip.

He wrote back to her as often. Terrible, spidery writing he had and she couldn't help noticing that his spelling – even for an American – left something to be desired. And when, after a few months, she had still not made up her mind, when the gaps between letters became longer, the letters themselves shorter, she began to notice how he nagged in his letters. Nat nags, she thought, and even – after she described the riverside picnic to him and his reply had included the phrase *the behavior of my future wife* – nasty nagging nit-picking Nat.

At the riverside picnic, a party she had been invited to by one of her Post Office colleagues, she had spent some time conversing with a man called Roland. Roland. She tried it on her tongue. It started with a curl like her own name and then flipped forward with a fishy flip like her own heart when he took her hand to help her up. He asked her to a dance. He was a teacher, a word-lover too, a reader – and even an occasional writer – of poetry. She said yes and bought herself a new blue dress and shoes out of her saved-up American money.

Roland and Rose, she practised and oh it sounded dignified, so much better than Rose and Nat which made her think of a little pest hovering over a fragrant flower. She had several dates with Roland over the following summer weeks, dates that went unmentioned in her letters to Nat.

'I love you, Rose,' Roland said one night. They were standing on the very bridge she had stood upon with Nat, looking at the same moon reflected in the same water. She told him about her word collections. 'You have the ear of a poet,' he said, between kisses. 'I wish you could be my wife.'

Bloom was his surname. 'Rose Bloom,' she whispered to herself that night, lying with the curtains open so that she could see the – almost rhyming – moon. 'Rose and Roland. Mrs Roland Bloom.'

She wrote a final letter to Nat. She considered returning the pen that sat so intimately in her hand like a warm red part of him. But she demurred. She thought Roland would admire the pen, man of words that he was.

And oh he did. 'What a splendid pen,' he breathed, fingering it. And, 'May I?' trying it out on the back of an envelope, signing his flourishing name.

She told him that Nat had given it to her. 'My American – almost – fiancé,' she said, wanting him to realize that he wasn't the only one, that she had had a choice.

'His loss is my gain,' Roland said in his predictable, gentlemanly way.

They toured Cornwall with Roland's motorbike and sidecar for their honeymoon. It was a week of cream teas and creaming seas, warm arms and glow-worms, and every night the waxing moon, glimmering down at them with a dim grin upon its fattening face.

Roland borrowed Rose's pen to write his postcards home. 'Best wishes, Roland and Rose,' he wrote in his flowing hand, even to people she had never met. She liked Roland to borrow the pen, thrilled to see it in his hand, was proud to have something he admired.

After the honeymoon, he often borrowed the pen to mark exercise books or sometimes to write poetry with. One evening she sat watching him work, watching the pen travelling smoothly across a sheet of paper, when suddenly he looked up, caught her gaze.

'Tell me about this Nat chap,' he said.

'I've told you.'

'He must have thought one hell of a lot of you.' He looked musingly at the pen.

'Well, yes he did.'

'And you him.'

'Yes . . . but you know, as soon as *we* met . . .'

'I never asked you, Rose, because it didn't – doesn't – matter . . . but you and he, did you . . .'

Rose looked down.

'None of my business,' he said quickly. He gave her back the pen before they went to bed and she replaced it, as she always did, in its leatherette box. He watched her undress and then he took her in his arms in a forceful way that made her gasp, surprised and almost afraid of this new side of him, and he made love to her in a hard, impersonal, almost brutal way he had never done before.

In the morning the atmosphere was uneasy. They were polite but their eyes never met. They ate their eggs quickly and just before he left the house, Roland said: 'May I borrow your pen today?'

'Of course.'

Roland put the pen in his briefcase and kissed her brusquely, left her feeling bruised, confused.

On her way home from work she bought pork chops, his favourite, and big Bramley apples to bake with brown sugar and sultanas. Over dinner he was quiet. Afterwards, as they washed up in their tiny elbow-bumping kitchen, he sighed and said: 'Rosie, I've a confession to make.'

'Oh?'

'I'm most terribly sorry but I've lost your pen.' And he did look sorry, almost as if he might cry. She put down the dish she was drying and put her arms round him.

'It doesn't matter,' she said, 'it was only a pen.' At that moment she truly didn't mind about the pen, she was only grateful to get his tenderness back. And when, forty years later, Roland died, when she and her daughter Lily were sorting through a box of his things and Lily came across the pen, concealed in the spine of a book, Rose said nothing much.

'You have it,' she offered her daughter, but Lily had no use for such an old-fashioned pen.

'Give me a Biro any day,' she laughed.

Late on the night of the funeral, when all the guests had gone home, Rose held the pen in her hand again, filled its belly with ink and did one of her lists: *whimper*, *weep*, *wail*, she wrote, *woe*, *widow*. *Woe*.

Pepper and Leo

George V. Higgins

G EORGE V. HIGGINS is a Boston University professor and boasts a chequered past as prosecutor,
defence lawyer and AP reporter, in addition to his
authorship of twenty-one novels including *The
Friends of Eddie Coyle*. His newest, forthcoming from
Little, Brown, is *Swan Boats at Four*.

Pepper Lonergan at forty-three, sole waitress for the booths at Cannonball's, was the kind of woman that Leo always said you wished you never had to go home to after a hard day on the job. Leo was the barkeep. 'And that's really a hell of a thing, don't you think? When a man doesn't want to go back to his own home after he's put in a full day's work?' Leo didn't mention her name when he said things like that, but he'd be looking right at Pepper when he did it; killing time while the regulars drank up the round they were on and started asking for refills, wiping the bar with that wet rag he had and reaming her out, right to her face; in front of the whole bunch of them.

'I had a good friend once, that did that, and my God if his life wasn't in Hell, it wouldn't've been anywhere at all. But that's what you have to do, you make that kind of mistake. "Two beers at Cannonball's – *oh*-kay, you can do that. Waste your time and our money, money that we haven't got, talking sports with the other bozos in there: if that's what you want to do, okay, go and do it. But then you get your ass home here, you hear me? You stay and you get drunk with Lindy and them?"'

Lindy had been one of the regulars for a very long time. Lindy'd never gotten married, so he stayed at Cannonball's late as he wanted, drank as much as he liked. Then his mother got sick back home in St Louis, which was where Lindy was from, and he went home to take care of her. They never saw him again. 'If that's what you wanna do, fine. But then don't bother coming back here. I'm not gonna take care of you. You can just sleep it off somewhere else.' Leo said if you were married to Pepper like Clarence'd been – and still was, if you wanted to get technical about it – you would've called those couple hours that you spent in Cannonball's 'the best part of the day, and you'd've been right as rain. You went and did this thing when you were young and horny, and now you're stuck with it. You married her when you were young, of your own free will – if hard-ons're free will – and now you can't see your way clear to gettin' out of it: bitch'd wreck you, you so much's cleared your throat and looked like you might try it.'

Leo was right: Pepper was not an easy woman. And even though Clarence'd never said anything about it, except once or twice when he'd had four beers or six and got to feeling sorry for himself, all his friends knew it and felt sorry for him, too. And he knew that. Which made it even worse, having them feel sorry for him, that he had to go home, and then having to go home on top of that.

But he wasn't doing it any more. Pepper no longer had a live-in husband who had to go home and face her every night. He'd gotten an Irish divorce for himself one night six years or so ago: 'Just goin' down the corner for a pack of cigarettes,' he'd told her, and he never came back. Pepper's disposition never'd been sweet before that, judging by what he'd had to say, but once he'd headed for the tall timber, she turned downright impossible.

I think it was partly not knowing where she stood in the world. She still had a legal husband. Nobody'd gone to court and filed for a divorce, so they were still man and wife. So Clarence must've owed her some kind of financial support, but nobody knew how much it was. They'd never agreed to an amount and so no judge'd ever stepped in and said, 'Well, since you two can't agree on this, this is what it's going to be'; set a figure for them neither one of them would've liked one bit. But it wouldn't've mattered, Clarence being long gone and hard to find. If there'd been a set amount, she wouldn't've known where to look for him to pay up.

It went on like that for over a year almost every afternoon, unless it got real busy, until the day that Leo really hit a nerve. He still didn't use her name, but when he said she could've divorced

Clarence after he was gone, on the grounds of desertion, she didn't like the guy that much, there wasn't much doubt who he meant.

'Oh, really,' she says, real sarcastic, 'and if I do, and they say that's what he is, a deserter, it is like in the army? Do they hunt him down and shoot him? Because that's what the bastard deserves.'

That sort of got to Leo, caught him flatfooted; he really got kind of flustered. She'd never come back at him like that before. He said – like all he was trying to do was just help her out – well then, maybe she could have Clarence declared legally dead. 'Which he probably would've been by now, if he'd've stayed with you,' and then take his share of what they owned together that he'd left behind.

'Like what?' she shoots right back. 'His half the rent that I pay by myself, onna one-bedroom apartment? His half a beaten-up Ford Escort that I bought seven years ago? I made all the payments, he didn't have no half. So, wise ass, what would I get, then, if I got his half? His half, exactly, of what? Half what he lost, betting on football with you guys? His half of very damned little, you ask me, because that's what the whole of it is: nothing but a big little, it costs so damned much to live now.'

'Especially,' Leo said, 'when you're leavin', what, fifty, hundred bucks a week? At the Indian casino, down in Connecticut there.'

'Oh, just leave me alone, Leo, willya, all right?' Pepper said. 'I work very hard, as you very well know. I got a right to have some relaxation, take a bus and go down and play the bingo anna slots, if that's what I want to do. I'm all by myself in this thing now you know – you maybe got that, at last? I'm not hurting nobody else that's depending on me for support.'

Nobody else in the place made a sound during all this. Could've been a game on – nobody would've been watching. Nothing, just silence. It seemed like it lasted half an hour. The regulars weren't drinking or talking to each other, which was what they went in there to do; just looking down into the beers, pretending they'd all gone deaf. And Leo's wiping and wiping, that bar-rag is part of his arm, and finally he says: 'Well, I'm sorry, Pepper. I guess this time I went too far.'

The regulars started to breathe again and loosen up, and Pepper said: 'Uh, uh, Leo, not enough. That won't do it, pal.' They all stopped breathing again. 'You been ridin' my ass since the day I came in here, I got laid off and used up my unemployment, and that's over a year ago now. And you know somethin'? I still don't know why this is, that you're beatin' the shit outta me.

'I thought when you called and gave me this job, it was you felt sorry for me. Here I was, by myself, out at work, out of money; the next thing I'm going have to go on relief, and you called. And I thought: "Well damn, I was *wrong* about Leo, all these years that I hated his guts. The guy does have some kindness in him. Whaddaya think about that?"

'So I come in and I go to work. I'm *grateful*. And I'm gonna *prove* it to you: by being a damned-good hard worker. Servin' and busin' six booths by myself? This isn't no picnic you give me, but the hell, I get to keep all the tips. So I figured that's you, being kind. And all of the crap you dish out all the time, well that's just your way of hidin' that fact.

'Now I'm not sure any more. There's got to be something more to it. So now lemme just ask you, if that's all right: what is it that you want from me? You want to get into my pants, is that it? This's been your idea all along? It isn't enough, I tend the six booths; I also got to ask you into my bed? Because that wasn't in the job that I took, and I wouldn't've taken that job. So tell me, was that what it was?'

Leo wiped the rag on the bar.

'Leo?' she says. 'Answer me.'

Finally he mumbles something none of the regulars could make out, but apparently she could.

'Leo, Leo,' she said, 'don't ever take up bowlin'. You got to have balls for that, too.'

Graceland

*Elvis Presley: born 8 January 1935;
died 16 August 1977*

———◆———

William Bedford

WILLIAM BEDFORD lives in Grimsby with his wife and two young children and has published three volumes of poetry, as well as his journalism and two children's novels. His short stories have been widely published and broadcast, and his adult novels include *Happiland*, *All Shook Up* and *Catwalking*. The latest, *The Lost Mariner*, is published in September by Little, Brown.

Jamie spent hours alone in the loft, keeping out of his father's way. He cleared the floor and sat in the quiet, listening to the birds scrabbling on the tiles, the summer rain. He liked to listen to the rain at night while his father sat in the kitchen, marking essays. When it was dark, he thought about his mother, remembering the way things had been before she died.

The record player was the first thing he found. It was grey, with a red lid, and there was a stack of old 78s beside it on the floor. He wiped the dust off one of the records and looked at the label. The white cardboard cover was torn, and when he held the cover to the light, he felt shocked, recognizing his father's neat handwriting: 'To Sandra, my love forever, David.' It was dated summer 1956.

Sometimes she sang when she was doing the washing-up, her arms shimmering with soapsuds, her hair damp from the rising steam. 'Get out of that chair, rattle them pots and pans,' she giggled helplessly, and his father would shout from the lounge: '*Those* pots and pans,' as if she was one of his pupils. 'It's *those* pots and pans, Sandra. Do try and teach the boy to speak properly.' Then his father would turn the television up and pretend to be reading, and his mother would bite her lip, trying not to laugh.

He carried the record player downstairs one afternoon when his father was out at school. When he put one of the records on, the crackling sound made him jump. He felt a strange excitement. The record was 'My Baby Left Me'. He listened, hypnotized by the voice, and when the record finished, lifted the needle back to the beginning. He imagined his mother doing the same thing, thirty years ago.

He played the records every afternoon. His mother had collected pictures of Elvis Presley, and there were several long-playing albums with photographs of the singer on the cover. The back of one of the albums was signed by both his parents, their names joined together in an enormous pink heart. There was a photograph hidden inside the sleeve showing a young girl in a flared skirt and white gloves, a boy with thick-soled shoes and greased-back hair. With a shock, he realized it was his parents.

The afternoon his father came into the room, Jamie was listening to 'Heartbreak Hotel'. His father stood in the doorway, staring at the albums spread around the floor. Jamie thought he was going to lose his temper, but he put his hand quickly to his forehead and then walked out of the room. When Jamie went outside, his father was standing on the lawn, staring at the overgrown garden.

'I used to work on a fairground,' his father said when Jamie touched his arm. 'In the summer holidays. I got the sack for letting your mother have free candyfloss.'

Jamie held his breath. 'I didn't know that,' he said, reluctant to stop his father talking.

'No,' his father answered vaguely. 'I suppose not.' He turned to go back into the house.

'I didn't know anything,' Jamie said desperately. 'You never told me.'

His father didn't hear him. He was walking away. In the morning, the records were stacked in a neat pile behind the sofa with the record player. 'We could sell those,' his father said absentmindedly.

He found the shop one Saturday afternoon when he was wandering aimlessly around town. He peered through the windows, and saw the stacks of records, photographs and old magazines. The shop sold memorabilia from the Fifties. He went inside and heard

'Mystery Train' echoing tinnily from a room upstairs. There were photographs of the singer covering every wall. He almost jumped when the record finished and he heard footsteps clattering on the wooden stairs.

The woman seemed surprised to find him in the shop. 'You lost, sweetheart?' she asked in a rasping voice. She was smoking a cigarette, carrying a pile of records. She laughed when she saw his startled blush, but the laugh turned into a racking cough. When she recovered, she dumped the records on the counter and winked at Jamie. 'Don't even think about it,' she said, waving the cigarette in his face and then grinding it into the floor with the heel of her shoe.

He visited the shop most afternoons. The woman was called Deborah. When he told her about his mother's records, she listened quietly, asking him about the labels, laughing when he described the tracks. She had them all in the shop but seemed to like hearing him talk about them.

'Why are you interested?' he asked her one Saturday afternoon.

'A new generation,' Deborah said with her hacking cough. Her eyes were shining. 'Or new customers,' she added ironically, refusing to take herself seriously.

'I wouldn't sell them,' Jamie said immediately.

She smiled and ruffled his hair. 'No, love.'

'I wouldn't.'

'I know,' she laughed. 'I wouldn't buy them!'

It was August when Jamie took 'Blue Suede Shoes' to show Deborah. She read the label, and the handwritten message scrawled on the white cover, and then lit a cigarette, blowing smoke rings over their heads. She seemed surprised, vaguely upset. Jamie watched the smoke rings drifting around the shop. 'I learnt that at school,' Deborah grinned at him. 'That and kissing. Only useful things they ever taught me,' she added with her croaking laugh.

A few days later, she told him about the bonfire. 'You want to bring your father,' she said. 'We do it every year. On the anniversary. Play a few records. He might know somebody.'

Jamie shook his head doubtfully. He wasn't sure his father even heard the words when he spoke to him. 'He won't go,' he said unhappily.

'He won't *let go*, you mean,' Deborah said.

He watched her lighting a cigarette. 'What do you mean?' he asked.

She smiled. 'These will be the death of me,' she said, staring at the cigarette.

'Then why don't you stop?' Jamie said angrily.

Deborah flinched, then laughed abruptly. 'You'll come, will you?' she said.

'What?'

'To the bonfire, on the foreshore? You'll come?'

On the night of the anniversary, he left a note for his father, and rode his bicycle down to the foreshore. There were dozens of people gathered round the bonfire, and somebody was playing music on a ghetto blaster. Jamie recognized 'Mystery Train' and 'My Baby Left Me'. A group of youngsters danced to the loud music. When 'Don't Be Cruel' throbbed into the warm night air, more couples began dancing, clapping their hands and singing to the music. They all seemed to know the words. Jamie went and stood close to Deborah. She was holding hands with one of the men. He had blue tattoos on his arms. In the darkness she put her other hand on Jamie's shoulder.

The fire was burning quite low when everybody gathered in a circle.

Jamie didn't know what they were doing. They stood quietly and held hands. Deborah put the ghetto blaster in the middle of the circle and pressed the play button. It was a song he hadn't heard before: 'Young and Beautiful'. He listened to the words, the deep gospel rhythms of the backing group, the simple piano. When the song finished, there was a brief silence, and then one of the women in the group started talking.

'I went to Graceland with my husband,' the woman said. 'It was a farm originally. You can see the old barn, and the horses. They keep the horses so it's like the countryside. He never left Memphis. He never left home. They have a memorial garden in the grounds where you can sit and listen to yourself remembering. You don't get much chance for remembering with so much noise around. They have a service, with candles. They play that record we just heard and people walk round with candles, flickering in the dark. He never sang anything better than "Young and Beautiful",' the woman went on. 'Not in my opinion. All those candles flickering in the darkness. You knew he was there. The people you love are always there.'

In his rage, Jamie had to cry out. 'No' he shouted. 'It's not true.' He broke free of Deborah's hand and ran clumsily towards the tideline. He could hear voices calling in the darkness, the harsh cries of alarmed seagulls. There were shadows lurching round the flames of the fire. 'It's not true,' he shouted as he struggled through the heavy sand. 'It's not true,' he kept saying as the salt filled his mouth.

His father found him by one of the groynes. He had gone to sleep, nestled against the wooden breakwater. His shoes were wet through and his hair was matted with sand. 'You look a sight,' his father said, settling down on the sand beside him.

'How did you know?' Jamie asked.

'Deborah fetched me.'

They sat together, their backs against the breakwater, listening to the tide lap up the shores. The sky was brilliant with stars. Down the beach, they could see the fire burning. A figure stood alone at the edge of the fire, throwing driftwood into the dying flames.

'It isn't true,' Jamie said quietly.

'What isn't?' his father asked.

'What the woman said. About Graceland.'

His father watched him, waiting, leaning forward briefly to brush the hair out of his eyes. 'I wasn't there,' he reminded Jamie. 'What did she say?'

Jamie thought for a long time, but then stood up and said it didn't matter. 'We should go back,' he told his father.

His father nodded. He held out his hand so that Jamie could help him up. 'Deborah's waiting,' he said, nodding towards the fire. They walked back towards the dying embers.

'We could sell the records,' Jamie said suddenly.

211

His father laughed. 'She wouldn't buy them,' he said.

'What!'

'I know!' his father insisted.

'Why not?'

'She's a nice woman. She's your friend.'

They reached the fire and Deborah smiled at them, throwing more driftwood on to the flames. When the wood was burning, she took a packet of cigarettes from her jeans and offered one to Jamie's father. He shook his head. 'You didn't tell your dad you were here,' she said gruffly.

'I left a note,' Jamie said. Deborah laughed. She had no right to laugh. 'I want to sell the records,' Jamie repeated, glaring at Deborah.

She shrugged and looked at his father. 'Really?' she asked.

Jamie's father was smiling.

'They're not for sale,' he said quietly.

With a sigh, Deborah took a long drag at her cigarette and then tossed it into the fire. The cigarette flared and disappeared in the flames. She grinned at Jamie.

'Who said I wanted to buy them?' she said with her harsh laugh.

Lippy Kid

Hilary Mantel

HILARY MANTEL was born in Derbyshire in 1952. She has been a book and film critic and since 1985 has published seven novels, the settings of which include Saudi Arabia, Southern Africa in the 1950s and Paris during the Revolution. Her latest book is *An Experiment in Love* (Viking, 1995).

The bags were almost packed. Only the bananas were left. Maria's bare brown arm stretched back for them, but the checkout woman frowned. 'What are these?'

Polly gave a derisive yelp. 'A grown-up, and she doesn't know fruit. Didn't you go to school?'

The woman glared. 'I mean,' she said, 'are they West Indian?'

Polly rolled her big blue eyes. She unleashed another chortle. Her mother paid and towed her away. Lippy kid, she said, smiling to herself.

Three fat, wobbling bags hung from one wrist; Polly hung from the other. Polly was four now, but she was diminutive, looked just a toddler with her plump waddle and her blonde curls. When she was alone with her mother she looked fifty; her age hid behind her eyes, and you had to know where to look for it.

'Sour baggage,' Maria said. She meant the cashier, but there was also the baggage that dragged at her arm, the cauliflower and the soft drinks in cans and the huge bargain pack of detergent. Sometimes she missed the buggy, Polly safely strapped in with a bag tucked beside her and one hooked on the handle. School next year, she thought. For part of the day at least, two hands free.

She knew already how it would be. At the school gate, the other mums would think she was Polly's nanny, or a foreign au pair. It wasn't just her dark skin, dark hair; it was that she never looked sufficiently proprietorial. She'd started to notice, in the Press, those

215

stories about hospital mix-ups. No question is too silly or too small, the midwife had said. She had never braced herself to ask: are you sure this little girl is mine?

They were at the end of the High Street now. A tallow-coloured boy was crouching on a blanket outside the hi-fi shop. HOMELESS AND HUNGRY, PLEASE HELP. His baseball cap was upturned beside him, and his eyes were on the shoppers' feet.

'Is that a West Indian?' Polly said.

Thank God she can't read. 'You know it isn't.'

'Sour baggage,' Polly said to her. 'Here, have a HoJo.' She held out a tube of sweets, the wrapper torn back and the top one missing.

Maria swung around and brought the child to a halt. 'Where did you get those?'

'Off a shelf in the shop.'

'Polly! It's stealing! You know that!'

'Nobody stopped me,' Polly said. She prised out the top HoJo and popped it in her mouth. 'Original HoJos and New FrutyJos,' she said, in someone else's voice. 'The chocolate-covered treat with a real surprise at the centre.'

Maria dumped her bags at her feet. She took the child by the shoulders. She wanted to shake her. I despise, I despise, she thought, mums who make scenes in public. They were blocking the pavement. A gossiping pair split and skirted them. 'Polly, when people steal, shops call the police. Now you know that, don't you? How could you, sweetheart? I would have bought them for you.'

'You'd have said, you'll have no teeth left,' Polly pointed out.

I should take her back to the shop, Maria thought. March her into the manager's office and make her say sorry and pay the money. It would frighten her, but she'd never forget it and she'd never do it again. Her glance darted back down the street. All that would take half an hour, half an hour minimum; Polly was due at her playgroup, and she herself had to be at work this afternoon. She looked at the chewy bulge in Polly's cheek, and the strings of goo that cat's-cradled her tiny milk teeth. She snatched the tube from Polly's hand, and with a flick of her wrist sent it spinning into a litter bin.

For a moment, Polly stared after the HoJos. Then she took a deep breath and yelled. 'Go away, you sour baggage. *You're not my mother.*'

Heads flicked. Steps faltered. Amazing, the noise that could come out of Polly's little body, the keening, the rise-and-fall wail. She twisted away from Maria, her fists flailing, tears springing out of her eyes. She was taking possession of the pavement like a diva embarking on the final act. A crowd was collecting.

'But I am, I am her mother.' Maria flung out her arms. A wild thought, that she might be accused of kidnapping Polly . . .

'Well, if you are, you ought to be ashamed of yourself,' a woman said.

Suddenly, Polly cut off in mid-wail. It was as if her plug had been pulled. She was staring past Maria to the beggar. The boy was levering himself from the pavement; an arthritic limp brought him to the litter bin. One arm plunged in; it came out, the HoJos in his fist. Polly watched, her eyes popping. The boy's fingers fumbled with the wrapper. His hands shook. He aimed a sweet in the rough direction of his mouth and at the third attempt he got it in.

Then it began in earnest. A roar, a petrifying roar, emerged from Polly's infant gut; she burst across the pavement, pointing to the beggar. 'Call the *police*, call the *police*.' The boy had collapsed on to his blanket. He moved his head ponderously, as if trying to focus on the source of the noise. His mouth gaped open; the HoJo stirred and melted on the tip of his tongue. Polly began to sob. 'Call the *police*, call the *police*.'

Now the sandwich queue at the bread shop reversed itself, and streamed back on to the pavement. A car and a van drew up at the kerb and strange women threw off their seat belts with jaws set. Maria was shouldered away, forced backwards. For a moment she lost sight of Polly. Frantic, she tried to bat aside the hot summer bodies that penned her in.

A stubble-headed man in a black vest came out of the hi-fi shop, shouting 'Hoi, hoi!' – meaning nothing, just adding to the din. Music blasted out of the shop's open doorway. Polly's cries soared effortlessly above it. Maria fought to the front of the crowd. Polly saw her. Maria's hand stretched out. *'You're not my mother,'* Polly

217

snarled; snarled it at top volume, as if she had come with a built-in amplifier.

The beggar had staggered to his feet. He looked bewildered. A stout woman held out her arms and Polly rushed into them. She let herself be lifted into the woman's arms. A man's hand dug into Maria's bare arm. 'She says you're not her mother.' He was dragging her back, bruising her. She stared into his mild grandfatherly face.

'Why don't you get a job?' the stubble-headed man demanded. His finger stabbed the beggar's shoulder. 'Go on, why don't you get a job?' He seemed to be waiting to see it happen, this very minute.

Polly's face was scarlet, her voice hiccuping. She'll have a convulsion, Maria thought, a fit here in the street. The grandfatherly man had now twisted her arm behind her back. 'Yeah, get a job,' he said. 'And you, bitch, get back to bloody España. Or is it fucking Italia?'

'It's child abuse, if you want to know what I think,' a woman said.

Another voice: 'Yes. Jamie Bulger.'

It was at that point, confronted by stubble-head's jeering face, that the beggar decided to spit. It was pathetic, anyone could see that; without strength or aggression, it came out a baby dribble, saliva dripping on to his chest. Stubble-head's pale biceps twitched, just once. He raised his fist and crashed it into the point of the beggar's jaw.

The boy reeled backwards, fell full-length on the pavement. Someone screamed. His skull crashed into Maria's abandoned shopping, sending tins rolling around scuffling feet. Two people bent down and began to claw them into their own shopping bags. 'Looters should be shot,' somebody yelled. Maria twisted her head, stared into the eyes of the man holding her, stamped hard on his foot. The momentary shock was enough. 'Get an ambulance,' someone was calling.

As she dived towards Polly, she saw for a moment the baffled look in the child's eyes. Polly did her bit; her feet lashed the ribs of the stout woman who rocked her, and then they were away, Maria's strong brown legs in their trainers pounding the pavement, the child clasped to her body, legs around her waist and arms around her neck: one fleeing entity with two sobbing heads.

When her heart and lungs gave out, she stopped. Dumped Polly on her feet, bent over, hands splayed on her shins, fighting for breath. They were in a quiet avenue, nowhere they'd ever been. Her breath rasped; she heard birdsong. She straightened up. Dappled sunlight flitted across Polly's face; leaf-shadow moving, a thrush singing on a gate. Maria crouched, took out a crumpled tissue. Scrubbing at Polly's face, she tried to uncover the baby-smile beneath the chocolate and mucus and dribble. Polly grinned and raised her fist, as if in salute to the events of the day.

'What's that you've got there?' Maria said. She dabbed her own saliva on to her daughter's jaw, working it round and round.

Polly raised her fist again. A disintegrating HoJo leaked its juices between her fingers, liquid and brown like running blood.

Since this happened, a year has passed. Polly's father has left his wife and moved in with Maria. Polly has started school and Maria no longer worries that she belongs to someone else. They talk about selling the flat and moving to a safer area, where tweetie-birds vie with the noise of the M25 and only the roar of Concorde shatters the evening peace.

Sometimes Polly's father takes Maria to dinner parties, where she joins in the banter. When the wine is in, the wit is out, she will lean on her elbow and quote Margaret Thatcher, telling the whole dinner table: 'There is no such thing as society.'

The Voice of Mo

Paul Bailey

PAUL BAILEY was a Literary Fellow at the Universities of Newcastle and Durham, and a recipient of the E. M. Forster Award. His books include *A Distant Likeness*, *Peter Smart's Confessions*, *Old Soldiers*, *Trespasses* and *Gabriel's Lament*. His most recent novel is *Sugar Cane*. He is currently researching a biography of the painter Francis Bacon, and is working on a novel.

I was Marjorie when I set off on the road to Damascus – Damascus, East Sussex, I like to joke – but I became Mo after I had my revelation. I wasn't on a real road, I need hardly say, it was more of a metaphorical one, and my revelation wasn't of the blinding kind. I mean, I didn't fall to the earth with a great light from heaven shining on me – but I have to tell you I heard a voice. Guess whose it was? It was mine. It was the voice of Mo I was hearing, the voice of the woman inside the woman the world knew as Marjorie. I stopped and listened to her, and I loved the sound she was making. And the sense, too: she made such sense to me.

That was ten years ago. Today I am celebrating Mo's tenth anniversary, and if the weather stays fine, my like-minded friends and I will have our little party alfresco in the garden. Yes, it was on June the fourth that I first said goodbye to Marjoriedom and informed the man I had married that I'd changed for the better, and that if he addressed me as Marje or Marjorie he would receive no answer. I saw the last of him a month later and in that same sweet year the other man from the age of Marjorie vanished from my life. To tell the truth, and it is only the truth Mo's true voice tells, I sent him on his way with the most honest words I had ever spoken. I said to the callow youth to whom I had given birth that I had spent far too long imagining there were hidden depths to his character, depths that would partially justify his ignorant and hostile behaviour, and that now I understood he had no depth, let alone depths, at all.

'What I see of you, Timothy, is what you are,' I told him. 'You are shallow. You are transparent. You will never be otherwise.'

The relief I felt at allowing the thought to escape was immense, was overpowering. I was filled with a strange new sense of happiness. I expected him to scream his oh-so-familiar abuse at me, but for once he was silent. I think he must have realized that no words of his could match those he'd been privileged to hear from his hated mother.

With the pair of them gone, what remained of Marjorie went as well. I moved from the house and village where she had passed her existence, and with the money – the blood money, the guilty money – a, certain lord and master settled on his former slave, I bought this beautiful haven. There's no trace of them here, and none of her, because the clothes I wear and the food I eat and the bed I sleep in are Mo's and nobody else's. That's how it has to be. When I was Marjorie, the smell of men was with me in every room, and no amount of lavender polish on the chairs and tables could ever quite kill it off. Marjorie, I have to tell you, was a carnivore among carnivores, and it's a medical fact that meat causes men to sweat differently from women. The odour is stronger.

I mustn't give the impression that I'm entirely responsible for what I like to call my conversion. The truth is, there was – there is – a book. If you haven't read *Daring to Know Yourself: Confrontations with Your Inner Being* by Susan J. Wilkins Bakker, you should. Susan – we're on Susan and Mo terms, since we correspond with each other regularly; Susan – as I was saying – advises you to find the person you want to be by digging deep inside. It's partly thanks to Susan – and my own initiative, I need hardly add – that I dug deep and found the Mo who was buried beneath the surface of Marjorie. Susan's writing has granted me the courage to face the truth. And facing the truth, I have to tell you, requires courage. It does.

You're a fool if you haven't gleaned from what I've been telling you that mine's a meatless diet. I've slammed the dairy door behind me, too, and banned eggs, milk and cheese from my kitchen. I drink herbal tea and I bake bread with rye flour. Fruit and nuts and the vegetables I grow organically are my staples, and I don't have to look at my reflection in the mirror to discover that my eyes are sparkling. Of course they are. They have no alternative but to sparkle. They are lit, you see, from within, from the source of my innermost self. They are the windows of – yes, indeed – my soul.

Everyone's eyes ought to be windows, but in too many cases they are shutters instead. Shutters bar the view; shutters keep the light out. Remember that simple truth. Marjorie had shutters, I can tell you, or perhaps blinds would be more accurate, and they certainly prevented the light of truth getting in. In her book, Susan describes the dark journey to the light of truth as a process of 'personal interior archaeology', or p.i.a. You dig and dig, patiently, until you come upon the buried treasure that is you. I have to tell you I had patience, especially when they – Marjorie's husband, Marjorie's son – were scoffing at my efforts. The day Mo's true voice spoke to me – the voice you're listening to now, I don't need to remind you – I really put the pair of them in a panic. The cowards fled.

I have to correct the statement you made to me earlier when you rang and asked for an interview. The mother of the famous actor whose name you mentioned is Mrs Marjorie Barrett, the wife of Mr Charles Barrett. I have no dealings with her, and certainly not with him, and as far as the famous Timothy is concerned, I am not concerned in the slightest. I am plain Mo Parker, and I live at peace with myself. That is of no importance to you, but I do assure you it is of vital importance to me. The famous Timothy Barrett may have announced that his mother 'almost succeeded in crushing his spirit' but actors tend to say such things. They exaggerate. They are shallow, you see, and that is why they act. They have no depths of their own, I have to tell you, so they borrow other people's. Unluckily for you, Marjorie Barrett isn't here to contradict me. She would have said, 'My son isn't shallow. He's the deepest of boys,' had she been sitting where I am. But Marjorie Barrett was a liar, that was her trouble, the cross she had to bear. The shuttered Marjorie Barrett was the most terrible liar.

Which I am not. I am, I have to tell you, the reverse. I could have told you not to come, and warned you that you would be wasting your time. But you haven't wasted it. You have been honoured with the truth. You have heard a little of my, Mo's, story. I saw you jot down the title of Susan J. Wilkins Bakker's book, which I sincerely recommend to you. A course in p.i.a. might change your life as it helped to change mine. When I was imprisoned in Marjorie Barrett, I had hopes – vague hopes – of release. Of parole, I like to joke. I don't know if you are nurturing hopes of release from whosoever you are called – Kate Something, I believe you said – but if you aren't, you ought to be. I can see that there is a good deal wrong with your present life, even if you can't. You particularly need to lose weight.

I am not in the least distressed, I have to tell you, by the obvious fact that for the past hour you have been trying not to laugh at me. Please have hysterics, if you wish. You're itching to write a clever piece about the crank, the madwoman who in a previous manifestation was the mother of the famous young actor, the Hamlet of Hamlets, Timothy Barrett. The crank hasn't disappointed you, has she? Shake your head until it drops off, but you won't convince me, Mo Parker, to the contrary. Marjorie Barrett wouldn't have entertained you half as much, wouldn't have afforded you such wonderful copy. She was as sane as you suppose you are.

And now, you can go. I shan't beg you to excuse me, as poor Marjorie would have done. I'm telling you to go. My like-minded friends will be arriving at six to celebrate Mo's tenth anniversary, and I have snacks and special drinks to prepare.

Down the Tube

Lucy Ellmann

L<small>UCY</small> E<small>LLMANN</small> has written two novels, *Sweet Desserts* (winner of the Guardian Fiction Prize) and *Varying Degrees of Hopelessness*, some short stories and assorted journalism, mainly by eating biscuits. She is now a hermit and lives somewhere in England.

I had stupidly agreed to go to lunch with the guy. I'd known him vaguely for some time, and found him rude. Of course I'm continually tormented by remissness in others, as I have better manners than almost anyone I know, but Donald was a particular trial. Until our last meeting, that is, when he was all charm, attentiveness and lust. He had a misshapen weathered face (possibly the result of too much booze) and irredeemably skinny legs which no trousers seemed able to show to advantage. To his credit, he was tall. I was not disposed to like him.

As my office was near King's Cross, he proposed we meet up on the Cruise Line – he was a member. I'd heard about these new 'leisure' trains that run on the Circle Line, and had seen them pass by, but had never been on one. It was my little stand against privatization. I'd watched them privatize oil, gas, water, air traffic controllers, buses, British Rail, roads, pavements and bridges, schools, libraries, ambulances, fire stations and the poor old dustmen, telephones, the Royal Mail, the NHS, the BBC and nuclear power. I'd even endured the incessant advertising. But I'd always baulked at the sell-off of the Tube. It seemed a crazy idea to me, pampered businessmen luxuriating underground!

But I admit I was curious – like a vegetarian longing to be offered a bacon sandwich. I got myself to the Circle Line platform at the appointed hour (it was sort of crucial to catch the train Donald was *on*) and stared for some time at the bored faces around me:

shoppers, tourists, herds of children off on school trips, shorties, fatties and all the other untouchables of this world. There were women with colourful basket-style handbags forever slipping off their shoulders, and three men in a row all sporting joined-up eyebrows. One was reading a pink newspaper, in Italian. I wondered if any of these would be catching the Cruise Line. Unlikely. They all looked keen on getting from A to B.

The Cruise Line was announced and edged austerely towards us, to the usual accompaniment of murmured jeers and titters. Some well-groomed passengers behind heavy-curtained windows were carried goofily by, stiffly avoiding our gaze. A semi-bald girl near me, with a wedge of bleached blond hair emanating from her forehead, was moved to taunt: 'Bloody snobs. Come the revolution you won't want to be caught sitting in there!' A few people laughed approvingly at her boldness, while I sneaked unobtrusively aboard the Bar Car.

It was like something out of the Athenaeum – reeking of Empire, tea plantations, gunboats and the failure of the Peasants' Revolt. A serf came straight up to me and asked: 'Are you a member?'

'No, but *he* is,' I said, pointing to Donald whom I'd located sunk up to his chin in a leatherbound chair. My guestdom was apparently confirmed during a brief consultation, as I was allowed to join him. He was hardly *there*, shrouded in a newspaper (he'd been doing *The Times* crossword). Only a hand stuck out, holding a whisky. My heart sank: nothing I hate more in a man than an addiction to *The Times* crossword. All smiles, he invited me to sit down. And the train set off on its trail through the tunnels of London, sparks flying and wheels singing to the rats below.

After a drink, to postpone further faltering conversation we headed for the dining car. To reach it we had to pass through a dingy smoking room, a games room where a few old geezers were playing chess on magnetic boards, a curiously soundproof reading-room, the Arcadia (full of computer games and fruit machines), and a cafeteria in which every chair had its own table and TV set. I assumed this was where we would eat, not speaking, just watching TV, and then go our separate ways. Enough was enough, after all. But Donald proceeded to a sumptuous dining car. Here the tables were for two or four and each nestled in its own private nook next to windows almost hidden by maroon chenille curtains, trimmed with tassels. (There were few windows anywhere else on the train – what was there to see?) I sank into a nook and began to plough through the menu. In the end I settled on a live lobster from a tank swaying in the middle of the carriage; its existence seemed not dissimilar to being at the bottom of the ocean, but I still thought the creature would be better off dead.

By now Donald had started mumbling in a resentful tone about his childhood.

'We lived in Japan until I was eight. Fools to come back.'

'Why did you?' I asked, rather wishing he hadn't.

'To prepare for my father's prostate operation,' he growled. 'The result of which was that they had separate bedrooms from then on. He wasn't really *there* for anyone. In pain, I suppose.'

I was having lunch with a sulky eight-year-old. The conversation was a depressing contrast to all that dubious splendour. Some great oafs guffawed behind us at an inaudible dirty joke. And I thought the rich are as seedy as the poor, in their own way.

Donald's monologue had moved on to his mother, who was apparently now dying in some hospital out in the Home Counties. His attitude towards this event was somehow more than just fearful. It was shifty. And I suddenly suspected his present upsurge of libido was connected with it. The imminent loss of his mother had impelled him to start dating again! One woman to be replaced by another. I was probably one of a number he was frantically sampling.

I'm usually not overly critical of men with only an ego to their name, men of lugubrious turns of phrase, men purpled by plaintiveness. In fact I'm all too prone to forget their faults and go out with them repeatedly. I've slept with plenty of people who failed me as dinner companions. Despite the fact that modern-day erections are said to be half their former size (due to the effects of pollution), I still find that most will do. But even I was beginning to have serious doubts about Donald.

'I came from America at the age of thirteen,' I told him, butting in deliberately. 'I never really got my bearings, never felt I belonged. I have an empathy with excluded people . . .' I noticed he was not listening at all. He was busy removing something he didn't like from his hollandaise sauce. This is why women are so silent in restaurants. Why compete with the hollandaise?

Looking out of the window I discovered we'd gone full circle and were back at King's Cross. But unbelievably, the station was full of smoke. The place was on fire! People were running in all directions, some towards the Cruise Line train, hoping to escape by getting on it. I was paralyzed at first. Then I realized the Cruise Line wasn't going to stop. I leapt out of my chair, searching for an emergency cord, while the train simply speeded up. I was flabbergasted. An announcement came over the loudspeaker: 'Due to technical difficulties, the Cruise – Line will not be stopping at King's Cross . . .' I held on to our table to steady myself.

'*Did you see that?*' I yelled at Donald.

He hadn't noticed anything, too busy filling out charity forms – making a small contribution to a charity gave you a discount on the meal. What a guy.

Observing that I was somewhat distraught, he decided to take me on a tour of the rest of the train. I dumbly followed him, through the sauna and massage car, through the exercise room, through the virtual reality cinema, through the ice-cream parlour and the dance-hall, and then up some steps to the eponymous promenade deck with its excellent sea views (murals), deck-chairs, shuttlecock, and the sound of waves and seagulls, piped in.

Here, Donald was jostled by an uncouth youth. He turned to confront the boy, but a dowdy ginger-haired woman stepped up and declared: 'I do hope he isn't bothering you. I'm a Probation Officer and – he's in my charge.' Donald snorted impatiently at her behind, as she bustled the kid down to the lower deck. He then grumpily explained to me the humanitarian policy on the Cruise Line, of allowing the occasional juvenile delinquent on board for a day, supposedly to give them a taste for the good life.

'The straight and narrow, huh?' I asked. 'Revelation on a Tube train!'

A man nearby chipped in, 'I favour the short sharp shock myself! Throw them on to the tracks. That'd soon sort them out.'

'Some people actually consider it a privilege to be run over by a Cruise Line,' offered Donald. 'Really. Suicides prefer it – more publicity, I suppose. Oh, um, would you excuse me? (Looking at his watch) I must call my mother.' And he was off, leaving me in the hands of the resident bigot! I waited ten minutes, maintaining total silence, then set off to find him. All I wanted to do was say 'goodbye' so that I could *go*.

Nothing had a sign on it in this train, so you never knew what room or car you were entering. Well, the elite knew, but I didn't. I journeyed through several carriages, opening doors, haunted throughout by an easy-listening version of 'Chattanooga Choo-Choo' (minus the lyrics). Finally, I found myself in what appeared to be a couchette car. I opened one door and to my shame detected, within extensive yellow silk bedding, a copulating couple. I hurried on. At the end of the corridor I saw a doorway, cut off only by strings of beads. I parted them. Inside was a comical boudoir, laid out in the style of a Wild West bordello. Suddenly, I wondered if there was any truth to the ancient rumour that Cruise Line trains were equipped with brothel facilities – a point on which members were notably silent. I advanced further into the boudoir now, and was amazed to hear Donald's voice coming from round a corner.

I peered round. There were those objectionable legs of his, seen from the back, in their long wrinkled trousers. He was talking, as promised, to his mother on the phone – in an irritable tone of voice. But my eyes were drawn to the trousers. They seemed to shift steadily up and down in an unmistakable thrusting motion. I think I glimpsed a woman's head – a lot of hair. He was having it away with some damsel while talking to his dying mother on the phone!

I strode back through the train, and waited behind the Probation Officer and hooligan for the thing to stop. When it did, we were disgorged at Gloucester Road. Comforting, but not comforting enough. I transferred to the Piccadilly Line, got a train to Heathrow and boarded the next plane to Cuba, the only communist country left.

Love is free here.

Shared Credit

Frederic Raphael

FREDERIC RAPHAEL was born in Chicago in 1931 and educated at Cambridge. His novels include *The Glittering Prizes*, *After the War* and *A Double Life*. His latest novel, *Old Scores*, will be published later this year. He won an Oscar for Best Original Screenplay for *Darling* in 1965. He is a fellow of the Royal Society of Literature and divides his time between France and England.

I never saw a film on which Noah Benjamin had sole credit, even though he was seldom unemployed. Noah was a rewrite-man. He was brought in, at the last moment, by producers who had had enough of off-the-wall originality and had decided that what was needed was another writer. When he wanted to spur me to one more effort, Gino Armadei would sometimes mutter: 'I don't know, perhaps what we need now is a Noah Benjamin.'

If Noah was never *the* Noah Benjamin he did not complain. Writing was a living for him, not a vocation. He left literature to his best friend, Saul Levinson, with whom he had travelled from Hollywood in search of a promising land where Senator McCarthy subpoenas carried no clout. By the time I met them, in the sixties, Saul was said to be writing the great *un*American novel: the mordant last word on the Black List. Noah regarded his friend's talent without envy: he was a modest star who seemed genuinely to look forward to being eclipsed by a brighter one.

Saul was made of different stuff: if he ever had a kind word to say about anyone, he always thought better of it. Noah was his favourite and willing butt. On one occasion at the bar in the White Elephant, I remember, Noah told us that he had been asked to polish a script of *Mayerling*; Ray wanted it to have a happy ending. 'But I think I've probably got better things to do,' he said.

'Come on!' Saul said. 'You never did a better thing in your whole life.'

Noah flushed, as if at an undeserved compliment, and went to the bar to pay for Saul's round of drinks. He left before we had drunk them: 'Maddy is waiting,' he explained. Maddy was Madeline, his beautiful blonde ex-actress wife, whom Saul had more than once remarked was the well-stacked proof that her husband must have some talent, even if it was not for writing.

The couple had met on the set of *Anna K*, after Noah had been hired to devise a more sympathetic (and cheaper) way for her to betray her husband in a nouvelle vague version of *Anna Karenina*, set in Khrushchev's Moscow. To everyone's astonishment, she renounced her career in order, as she put it, to 'be with Noah'.

Meanwhile, Saul had been divorced by Roxanne, his childhood sweetheart and the mother of his four daughters. He was often at the Benjamins' house. He found it a little embarrassing that his friend was so idiotically happy, but a novelist had to be tolerant when he had no place else to go.

Noah's career might not be gaudy with rewards, but it was financially very rewarding: by the mid-sixties, the Benjamins had a house in Wilton Place and a six-cylinder Jensen at the yellow door. Only one thing was missing in their happy lives: Maddy had problems conceiving a baby. Their specialist ran some tests and then he advised them to try going somewhere quiet, by the sea. Noah rented a villa at Le Canadel and planned an undisturbed summer where they could be just the two of them.

However, when Saul Levinson turned down a fat script job, because the novel – working title *Are You Or Have You Ever Been?* – had to come first, Noah asked Maddy if she could bear the thought of inviting him to Le Canadel to stay with them.

'Not really,' she said.

'He can have the staff quarters,' Noah said. 'He wouldn't need to come near us.'

'I love you, Noah,' she said. 'You're such a *schmuck*.'

'We won't ask him then,' Noah said. But he did. What else could he do after hearing that Saul had escaped Gino's prehensile overtures by suggesting that he give Noah a chance to do a *first* draft screenplay for once?

At first, their guest joined the Benjamins regularly for dinner on the marble terrace overlooking the sea and the railway line (not mentioned in the brochure), but then, one day, he surprised Maddy naked, at the swimming pool and made an unwise remark. She replied with a selection of unexpectedly acute hypotheses concerning why Roxanne and his daughters now preferred the company of a very handsome, very rich Lebanese. The Benjamins' house-guest thereupon became reclusively monastic.

Noah reduced his first draft of Gino's script to 117 pages – what film producer ever appreciated generosity - and express mailed them to Gino. After ten days, he was abruptly invited to come to London to discuss the scenes that did not work. Taking the summons in dolefully good part, he told Maddy that he would be gone for two weeks and not a day over; if she seriously needed anything she really should *not* hesitate to call on Saul.

Noah took a cab to Nice to catch the plane. Gino's comments were not pithy, but Noah's professionalism – and his desire to get back to Maddy – made sure that their conferences were less meandering than usual. He worked so hard on the rewrites that he was able to deliver the new scenes within a week. Before Gino could find an unreasonable reason to keep him on hand, Noah flagged a cab and just managed to catch the evening flight to Nice. He could imagine how surprised Maddy would be to see him.

He took a taxi from Nice along the moonlit corniche road to Le Canadel. At the wrought-iron gate across the drive up to the villa, he paid off the driver and ambled towards the front door, jiggling his keys and savouring the zest of the pine trees and the prospect of Maddy. There was no light over the garage, where Saul usually worked late, and he wondered, with a lift of excitement, whether The Novel had at last reached term. Imagine if its creator was sleeping the sleep of that rare being, an author who had been true to his promise!

He crept up the soundless marble stairs and eased open the door of the bedroom. It might have been Gerry Fisher who had artfully lit the scene of the naked couple lying, glisteningly spent, on the uncovered bed. Noah stood in the doorway for a while and then, breathing carefully through his nose, he turned and went out and closed the door on his wife and his friend.

He stood for a while in the hall. Then he took another long breath and walked out of the house and locked the door behind him. He had only a light bag with him and the night was cool. He found a taxi in Le Lavandou which took him back to Nice airport. There was no problem about a seat on the early flight to London.

Once back in Wilton Place, he called Gino – who had no idea that he had ever left London – and was told that the new scenes were much better, except for one, which was, Gino had to say, much worse. It took only a few hours to fix it, so Noah was able to call Maddy and say that he would be on the evening plane.

She was at Nice airport with the Jensen. She kissed him keenly and said that she had some news which she hoped would not upset him: Saul Levinson had finished his novel and had moved out. A senior editor from Simon & Schuster was staying at the Hotel du Cap and had wanted to see him right away. 'So . . . you can imagine: whoosh, right?'

'I can imagine,' Noah said.

They went back to the empty villa and swam together in the pretty pool and then he took her to bed, for a long time. When he had finally finished, she said, 'Wow!'

'Does that beat "whoosh"?' he said.

After they had returned to London, Noah's agent called to say that Gino was going into production with 'The Big One'. Noah went out and bought Maddy that red Mini Cooper. A month later, she told him that she was officially pregnant. They could not tell whose tears were whose. When she said that she wanted to talk to him, he kissed her to silence and then asked her what they were going to call the baby. She said she loved him, but there really was something he ought to know. He said that he knew that she was pregnant and that he knew she loved him and that was enough for anybody to know.

He gave us the news at a poker game that night. Saul Levinson was now both rich and successful; a huge section of *Are You Or Have You Ever Been?* was going to be serialized in the *New Yorker*. However, success had not changed him: he was still drunk and bloody-minded. At two-thirty in the morning, Noah outbluffed him with over £100 on the table, it was not much, but – in those days – it was money, and Saul had lost it. 'Bluff, bluff, bluff,' he said. 'That's all you know, isn't it, Benjamin?'

'Take it easy, Saul,' I said. I felt bad, because Gino had asked me to do a polish on Noah's script.

'So Maddy's pregnant, is she?'

'Three months,' Noah said.

'Good old Riviera nights!' Saul said. 'Bet you that hundred quid it's a girl.'

'I like girls,' Noah said.

When Bathsheba was born, I was working on the script of *Are You Or Have You Ever Been?*; Saul said he was tired of the whole overpraised thing (he could not even take his own success graciously), but he consented to point out, over a drink where I had been incompetent or downright crass. It was then that I asked him why he had bet on the baby being a girl.

'All my kids are girls,' he said. 'Come on, be your age: I was staying with them all summer pretty well.'

I said, 'You're a pretty thorough going sonofabitch really, aren't you?'

'Am I? She desperately wanted a kid. He couldn't give her one. And you know what they say in business if things don't work out, you can always get another writer. He's never going to know, is he?'

The Lantern at the Rock
A Ballad in Prose

George Mackay Brown

GEORGE MACKAY BROWN was born in 1921 and has lived always in Orkney. He has written six books of short stories, six novels, and several books of verse, in addition to plays and essays. He studied English Literature at Edinburgh University. Though he is a state pensioner, he continues to write for three hours a day. His latest novel, *Beside the Ocean of Time*, was shortlisted for the 1995 Booker Prize.

A ship from Sweden struck the rock Hellyar in the darkness of a winter night. The ship *Sverige* sank at once and all on board were lost. The islanders salvaged much goods and gear and timber from the wreck, especially many hogsheads of spirits.

There was much drunkenness and bad behaviour on the island that winter. Little work was done. There was fighting and stealing and quarrelling in the houses.

The morning after the wreck a woman called Brenda had gone out to feed the ox in the byre. She heard a cry from the cave. There she found a boy with a broken leg. She could not understand the words he spoke. Brenda carried him up to her croft.

Her man Sigurd was in bed in a stupor of drink. The first of the barrels had been broached.

Brenda set down the Swedish boy at the fire, and she gave him a bowl of hot broth. He shivered for a while. Then he wept. He looked long into the fire.

Brenda bent down to stir the burning peats.

The boy put his cold mouth to her cheek.

It was said in the islands roundabout, it was no natural shipwreck. The winds were all bound up and laid by that night. The ship had been lured on to the rocks with a false lantern; so the jealous neighbouring islands said.

The islanders, at the end of winter, painfully sobering up among the empty hogsheads hidden in a cave (where the excise-men couldn't find them) denied it, but in low voices, with shifting eyes. A few of the island men, taunted at the Hamnavoe horsefair, turned away with red faces.

'They'll all be hung, once the truth comes out,' said the jovial horse-dealer in Hamnavoe.

The islanders who heard that rough-tongued taunting man stood with blanched faces.

For them, it was not the happiest horse fair. Generally, the horse-fair is a time of laughter and fiddling and dancing.

That evening they went down early to their yoles and sailed home.

The boy's leg was badly set by Madda, the island midwife and shrouder of the dead. It seemed he might never walk again. But three weeks after Yule he could hirple here and there about the crofthouse, holding on to a sill, a chair, the table.

He was a winsome fair-haired boy, called Tord.

He was well-looked after by Brenda, who had no children herself. Most of the village women looked in at the croft, that winter, from time to time, to see the boy. They were all greatly taken by his beauty and courtesy. 'A great pity it is,' they said, 'that the boy will never be able to walk, or do for himself. Brenda has taken a burden on her. Still, he will be a light in that poor barren croft.'

But Sigurd her man could not stand the boy. 'I'll speak to some skipper in Hamnavoe,' he said often, 'a Baltic-bound skipper. He'll ship the foreign creature back home. If he was able to help me about the croft, at ploughing and peat-cutting! My wife is a fool. Some years we can hardly feed ourselves.'

As spring came on, the boy Tord limped outside and sat in the sun on a low wall, looking out to sea.

He quickly gathered enough words to make himself understood to the islanders.

He called a greeting to them as they went down to their boats and returned at evening, the women carrying the baskets of fish. Few of the island men turned their faces to him. But the women put down their heavy baskets of gutted and cleaned fish and waved: 'Tord! Tord . . . !'

After plough-time and seed-time, the islanders waited for the warm rains and the sun.

There had been a March drought for weeks but no one was worried. The islands are never short of rain.

One morning, Sigurd went to the door of his croft and he called out cheerfully enough (for he was a morose man): 'Brenda, there's a big rain-cloud in the west. And not before time.'

The wind was blowing dust about the island.

Then the wind changed and the huge rain-bearing cloud discharged fructifying rain on all the neighbouring islands.

A few drops fell on this island, no more. The sun shone. The wind changed and blew sterile dust about the braes and dykes.

'Tomorrow or the day after,' said the island folk. 'Then the rain will come.'

But the rain was slow in blessing the island with its lucency and fertile green flushings.

The islands around had rain in plenty. Their burns were full of songs, their wells were abrim. A sweet new tender green covered their ploughlands, and their cows waded knee-deep in the pastures.

Barren dust blew about the island of the ship-wrecking. The cattle and sheep and swine on the hills grew thin and bony. And the oats and barley came up thin and poor, and drooped their heads in the dust.

'The rain must come,' cried the islanders.

But the rain did not come. Days and weeks passed, and the rain fell on all the Orkneys except this one island.

Now they were taking buckets from the dregs of the island wells. The wooden buckets trundled on the stone floors of the well, and came up with worms and mud and roots in them.

The island men rowed across the sounds to the other islands, to buy water. They were given a bucket of water here, a pailful there, to wet the throats of the dying old man and the young woman with the newborn ailing child.

They tried to steal water at night from the wells and waterfalls of neighbouring islands. Stones came out of the darkness and drove them back to their small boats.

Thunder flashed and cleared its throat and grumbled all round the island, and splashed its dowers of rain on every island but this one.

One midnight Tord was lying awake in his corner. He heard the rough snores of Sigurd. There came a sigh from Brenda. Tord could see by the light of the stars and the hearthglow that Brenda got out of bed and stood under Sigurd's lantern that hung on the wall. Some men said that this was the lantern that had lured the Swedish ship ashore.

Brenda said: 'The lantern is a good light, daughter of the sun and moon and stars. By its glimmer we feed the ox in the byre and read a chapter of the Good Book. We have made it a vessel of darkness and shipwreck.'

Then Brenda went back to bed, and Tord could tell by her soft regular breathing that she was asleep.

Next morning Tord was sitting at the end of the house, in the sun. Sigurd had gone fishing. (There had been poor fishing that summer also. Men could not remember thinner poorer catches.)

Brenda was out in the yard, throwing oats to the hens. The scrawny cock raged with thirst, a dry half-hearted carillon. Here and there on the horizon, the islanders were pulling in barren lines.

Brenda was chanting slowly, as if in a dream: 'We have taken on ourselves a curse of salt water. Now its sister, the sweet rain, is turning its face from us.

That same evening, under the first star, the oldest man in the island died. The girl and her child died at sunset.

'Do you walk in your sleep, mother?' said Tord to Brenda. 'Do you walk and speak among your dreams?'

'Never,' said Brenda. 'And I'm not your mother. Your mother is up there, under the green mound, with your father the skipper and the drowned sailors.'

'I know that,' said Tord. 'I go up there and talk to her. But you are my mother now.'

'Eat your bannock and egg,' said Brenda. 'I hear the boats scraping on the shingle below. I will try to be a mother to you, boy.'

The Lantern at the Rock

* * *

'Why are you forever speaking in your sleep?' said Sigurd to his wife. 'Why do you get up out of bed so often and wander here and there speaking nonsense and then come back to bed again?'

'I sleep from sunset to dawn without a break,' said Brenda. 'I have a clear conscience, not like some men in this island.'

But one night, when Brenda was saying her prayers in the chair beside the hearth, she thought she saw a moving glimmer on the hillside.

She opened the door and looked towards the hill. A cripple boy with a lantern was standing beside the mound where the Swedish sailors were buried. He gestured, the lantern threw yellow splashes of light about his face and hands. Soon he was surrounded by the drowned people. Tord turned towards the kirk and the kirkyard and began to hirple in that direction. The Swedes followed. When they came to the kirkyard they all stood among the tombstones. Tord hung the lantern over the new-buried, the old man and the girl with her infant. Then the sea-dead held up their hands in forgiveness and blessing upon the earth-dead.

A drop of rain water hit Brenda's hand. It tasted like honey.

She hurried into bed and buried her head in the blankets. Sigurd snored like a saw rasping through wood.

A while later, when the early summer dawn was coming in at the east window, Brenda sat up and looked about her. Tord was in his bed in the corner, and the lantern was hanging on its nail at the wall.

She touched it, the glass was warm.

There was a new sound in the island, a surging and throbbing. Brenda went out into tumults of rain. She stood there a long while, her face and her hands shining.

The rain fell and fell on the living and the dead, all that day till sunset.

When Sigurd and Brenda died, many years later, Tord inherited the croft and the fishing boat.

He walked with a limp all his life but he was strong and capable and after a year or two the islanders accepted him as one of themselves.

He married an island girl and they had four children.

When they were young, those children brought first spring flowers to the green mound where the Swedish crew slept in peace.

Forward to Fundamentals

Michael Carson

MICHAEL CARSON was born in Merseyside just after the Second World War. Educated at Catholic schools, he then became a novice in a religious order. After leaving university, he took up a career as a teacher of English as a foreign language and has worked in various countries, including Saudi Arabia, Brunei and Iran. He has written four novels, *Sucking Sherbet Lemons*, *Friends and Infidels*, *Coming Up Roses* and *Stripping Penguins Bare* (available from Black Swan).

'Where is Malin Head and bloody Bailey anyway, is what I'd like to know?' said Flo, who was listening to the shipping forecast while lighting the gas under the cauldron of gruel. Then she reached for her hand-knitted duster and cleaned old dinner off the kids' manacles.

'Search me,' I said. 'Somewhere all at sea, I expect.' Like the rest of us.

In a loud voice, louder than the echoey dinner-room liked, Flo said: 'I've a good mind to write a letter to the shipping forecast people, Pet. It's about time they went forward to fundamentals like the rest of us. I don't know how they've got away with gobbledy-gook all these years.'

Ships still pass in the night, I thought, but didn't say anything. I took my mop and made a meandering river of wet behind me, like a snail who means well, parking myself at the glass door between the dinner-room and the upper corridor of St Lilley's Vocational Primary. 'There's a queue of kids outside the Patten room,' I said.

'It's Lower Third Chimney Sweeping, I expect, in for their pattening. I shouldn't be saying this, but Mr Grime can't control them. Have you seen the way they climb away from him up the practice flues? He hasn't got the knack. His lot always end up being pulled out by the head for a pattening. It's funny how some of the staff can keep peace-perfect-peace and others can't.'

253

'In the old days you liked to hear a bit of hubbub. Sign of life, you said,' I said.

But I don't think Flo heard me. She was polishing the chains that connect the manacles to the dinner-benches. 'You'd think the little horrors would have learnt by now!' she said.

'Well,' I said. 'I don't see the point of training chimney sweeps. There's no coal to put on the fires, and even if there was, nobody'd have enough money to buy it.'

Flo heard that. She looked around, then she aimed a harsh look in my direction. 'You'll go too far one day, Pet,' she said.

'Time to stir the gruel,' I told Flo and I mimed smoking a fag, just like Flo loved doing before we all went forward to fundamentals.

We were still not on speaking terms when the sound of thrashing and screams gave us the five-minute warning that the kids would be in for their gruel. Upper Second Dishwashing came in first, with Miss Crisp corralling them with her wooden spoon.

'Good afternoon, Miss Crisp!' I called, breaking the hard brown bread and throwing it into each bowl of gruel that Flo dished out with the same amazing speed that was mentioned in her MBE citation.

Miss Crisp nodded in the patronizing way that teachers have remembered how to do. She turned to her class. 'Sit!' she commanded. 'Manacles on left ankle! Click shut! Manacles on right ankle! Click shut! Hands on table!' She inspected the hands of her class. 'Fingers on lips!'

It's funny how people have changed since we went forward to fundamentals. When Miss Crisp first came to St Lilley's she was full of cunning ways to get the kids interested. You can see how long she's been here just from that. But in those days, before forward to fundamentals, she'd bring in maps and silver-paper-covered toilet rolls – remember them? – and things picked up on her walks in the countryside. You could walk in the countryside in those days, you see. And she'd have the kids make up plays about the quest for the silver-paper-covered toilet roll, only she would say that it was something really precious, like a jewel casket, and I'd pass the door of her class and the kids would be doing their projects and looking up, over, under and through everything for knowledge and asking questions and exploding into reading and – I have to look round, scared I'll get caught just thinking it – *happy*.

'They look happy, Miss Crisp,' I'd say.

'I hope so, Pet,' Miss Crisp would reply. She was always pleased when somebody noticed. 'I stay awake nights trying to come up with all sorts of activities that will *consume* the children. It's a hard battle to hold their interest when they have the telly and computer games at home and all I have is silver-paper-covered toilet rolls, and what I can forage. But, you know, Pet, I think it's working.'

'I'm sure it's working Miss Crisp,' I'd say. 'They're a bit of a handful in the dinner-room but they're happy. That's the main thing. I can remember when I was at school.'

'How was it for you?'

'It was – like you would say – *basic*, Miss Crisp.'

'Yes, basic's a good word for what it was,' Miss Crisp would reply. 'Were you afraid of the teachers?'

'I used to wet my knickers, Miss Crisp,' I'd say.

'It was *that* basic, was it, Pet?'

'Yes, Miss Crisp. I'd love to have been in your class. It might've made all the difference to me. I always wanted to be a nurse but my teachers kept telling me I was too stupid. Probably I was.'

'Nonsense! They robbed you of your self-esteem. Thank God, times have changed. Now learning is an adventure – well, as much of an adventure as I can make it with the slender resources available.'

'There are some who say there's not enough discipline,' I'd say – not knowing how it was going to go.

'Those are short memories, Pet. I remember teachers who made me feel small, pulled me out of my seat by the hair . . . you remember wetting your knickers. I vowed that when I became a teacher that it wouldn't be like that in my classroom.'

'Quite right, Miss Crisp.'

* * *

I was busy with these thoughts of bygone years – and trying to work out how Miss Crisp, and the rest of us, could have changed so much – while I threw hunks of bread into the bowls of gruel. I noticed that Miss Crisp had picked on a little brown boy. Nothing new in that. She was accusing him of having dirty fingernails that might be all right where he'd come from but were no good for St Lilley's. She hit him with her wooden spoon. The child sobbed and I saw water dripping off the bench and forming a puddle at his feet.

Don't ask me why, but my heart went out to him. Thinking that this wasn't like me, and definitely wasn't fundamentally correct, I picked up an old floor cloth and walked down the dinner-room as if I had an errand. I threw the cloth over the wet spot and gave the child a squeeze, leaning over the table to swat a bluebottle as I did so, to try and disguise the squeeze. Physical contact has been completely beyond the pale for years, of course. I heard Flo gasp behind me, saw the anger in Miss Crisp's eyes.

Luckily, Lower Third Thatching and Upper Fourth Gritting came in. The sounds of manacles, chains and barked commands drowned out the brown boy's cries as Miss Crisp laid into him again. She stood him up on the table so that everyone could see his wet patch. 'This will cost your mother a fine!' she said. 'What is her occupation?'

'Matchgirl. Third class. Unemployed,' the little boy replied.

Miss Crisp searched in her bag and produced her board-rubber. She slapped the child, once on each cheek. She left chalk-dust, the exact shape of two eclairs – remember them? – on each of his brown cheeks. He stood, marked and erect, accepting the sneers of children and teachers alike. He was joining polite society. I could tell. He seemed carved from stone.

After work I walked home across Westminster Bridge. There were several new heads on the poles. It was always a bit of a relief that they rang the changes. Well, you get tired of the same old faces, don't you? I was surprised to see every member of the heavy metal band 'Smoking Kills', gracing five poles, one after the other. Pop singers did not usually make it to Westminster Bridge. The members of the Forward to Fundamentals coalition government like to look out on good-looking heads. Usually unmarried mothers, ladies of the night and one or two of the prettier political reporters find their heads within sight of the House of Fundamentals. Pop stars end up on Blackfriars Bridge, if they're lucky, and quite a few grace the Thames Barrier. Chelsea Bridge is the exclusive preserve of sexual deviants, while those guilty of fraud occupy London Bridge.

I know all this because my hubby, Lionel, drives a tour bus. His route zigzags across London's bridges at a snail's pace while the world's tourists gawk. Lionel's lucky to have that job. Heads on poles are the biggest tourist attraction the capital has to offer – after public executions, of course.

People kept coming out of the darkness, flashing their hawkers' permits and asking me to buy National Lottery tickets. I make it a rule to buy one a day, but it's a problem because when you buy one you have hoards of other hawkers descending on you.

Years ago the National Lottery stopped becoming a way of financing good causes and became almost the last thing an ordinary person could do to earn a crust. No one knows where the money goes. It would be a scandal if there were such things as scandals any more. They no longer exist; just as TV, footpaths, laughter, hope for the future, no longer exist.

I turned up Blackfriars and decided to cut down by Smithfield Market to get home to Hackney. I passed the Old Bailey and I had this daft thought: if I could climb up and put Miss Crisp's silver-paper-covered toilet roll in one tray of Justice's scales and her wooden spoon in the other, what would be the result? Perhaps the scales would creak to equilibrium. Kindness and Kicks, Smiles and Tears, Romance and Discipline, all rolled up together into a well-meaning Golden Mean. I looked round to see if anyone could see me thinking that way. Then I shrugged at the pointlessness of the thought – probably my teachers were right – and returned my head to fundamentals. What, for instance, was I going to give Lionel for his supper?

I arrived home to find the School Inspectorate camped outside my door. The neighbourhood watch was out on the walkways, accusing me of things before somebody accused them. They've got the fundamentals down pat round our way.

'Miss Petula Bird? Dinner Lady second class?' the inspector asked.

'That's me,' I said.

'We have reason to believe that you have fondled a pupil in your care at St Lilley's Vocational Primary Institution. You are under arrest. Your rights and duties under the Subject's Charter have been posted to you. You must admit your crime into this tape recorder and then you will come with us.'

I snapped. Well, I might as well. I touched a child affectionately. It's the worst thing you can do. Everyone is agreed. Lionel has never told me where they put the heads of dinner ladies. He probably didn't want to depress me.

'Yes,' I said into the tape recorder. 'I admit it. I touched the child. He was miserable and I wanted to make him feel better. You see, I don't believe children are basically bad. I don't believe it. I *won't* believe it! They need love as well as discipline. If you ask me, it's time we went back to progress. Who told on me, anyway? Miss Crisp, I suppose.'

The inspector switched off the tape recorder. 'No. The child accused you,' he said.

Drawn from Life

Justin Cartwright

JUSTIN CARTWRIGHT was born in South Africa. He was educated there and at Oxford University. He has lived in London all his adult life. He has written six novels and has been shortlisted for many awards, including the Whitbread, twice, the Sunday Express, the James Tait Black, the CNA (winner) and the M Net (winner 1994). His most recent novel is *Masai Dreaming* and his new novel, *In Every Face I Meet*, will be published by Sceptre in September 1995.

Horses occupy a particular place in the affections of those English who live in the country: they love their long, fragile legs, their inquisitive, whiskery muzzles, their mobile, tubular ears, their sensitive skin, their big, gentle eyes and their coarse manes. They love the ritual associated with horses; the saddle soap and the dubbin, the linseed oil and the bandages, are the liturgical apparatus. They love the way horses steam when they are wet and when they are hot. They love the scents of tack, saddle blankets, New Zealand rugs, hacking-jackets and jodhpur boots. They are reassured by the sight of polo-sticks, hunting crops and whips in a huge old vase in the hall. And, of course, they love horse paintings.

The greatest horse painter who ever lived, the English Leonardo, was George Stubbs. Stubbs was the sort of man who, when it would have been a lot simpler to use some tact, spoke his mind. But he had spent many, many hours dissecting horses and remained true to the knowledge he gained in this way. He refused to nod to changing fashion. To him, things were painted from life. That is what painting was. To most Englishmen, that is still what painting is.

When Colonel Gabriel Torrington died at the age of ninety-two, the family solicitor, Barnaby Fisher, who was sorting out the colonel's papers, found a portfolio of drawings by Stubbs in a cupboard next to a box file containing the estate's milking records since 1932. There were twenty-five sketches and drawings of horses

261

on a fine-weave paper. Although he knew nothing about art, Mr Fisher had heard of Stubbs. He summoned the two women who worked in the house, Mrs Green and Mrs Jenkins. They had formed a shrewd alliance, over the years. Because of their familiarity with the colonel's housekeeping, they had an unspoken status in the village. They kept the colonel's secrets and disseminated his opinions when it suited them. They saw themselves as carrying on a duty of continuity to the big house, the land, and the way things had always been, despite the encroachment of the Country Museum and the Little Chef just beyond the park wall. Although they were quite different in shape, one tall and thin and the other broad and sturdy, their faces were similar, bleached like boats that have been left out in all weathers.

Mr Fisher shuffled some papers importantly. The women stood at the door of the colonel's study in their nylon housecoats. He didn't invite them to sit.

'As you know, Colonel Torrington has left you some money in his will.'

'Yes sir.'

'He has also said that once the inventory is complete, you may take your pick of three objects from the house. Excluding, of course, anything of outstanding artistic significance. That will be the province of the National Trust and Sotheby's when they come to value everything. Do you understand?'

'Yes sir.'

'The question is, did the colonel suggest to you any items you might like? I ask this so that I can perhaps put them to one side, as the colonel asked me to.'

It seemed that the women had made up their minds, and had chosen some china (Mrs Green) and a walnut table (Mrs Jenkins) and some other trinkets. Mr Fisher made a fuss of noting their choices. There was no mention of the folder of drawings.

'Now, during the process of probate there must be absolutely no disturbance to the colonel's papers. I am sure you understand.'

Mr Fisher closed the door of the colonel's office. His grandfather had handled both the marriage settlement and then, so soon after, the painful legal work made necessary by Camilla Torrington's death. That was in 1929. Since that year, the colonel had lived as a near recluse. Only once, in 1953, had he left the grounds to attend a reception in Cirencester for the newly crowned Queen. Lady Camilla was a descendant of the Marquess of Rockingham, who was a patron of George Stubbs.

Mr Fisher, after a visit to the library in Cheltenham, came to the conclusion that the drawings were studies for Stubbs's *Whistlejacket*. *Whistlejacket* is Stubbs's most famous work, yet there is something strange about the painting. The horse is poised on its hind legs. There is a large blank space above its broad back where you might have expected a rider. It is an equestrian portrait, minus the equestrian. The equestrian intended was George III. The Marquess of Rockingham, who had commissioned the portrait in 1762, fell out of favour with the King and resigned as Lord of the Bedchamber. The painting was never finished. The Marquess had someone else in mind to paint the King and someone quite different to supply the background. All his life Stubbs suffered from the widely expressed opinion that he was only a painter of horses.

That afternoon, Mr Fisher had a meeting with his bank manager. Mr Fisher had borrowed £800,000 to develop an old people's home with the eager connivance of the bank. But there had been delays and a surprising lack of interest considering the quantities of elderly people in Cheltenham. Mr Fisher explained the economies he had made: he had axed the colonic irrigation facility and cancelled the hydrotherapy bath. The bank manager took notes ominously.

'When do you expect the take-up to be complete?' he asked.

'We're expecting renewed interest in the spring.'

The manager wrote slowly.

'I will have to pass this higher up,' he said. 'To extend the facility.'

'I am expecting a considerable legacy in the near future,' said Mr Fisher suddenly.

'Are we talking five figures?' asked the manager.

'Six.'

Geneva is a city where the ephemeral is turned into currency, Here, watch companies sponsor exhibitions of paintings and orchestras play for the glory of banks so that the bored and exiled are lulled into believing that they have a firm hold on the slippery world. Here, the right of the rich to be protected from the envy of police and tax inspectors is scrupulously protected.

Mr Fisher approached the offices of Hurlimann Frères, which overlooked a small island in the turbulent grey river rushing out of the lake. Under his arm was a parcel containing one of the drawings. The expert from Hurlimann was an Englishman, long resident abroad. The stripe in his suit and the gold signet ring on his finger were fatter than anything Mr Fisher had seen in Gloucestershire. He pointed Mr Fisher into his Louis-the-something office which had a perfectly framed view of the lake. His secretary, who looked to Mr Fisher like a Dior mannequin, brought coffee in wafer-thin china, almond biscuits on a silver tray, and a bowl of glimmering sugar crystals. Mr Fisher's secretary, Debbie, usually gave him Nescafé, with a Hobnob and two sugars, in an Injured Jockeys Fund mug.

'Shall we look at the pictures now?'

'Picture. Just the one. First I must stress that this is completely confidential. For the moment I am only looking for confirmation that these are drawings by George Stubbs.'

He handed the brown folder to the expert, who cut deftly through the masking tape with a silver penknife.

'My God,' he said. 'Jesus Christ Almighty.'

Mr Fisher wondered if the elegant fellow was undergoing a religious conversion right there.

'Whistlejacket.'

'I thought so. I looked him up in Cheltenham public library.'

'This is a preliminary study for Stubbs's paintings for the Marquess of Rockingham.'

'What is it worth? I mean what would it be worth, on the open market, so to speak.'

Mr Fisher had intended a little more prevarication, but the questions could not be suppressed. He could see only the mounting debts of his unpeopled old people's haven.

'What is it worth . . . Well.'

The expert was standing near the window now, so that the jet of water from the famous fountain appeared to spout directly from his head. His hands were trembling. 'Excuse me,' he said. 'How many drawings are there?'

'Twenty-five.'

'Good God. If they are all in the same condition there is no saying. It could depend on what museum wanted them most. But, and there are a lot of qualifications here, at least twelve million Swiss francs. Let's say about six million pounds at the current rate. Would you want to sell privately or at auction?'

Mr Fisher took a taxi to the airport. The expert had asked about the 'provenance' of the drawings. Mr Fisher thought he was asking if he had found them in the South of France. For a fee Hurlimann would set up a trust in the Netherlands Antilles, make the trust the owner of the drawings, make Mr Fisher, via a few Swiss companies, the beneficiary of the trust, and sell the drawings in a fog of anonymity. There were ways of doing these things. Many of the landed families in Gloucestershire had immense wealth, all safely tucked away in places which were no more than a few post boxes and a banana packing factory. Mr Fisher's brief visit to Geneva had expanded his horizons. Nowhere on these broadened horizons did he see sheltered accommodation, colonic irrigation, or Mrs Fisher.

It took Mr Fisher just over an hour to reach the manor from the airport. As he entered the long driveway it was already dark. In big cities there is always a glow rising like a dust-storm above the buildings, but here he could see only the bare trees flaring in the Volvo's headlights. He fumbled with the keys, pushing open the heavy, studded front door. He hurried to the colonel's study. As he reached it, the phone on the desk rang. He picked it up, startled.

'Yes.'

'Is that you, Mr Fisher?'

It was the gentle voice of Mrs Green.

'Oh yes. Yes. Did I disturb you?'

'No no. I saw the lights of your car. I just wanted to give you some very good news.'

'And what's that?'

'The man from the National Trust was here today. We showed him some drawings in the colonel's study. I hope you don't mind. We didn't touch the papers. He says that he believes that they are by

Stubbs. He thinks they could be worth a lot of money. He's taken them to the Tate Gallery for authentication.'

Mr Fisher could not speak for a moment. Then he said, 'George Stubbs. The one who painted horses. Jolly good.'

Mist

$\text{\textreferencemark}$

Richard Adams

One of my friends in the Lake District is a sheep-farmer called Dennis Williamson. It's some years ago now that through Dennis I met another hill-walker like myself, Alan Roberts. Alan and I have done many a walk since then. He has a sort of idiosyncrasy, if that's the right term. He won't walk in mist – not even a light mist. This can be a bit irritating.

One day, when we were both chatting to Dennis, I brought up the subject of mist on the high tops. I said that when I was alone and there wasn't much visibility, I could never overcome the idea that the surroundings were malignant, or at any rate unwelcoming. To my surprise, Dennis, a practical, straightforward hill farmer if ever there was one, endorsed me at once. 'Ay,' he said. 'Y'feel theer's soomthing oop theer as doosn't like yer, don't yer?'

After supper the following evening, Alan put down his Wainwright and said: 'Did you mean what you were saying to Dennis yesterday about there being some sort of malice in the mist?'

'Well, yes,' I answered. 'More than once, when I've been alone in mist, I've felt a sort of hostility in the surroundings.'

Alan said, 'I'd like to try and tell you about an experience I had – oh, several years ago now. Only I'm afraid you may think I'm a bit nutty.'

To this I said nothing, but simply waited for him to make a start.

'Some time ago,' he said, 'I had a year at a university in Virginia. We were fairly close to the Blue Ridge mountains and of course I wanted to get in as much walking as I could. Looking for friends to walk with, I came upon Don Hatherley and his girlfriend Carol. They knew a lot of the local trails and went out with me for some of the best walking I can remember.

'Neither Don or Carol had ever been out of America, and when I suggested that they ought to come over to walk in the Lake District they fairly jumped at the idea. We fixed that they were to come in September and stay at Wastdale Head.

'Their visit was a complete success. We did most of the best walks in the Lakes, and of course we went Wordsworthing at Rydal and Beatrix Pottering at Sawrey. The weather was perfect and no one could have asked for better conditions.

'My idea was to spend our last day doing the Scafell horseshoe: Crinkle Crags, Bow Fell, Scafell Pike, Scafell – the lot. I laid on a hired car to take us to Cockley Beck at the top of the Duddon Valley.

'Early next morning it was cloudy, with a fair bit of mist on Great Gable. At breakfast, however, Don and Carol were full of enthusiasm. The car dropped us at Cockley Beck at about ten o'clock. The first thing to do, of course, was to get up on to the Crinkle Crags by climbing Red How. It's a hard slog, but my two Americans went at it without a word of complaint. We did it in a little less than an hour, having come into some light mist about half-way up. On the top it was thicker, but as we set off northwards, there was at least seventy yards' visibility.

'When at length we came down off the Crinkles and reached Three Tarns – the saddle between the Crinkles and Bow Fell – the mist higher up had thickened. We couldn't see the summit of Bow Fell at all. I thought we should call it a day. I said so as firmly as I could. "You don't know how quickly mist can thicken on these tops. We ought to go down before it gets worse."

'"Ah, hell, Alan," said Don. "Bow Fell's one top I really want to climb. You'll be kicking yourself tomorrow if we chicken out now."

'I could see that if we went down and conditions didn't get any worse, they'd probably not forget that my silly caution had spoilt their last day. Besides, as Don pointed out, it would be a long trudge back if we didn't go by Scafell. In the end I gave way.

'We had no trouble getting to the top of Bow Fell, but once there we found thick mist all round us. If we were going to reach the Esk Hause it would be a matter of making our way from cairn to cairn – if indeed we were even going to be able to see from cairn to cairn. I felt thoroughly demoralized. The mist had really penetrated me: my socks were wet, my trousers, my anorak and my woollen cap. When we came to the Esk Hause, I more or less pleaded that we should go down to Sprinkling Tarn and then round to Wastdale Head under Great Gable. But Don would have none of it.

'"Alan, you told me that Scafell Pike's the highest top in England. It'll take more than a bit of mist to stop me now."

'It was clear to me that if I set out for Sprinkling Tarn, I'd go alone, for Carol would certainly do whatever Don did. I wasn't ready to quarrel with such close friends. I nodded, and we set off up the slope leading northwest in the general direction of Scafell Pike.

'I knew that quite soon we had to change direction left. In normal conditions, with cairns marking the path, it would have been a simple matter. But in this mist one could hardly follow the path for five yards. Soon I realized that we were off it and had, if anything, veered to the right. The mist now seemed almost tangible, enveloping each of us separately like blankets.

'"I guess we haven't been too clever," said Don. "Maybe we'all ought to go back to the Hause. You reckon?"

'It was at this moment that I grasped how serious our plight really was. We were as good as lost in thick mist on Great End. Great End, the northernmost height of the Scafell range, is notorious as a killer. The books warn you off it. A number of people have fallen to death from its north face, for the precipices begin by looking like footpaths and then suddenly drop sheer.

'"Don," I said, "in a mist like this, on Great End, there really is danger. Let's sit down for ten minutes and think what's best to be done."

'I sat down, closed my eyes and tried not to panic. In theory, of course, one ought to be able, on a compass bearing, to walk in any direction over relatively open ground in the thickest of mists. But in practice – especially without much experience and in a dangerous place – it's not so simple. However, we'd have to try it. There was nothing else to be done. I was just going to say this, when Don clutched my sleeve. I opened my eyes to see him and Carol staring past me into the mist.'

Alan paused. Then he looked up directly at me.

'You'll have to take my word for what I'm going to tell you now. I admit I was badly demoralized and I entirely agree that in thick mist people can be prone to strange ideas. But if Don and Carol were here now, they'd bear me out.

'About thirty feet away, I made out – or thought I could make out – a figure. It was no more than a dark shape in the murk; but a human shape, or so it seemed to me.

'Yet how could it be human? This figure was huge beyond belief. If it was man it must have been well over six and a half feet tall, and broad in proportion; and it must have approached us in that stony place without a sound. It was standing perfectly still and I knew that it was facing us.

'We couldn't move or speak. We huddled on the stones, gripping one another's arms and looking up. As we continued staring, the figure seemed (I can only say seemed) to raise one outstretched arm to shoulder height. After a moment I realized that it was pointing.

'Without a word we stood up and slunk away into the mist. When we'd stumbled perhaps a hundred yards, we came to a cairn and a footpath. The path ran south-west, more or less. We followed it.

'We groped our way along that path for more than half an hour. We met no one, and in some way or other I felt that we were still in the power of whatever we'd encountered. But had we been directed out of danger; or were we intruders to be got rid of? Certainly, we could have died in that mist, and we hadn't. But we all knew no benevolence had been extended to us.

'After how long I can't say, I realized that we were at the northern end of the Mickledore, the knife-edge that runs between Scafell Pike and Scafell. It's about two or three feet wide, with steep drops on either side, and perhaps two hundred yards long. But since I knew the place well, we were able to make our way more or less easily to the Scafell end. As we turned right to go down into Wastdale, the mist was as thick as ever. It wasn't until we'd passed the foot of Lord's Rake that we were out of it. We stopped and looked up at the impenetrable ceiling out of which we'd come, but still none of us spoke. After a moment Carol burst into passionate tears, sobbing on Don's shoulder.

'Forty minutes later we were back at Wastdale Head, drinking brandy.

'Later that evening, while Carol was having a bath, I went into their room, where Don was lying on the bed, still absorbed in Wainwright. I sat down and looked him firmly in the eye.

'"Look," I said. "We've *got* to believe that that was a real person – a human being. I refuse to consider any alternative."

'"Like 'Why didn't he speak?' you mean."

'"Yes, and 'Why—.'"

'"I got me a great idea," interrupted Don. "Let's never talk about it again, not to ourselves or to anybody else at all. I've already put it to Carol, and she agrees."

'After pondering for about half a minute, I nodded. "Yes, I agree too."'

Alan stopped and for a minute or two neither of us spoke. Then he said, 'Now you know why I won't go up in mist – even light mist.'

'Alan,' I answered, 'I believe every word you've told me, but I can't offer any explanation. That was a good idea of your American friend's. Let's not discuss it at all.'

Desert Island Discs

————◆————

Victoria Glendinning

VICTORIA GLENDINNING has written several best-selling and prize-winning biographies, including her life of Vita Sackville-West, which won the Whitbread award for best biography of 1983, and *Trollope*, which won the Whitbread Biography of the Year prize for 1992. She has written two novels, *The Grown-Ups* (1989) and *Electricity* (1995). She lives in London and Hertfordshire.

I get quite enough exposure. Too much, some would say. So I don't know why I was so worked up. But I guess absolutely everyone wants to go on *Desert Island Discs*. I certainly did. Frankly, I can't understand why I hadn't been asked before.

I wasn't, however, like the people who update their eight records mentally on an annual basis, because actually I hardly ever listen to music. Sue Lawley's researcher, who came round to check out my life-story, had to give me a hand. My wife Anita made some suggestions too. I think I struck a nice balance between rock – to represent my misspent youth – golden oldies, some bits of Mozart that Anita likes and, to end with, the theme tune of my TV show *The Man Who Likes Women* – which, obviously, I also chose as the one I'd take over all the others.

For a man like myself, famous for interviewing only women (and only famous women), it was odd having the tables turned. I felt, after the recording, that Sue Lawley hadn't really exploited the piquancy of the situation, though I was satisfied that I myself had performed pretty well. She asked me if I thought women were fundamentally different from men. I could see all sorts of PC pitfalls in that one, which I avoided by saying that I thought women were basically nicer, less selfish, and the better half of the human race.

It's a bit of a knife edge. On camera, I have to appear open to intimacy with women and yet remain what is called 'centred'. So I told Sue Lawley some stuff about being able to understand and empathize with all women by having a deep relationship with just one woman – which I don't think is strictly true, but I heard someone say it at a dinner-party once and it provoked a sort of respectful mutter of agreement round the table. Also, I thought it would please Anita.

Afterwards, I was photographed for the cover of the *Radio Times*. I was pleased about that. Good publicity is important right now, because there has been a nasty rumour in the press about my contract not being renewed. I just don't believe it. But there has been a bit of a chill in the air. Jealousy, the usual thing. Plus this mania for putting a stop to anything that's actually working. Plus a spot of bother with that uptight assistant producer. Sexual harassment, my arse. I thought we *liked* each other.

Desert Island Discs goes out on Sundays at midday, at 12.15 to be precise. I was away in Cheltenham that week, filming interviews with female authors at the Literature Festival. I have to confess that the Man Who Likes Women – and I really do – likes women who are writers rather less than other kinds. Women authors talk either too much or too little. Most of them fail to appreciate that viewers love my programme for its controlled flirtation, its verbal seduction. Also, I hadn't read the bloody books, and didn't have the time to get through all the paperwork my researchers gave me. So it was pretty tough going.

We had it all in the can by Thursday evening. I avoided the usual boozy post mortem with the production team, rang an old girlfriend in the area, and took her out to dinner. It was so good seeing her again that after I checked out of the hotel next day we met for lunch in a pub, drove around a while, and spent Friday night in one of these luscious Cotswold country-house hotels. The only bit of bad luck was that my car was broken into during the night – in the hotel car park, would you believe – and both the radio and the phone taken. I had to get the door fixed, report the incident to the police, and then drive my friend back to where she lives, miles west of Cheltenham.

When I finally got back to London very late on Saturday night, Anita was in bed and asleep, I was completely knackered. I didn't wake up till about eleven on the Sunday morning, so wasn't surprised to find her side of the bed already empty.

I had bought Anita a present in Cheltenham, between leaving the hotel and meeting my friend in the pub. It was a little gold heart with a diamond on it, to be worn as a pendant. Anita and I have been married six years. I feel very much at home with her, though the actual home is, strictly speaking, hers; I moved into her flat when I left Kirsty, my first wife. Kirsty, quite fairly, held on to the house and furniture. Anita's place is pretty cramped in comparison, though I have – had, I suppose I should say now – the spare bedroom as my office, with my own fax, telephone line and so on.

I virtually live on the telephone. I was desperate when I was going on *Desert Island Discs*, because I couldn't think what book I should choose, apart from the Bible and Shakespeare which you get anyway. I'm not a great reader. Then I had an inspiration. I would ask for two 'residential' volumes of the London telephone directory. And my one luxury could be a very powerful mobile phone. Then I could ring up all my friends. Anita laughed when I told her. Sue Lawley said on the programme that the island was so remote that a sufficiently powerful mobile phone had probably not yet been developed. But she let me have it.

I lay and luxuriated in the warm bed for another half hour or so. Then I dug out my jeans and a sweatshirt, slipped the pendant into my pocket, and went downstairs to the kitchen, longing for strong coffee.

Anita was sitting at the table.

'Good morning, darling. Dreadful that I was so late back. I had a whole chapter of disasters. Just wait till I tell you.'

Anita said nothing. She didn't even smile at me. In front of her was a pile of books: two fat tomes, and two telephone directories.

'Take these and go,' she said. 'Now. This minute. I've had enough.'

I just stared.

'Out. You're out. I want you OUT. Now.'

I thought she must have gone mad. I sat down opposite her and gave her my undivided attention. I know I was one hundred per cent sympathetic. I felt something awful must have happened to her.

'Stop *interviewing* me. You never rang to say when you'd be home, I haven't had a real conversation with you for days – weeks really – and now you start treating me like one of the women on your programme.'

That shouldn't have irritated me, but it did.

'You should be so lucky. I like the women on my programme, and they like me. You are treating me as if I were your worst enemy.'

Then it all came out, in a gale of tears and anger. Some young woman had telephoned me while I was away, using the house line instead of my work number. I can guess who it was. I had arranged to meet someone for a drink in London on the Friday night, and had forgotten to ring her and cancel. Anyway, Anita had become suspicious. She had gone up to my office and played back yards of indiscreet messages on my answering machine. She had read some silly faxes. She went through my mail. She had betrayed my trust, though it didn't seem quite the moment to bring that up. I feel sick when I think about it.

I told her I loved her, which is true. I gave her the little golden heart. She held it in her hand, looked at it, got up, and threw it in the bin under the sink.

'Go away and don't come back,' she said. 'You can send someone to collect your stuff tomorrow. No, not tomorrow, I've got too much to do and I won't be back till late. Tuesday.'

I kept on trying to explain to her.

'It's not even really my fault,' I said, meaning it. 'Because I'm sympathetic, and a good listener, and like women, I may inadvertently give them the wrong impression. I get sort of taken over, and can't control what happens next. And then it sometimes seems kind of unchivalrous not to go through with it.'

'Piss off,' said Anita.

She knew that would annoy me. I hate women to use coarse language, they seem to be letting themselves down.

Suddenly I looked at my watch. My *Desert Island Discs* would already have begun. Anita knew exactly what I was thinking.

'You can listen to it in the car,' she said. 'And take the Bible, Shakespeare, and your rotten telephone books.'

'My car radio's been nicked. And my car phone.'

She banged down the little kitchen radio on top of the books.

'You can have this as your one luxury, then. The batteries are on the way out, but still. Or would you rather have an umbrella instead? It's started to rain. And leave the latchkey.'

The little radio, its batteries failing, wouldn't work at all inside the car. In desperation, I drove aimlessly around until I saw a crummy little park. I dumped the car on a double yellow line – no option – ran with the radio to the nearest park bench, and switched it on. It was icy cold and pouring with rain. I was already soaking wet and shivering. The traffic roared by outside the park railings. Anita always listens to Classic FM when she is in the kitchen. I had to put my ear to the radio while I returned it to Radio 4.

And then what did I hear? I heard those bloody seagulls, the ritual acknowledgement to Roy Plomley, and a creamy voice saying: 'Sue Lawley's castaway next week will be . . .'

I had missed it.

I just sat there, for an hour, in the rain, in the middle of nowhere. My wallet and credit cards were still in the jacket of the suit I had worn for Cheltenham. I had nowhere to go. I hate being alone. I did not feel that either the Bible or Shakespeare were likely to be of much comfort to me. I got up from the bench at last, and returned to my car. It had been clamped.

I suppose I can listen to the repeat.

Growing Away

———◆——◆◆——◆———

David Cook

D AVID COOK has written eight novels, four of which have won prizes without making him rich. He has adapted three for TV and one for the cinema. His TV film of *Walter*, starring Sir Ian McKellen, won the Special Jury Prize at Monte Carlo; *Second Best*, starring William Hurt, won the Special Jury Prize at San Sebastian. He is currently writing a TV series for Patricia Routledge.

I exchanged mother for Eric thirty years ago, and did not feel the need to cry at her funeral. I was there for her last few days though – there with the hugs, the hand-holding and the reassuring smiles when her mind started to go and she thought the other hospital beds were whist tables laid out in the village hall, and kept asking her visitors what were trumps.

Sharing a hymn book, all I could think about was how comic she'd have found this conveyor-belt cremation, with a young man in fancy dress tripping over her name. One would have thought 'Gloria' would have come more easily to a man of the cloth. I'd wanted someone to recite 'The Green Eye of the Little Yellow God' because that was her party piece, but no one else thought it a good idea.

There she was, her body centre stage in a velvet-lined one-woman toboggan, her mind, reading mine as usual, sifting through my thoughts concerning the lack of tears, then wrapping word after word around each of her own thoughts, just as at Christmas she would construct huge joke parcels concealing the tiniest of presents. *'I never demanded tears. Demands never worked with you anyway, you know what you are. Any tears shed for me would be tears for yourself considering the closeness we once had.'* And she'd remind me what she went through giving birth to me, all that pain with her legs in the air while the German bombers hung heavy above, having their way with Preston Docks.

'Given those conditions, hardly surprising that what I produced turned out to be neither fish nor foul.'

'And Jean?'

'Jean was my Love Child.'

By this my mother did not mean that Jean had been born out of wedlock, simply that she was the product of love, whereas I had been a mistake, badly timed.

'Did she ever tell you that you were her Love Child?'

My fifty-six-year-old sister stops buttering bread, slowly puts the knife down, and turns to stare past my right ear. She has provided quiches and smoked turkey profusely for the funeral guests but is now preparing supper.

'Are you really the world's biggest arsehole, Michael, or just its understudy?' Seriously overweight, Jean stands among shiny ladles, sieves, whisks, all hanging within arm's reach, the flush of her cheeks reflecting the polished tiles of the kitchen floor. Her kitchen has been designed by specialists: it took weeks to decide from which French hillside those tiles should be quarried.

'Don't include me in your imagined conversations with the dead. Certainly not any you have with her.'

I fiddle in my pockets, making gestures of retreat. 'I'd better not stay for food,' while Jean, in broken down moccasins, shuffles away to turn both taps full on. The noise of gushing water covers my progress to the door. I turn to see her large shoulders in jarring movement up and down. I ache to go to her, but anger which, as usual, I cannot edit frightens and prevents me.

I am trying to keep count of the number of times Jean blinks while Mum is plaiting her hair. Jean has been told to stand still or it will hurt even more. I am six and Jean is eight-and-a-half. She is wearing plimsolls and short socks. The plimsolls should be black and the socks white, but both are grey. Her dress with the pink stripes is being worn over a woollen swimming costume to save weighing down the suitcase, and over the dress is her navy-blue school raincoat, which Jean says is threadbare, but Mum says that doesn't matter because it came from a good home. We have many clothes, and even some furniture, which once had good homes.

As ribbons are tied tightly into bows to prevent Jean's hair bursting out into a frizzy mess all over her screwed-up face, Mum tells her what she must do. Jean must sit on the suitcase while Mum ties it up with rope, then they will lift it into the pram which we use for collecting wood and cover it with a blanket. Jean must push the pram across the fields, so that the neighbours won't be given the satisfaction of telling the tradesmen that we were seen leaving with a suitcase. Jean blinks for the twenty-fourth time and looks to see if I'm still counting; Mum tells her to listen. Mum will give Jean half-an-hour's start, then she and I will slip out the back way and pretend we are going in a different direction. We'll meet at the level crossing where the woman who opens the gates will keep the old pram in her garden until we return. After that it's a train ride, then a walk to another road called the A One, then we wait for the right coach to take us to the seaside and a sandy beach.

Jean looks at the autumn rain running down the outside of the window and blinks twice, quickly. Mum says that two hundred miles to the north the weather could be different. When broadening your horizons, it's always a mistake to begin a journey wrong-footed by worry. Jean wriggles her toes inside her plimsolls.

In Jean's garden the sensors of security lights respond to my presence, first with a series of faint clicks from the tree tops, then with one harsh white light after another illuminating my way from the front door to the electrically operated gate. I stare into the darkness beyond the gate until Jean's husband takes me by the arm and guides me back into the house where Jean is whipping herself up into a soufflé.

Mum had written a note to let Dad know about our sudden need for broader horizons. She tries to decide where in the room he will be most likely to see it before rushing to the police station to announce our disappearance. The note must be destroyed when

Dad has read it in case Mrs Haythornwaite calls. Dad lacks the firm hand needed to keep Mrs Haythornwaite on the doorstep; without a firm hand, she edges into the kitchen to lean against the cooker and check when it was last cleaned.

Dad is to wire money to the Fleetwood General Post Office, so that we'll have something to spend in that land of sun and sand. Mum does not wish Mrs Haythornwaite to know about Dad's subbing his wages to send us holiday money. Some people lack imagination. Mrs Haythornwaite, who once refused Mum the loan of five shillings in case it spoiled their friendship, is such a person.

We reach the level crossing, where some trains halt but most do not, and there we wait. Then a short train ride, then another walk in fading daylight with headlights whooshing past us through pelting rain.

Travelling long distances at night is cheaper than by day. Broadening horizons is not about gawping at landscape through windows of tinted glass: it's getting the back seat and being able to spread out. It's Mum's whispered conversation in the semi-darkness with a woman whose own mother has been given blessed release and passed over into the spirit world. They talk of séances and a medium who looks like Clark Gable. At Newcastle-under-Lyme a male passenger staggers during the Comfort Stop. It is Mum's belief that he has left his wife or robbed his employer and is trying to forget. And in this, Mum says, he will not be helped if Jean and I keep staring.

We arrive before dawn to the smells of spilled diesel and damp overcoats. The coach manoeuvres across wet tarmac. The passengers disembark unsteadily into puddles for the first paddle of the holiday. Most have swollen feet. They hobble to the rear of the coach to reclaim their luggage, eyeing each other in the hope that none will break ranks and give the driver a tip. The hope is doomed: there is always one. The first piece of silver makes a furtive journey from pocket to hand, then hand to pocket with an exaggerated, 'That's most kind and thoughtful. We do our best, you know' for everyone to hear. All but my mother search for coins to exchange for their own property. Mum tells Jean to stop complaining about the tight plaits (which have given her a headache) and to pick up our suitcase.

Mum marches ahead of us towards the seafront while the other passengers pile into warm taxis or disappear down side streets to be met by accommodating landladies in slippers and curlers. These people lack imagination and are missing the opportunity to broaden their horizons. They will not huddle together on a wet bench, waiting for dawn to come up over the sea to the sound of an imaginary cinema organ. They will miss the life-enhancing excitement of waving to the driver of the day's first tram. Their breakfasts will be the breakfasts of landladies who pride themselves on breakfast: they will not be limited to sliced Wonderloaf and Stork margarine and they will not need to ask for more.

Jean asks for more. She has always asked for more. During these years of childhood Jean is often a very hungry 'Love Child'.

A hidden tape recorder played 'The Long and Winding Road' as Gloria's coffin jerked over rollers. I remembered what she'd always said when setting out on a journey: 'Best foot forward . . . Every tour a mystery . . . Always travel hopefully.' Then she had gone. There had been no tears from me and none from Jean.

I returned south to Eric. He had been to the travel agent and brought back brochures about discovering the Unknown Greece, and he had spread out on the kitchen table his latest personal pensions statements, showing all the accrued bonuses. He only has two years to go before retirement. Then we shall be certain of security.

Goodbye to Yonkers

Berlie Doherty

BERLIE DOHERTY was born in Liverpool and educated at Durham University. Besides being an
acclaimed writer of children's books – winning the
Carnegie Medal with *Granny Was a Buffer Girl* – she
has written radio plays and stories, theatre plays,
television stories and compiled anthologies. Her
novels for adults are *Requiem* and *The Vinegar Jar*.
She now lives in Sheffield.

Joe stares out of his window most of the time, at the leafy sanctuary that surrounds his house. He notes that the squirrels are getting more plentiful, and that most of the birds have gone clean away. When evening settles in he goes out to the wooden deck that he built years ago. Barbecues himself a meal. Saves washing the dishes, and anyway, he loves the smell of the smoke, likes to see the stars coming up. It's peaceful here. He's happy enough. His girls come now and again, but they're busy, they have good jobs in Manhattan. They nag him. They tell him he's aged fifteen years in the fifteen months since Dolly died. You ought to go out more, Dad. Join a club. Meet people. It's not good for you, being alone like this all day. Ah well. He's just filling in time now. They know that. He knows that. So what? It's quiet time. It's OK.

They last came on Mother's Day. Odd thing to do. Tried to re-create the sort of day Dolly would have made: blueberry pancakes and maple syrup and all, pretty flowers on the table. Brought a couple of friends with them too, an old man and his daughter, people from England come on holiday. Thought he'd like to meet them, talk about the old country. What do they know about my old country, Joe said. These guys are from England. That's not my country. 'Just wait till you meet them,' Mary-Anne said. 'That man is twenty years older than you and acts ten years younger. You should be ashamed . . .'

The old guy had never even been to Scotland, it turned out. Just up the A1. He'd never even been. And there Joe was, stuck between them on the settee where he slept nights, sitting upright between them like a hamburger making conversation about England while the girls fixed margaritas to drink and a Mexican dip for the tortilla chips. There'd be droppings all over the carpet. We'd be better outside on the deck, even if it is cold.

'What brought you to Yonkers?' the English woman asked him.

'Work,' Joe said. His eyes glazed, thinking back. Fifty years, was it? 'Nothing for me in Scotland. I was a miner. Hated that. Didn't tell anyone, not even my mother. Saved up my money and came to America.'

'Don't you miss it?'

'My bike. Missed my bike. Loved that old bike like nothing. Covered miles on it.'

'And you didn't bring it.'

'Bring a bike to New York?'

The girls protested that they'd had bikes when they were kids, cycled miles through the woods in Yonkers.

'You don't understand,' said Joe.

He wandered into the kitchen, tipped his margarita down the sink and found himself a can of Diet Coke in the fridge.

'What's the girl's name?' he asked Mary-Anne.

'Girl!' Mary-Anne laughed. 'She's older than me! Has grown-up kids and all.'

'You're all girls to me.'

'Your cataracts are getting worse. Time you got them fixed.'

Joe went out to his deck. He could hear the woodpecker drumming away. He lit his barbecue. Inside they were pouring more drinks, the old man telling stories. It was better out here, where he didn't have to talk. He'd never felt lonely out here. It had been his sanctuary. All that grieving for Dolly. This place was a comfort to him. On a sudden whim he went to the house and tapped on the mosquito grid over the door.

'Anybody want to hear a woodpecker?'

The English woman came out. He knew she would. The old man tried to follow but faltered at the steps, lost for someone to help him down. Joe ignored him. If the woman knew her father was behind her she gave no sign. She craned her neck, listening and smiling.

'Never heard that before,' she said.

'Comes most nights.'

'I can't see him though.'

'You won't. He's way up.'

She turned herself round, like a child dancing. 'You've so many trees here! I'm amazed.'

'You're amazed to find trees in America?'

'So near Manhattan. All that concrete. I thought that New York was all concrete and cars.'

'Time was,' said Joe, 'when you wouldn't find another house here. When I bought this place it was trees, trees, trees. Now they're throwing up houses all over. Woman over there has dug up her grass and put plastic lawn down so she don't have to cut it. She wanted my trees down! You wait till the fall. Then you'll see concrete in Yonkers.'

The old man joined them at last, helped down by Mary-Anne. 'Can't hear it,' he said.

They all stood still. A cat yawned round their legs, waiting for the cooking to start.

'Nope,' said Joe. 'Darn squirrels must have chased it.'

The woman went indoors. The old man stood with his arms folded watching Joe as he turned the steaks on the barbecue grill. The smoke made them both cough. The old guy had tears streaming down his cheeks.

'So how come you travel all this way to New York and you never even went to Scotland?' Joe asked him.

'It doesn't appeal to me,' the old man said. 'But New York! I had to see New York before I die. Not that I intend doing that yet. I'm only ninety-two, you know.'

'So you told me.'

'Don't do anything to excess. Don't drink much. Gave up smoking thirty years ago . . .' It had the air of practised litany, Joe thought. Reminded him of church.

'You've plenty of time to go to Scotland then.'

The flames spurted suddenly. The old man turned away, flapping the air in front of his face, and made for the steps.

'Haven't seen Paris yet,' he said, choking. 'Or Rome.'

'The girls will give you a glass of water,' Joe called.

Later, the meal eaten and the barbecue plates thrown in the garbage-can, the old man snoring in the rocker, and the girls upstairs fixing beds, the English woman said: 'Yonkers. It's a funny name for a place.'

'Dutch,' said Joe.

'That's another thing about New York,' she said. 'Everyone comes from somewhere else.'

'My daughters were born here. They're New Yorkers, sure enough.'

'You should go home,' she told him. 'It would be good for you.'

He couldn't sleep that night. He was downstairs on the couch, where he'd spent every night since Dolly died. He had not been upstairs since the morning he woke up to find her dead in bed beside him. The girls had given up pestering him about that. But that night he didn't even try to sleep. Thoughts of Scotland were wisping in and out of his mind, like the lines of half-remembered songs. He saw himself as a young man, pumping up hills on his bike, his back crouched over the handlebars and wind streaming through his hair. He saw again the blues and purples of the mountains, felt the air cold and sharp on his face.

By the time the women and the old man were up he was in the garden. He told them he didn't need breakfast. He couldn't eat. When his daughters came to tell him they were leaving he was brushing out his barbecue, a morning ritual.

'I'm glad you came,' he told the English visitors, and meant it.

'It's done you good,' Mary-Anne said. 'I can tell. You should meet more people.'

He waved them off. He knew the girls would worry about him now in his empty house. They'd cleared his fridge of old food and stocked him up with fresh. There was a plate of pancakes for him on the counter.

He worked all day in the garden. For the first time that year the rockery flowers emerged from their tangle of weeds. Dolly had chosen them. At the end of the day his mind was still racing. He couldn't sit down. He couldn't settle to anything, not even to lighting his barbecue.

'What the hell,' he thought. He went indoors and phoned Lora.

'I'm going home.'

'Home? What d'you mean?' Joe could register the concern in her voice.

'Scotland. Home to Scotland.'

'You're leaving Yonkers?'

The house was full again. What was the matter with them? They spent hours on the phone at their jobs, making all kinds of complicated arrangements with all kinds of important people. Couldn't they understand a clear and simple statement like that?

'What have I got to lose?'

'Us, Dad. Your family.'

'You don't understand. You're New Yorkers. How could you understand?'

'We'll take you over,' said Mary-Anne. 'You can have a holiday there with us. We'll all go. And then we'll bring you back.'

'What did I tell you! You don't understand.'

'What d'you think you're going to do when you get to Scotland, Dad? Ride your bicycle?'

The girls looked at one another, sighed, smiled ruefully, and started again. He was a stubborn old mule, Dolly had always said that. They finally came to understand that their father meant what he said. He was leaving.

He insisted on going into Manhattan on his own to fix up his flight.

'God bless him,' said Lora into her handkerchief. 'Him with his eyesight, too. It's a miracle, Mary-Anne.'

'Now of a sudden his house looks like Mom used to have it.'

297

They rang him the night before his departure. 'I can get there on my own,' he said. 'Do you think there was anyone here to meet me the day I arrived?'

Fifty years before, he thought. A young man with pockets full of hope and nothing else.

At last they left him alone. His flight tickets were on the music stand of the piano. He picked them up and leafed through them, checking them for the hundredth time.

'Edinburgh,' he thought. 'Tomorrow you'll be in Scotland, Joe.' Odd thing, that. Tomorrow he would say goodbye to Yonkers.

He went outside. It was dusk. The air was pungent with the scent of blossom. He lit his barbecue, cooked himself a meal. The old woodpecker drummed. He sat on the deck and rocked in his chair, eating the hamburger jammed into the breadroll. He drank his Coke. The stars bloomed.

When it was cold he went indoors and fastened up for the night. He looked round the rooms, turned off the lights and went upstairs, to the bedroom that he and Dolly had shared. The bed was still made up. He took off his clothes and slid in between the cold sheets. He lay in the darkness with his eyes wide open, and then he turned over on to his side.

'I've come home, Dolly,' he said.

Outside on the deck the charred papers scattered and drifted, like leaves in the fall.

Confession

Clare Boylan

C LARE BOYLAN was born and grew up in Dublin, and was an award-winning journalist before turning to fiction. Her short stories have been published in many countries, and she is also a successful novelist and editor, her novels including *Holy Pictures*, *Home Rule* and *Black Baby*. She recently edited *The Literary Companion to Cats*. 'Confession' is taken from her latest collection, *That Bad Woman*, which is published by Little, Brown.

The two girls ran between the aisles. They had a penny which they had decided to invest. They would light a candle and pray for Uncle Matt to come and visit, because he always gave them a shilling. They slowed down when they passed a pew which was full of people who shuffled on their knees to fill the gap left by a man who stepped off the end and vanished into a box.

'Where did he go?' Betty said to Fanny. Fanny did not know so she told Betty not to speak in church. Betty turned her attention to a kneeling woman whose bowed head was wrapped in a scarf. 'What's in there? Why is everyone going in there?' She clutched the carved end of the pew in case Fanny would drag her away. Her face was level with the kneeling woman's whose head rose so slowly that there was a moment when Betty feared that the scarf might not actually contain a face.

'It's the confession box,' she told Betty. 'We go in there for forgiveness.'

'Forgiveness for what?' Betty said.

'For when we have been wicked,' the woman smiled.

'What's wicked?' Betty said as Fanny dragged her away.

'She is. She eats children,' Fanny told her.

'You'd go to jail for that,' Betty said hopefully.

Fanny held her sister's hand. She lit the taper and touched a candle and the wick curled and sizzled and a black straggle of smoke grew out of it and then a bright eye of flame blazed and gazed at them.

'No one ever finds out,' Fanny whispered. 'She eats every bit of them, first the fingers and the eyes and then she nibbles off all the flesh. By then she is too full to stand so she sits down and belches to make some room and then, one by one, she crunches the bones. Last of all she eats the hair, holding it up and licking the stray hairs off her fingers.'

The moment she had said this Fanny forgot all about it, but for years afterwards Betty woke in the night to the muffled eager munching of bones, and then she would see the woman's face and have to watch her eating the hair which waved and straggled like the black smoke on the candle. The woman had had black hungry eyes that burned into Betty, and when she smiled she showed long, bone-crunching teeth and the red on her lips made a saw pattern in the wrinkles, as if the blood dripped down.

By now Fanny was going to confession. She had to take Betty because she had to take her everywhere, and Betty was made to kneel beside her in the line. When other people emerged they looked subdued, but Fanny always came out smiling. She held her joined hands over her face so that people would not see, but Betty saw and once or twice she saw her licking her lips.

'What happens when you go in there?' Betty said.

'It's a secret,' Fanny told her. 'I'm not allowed to say.' The younger sister became obsessed with the confession box and pestered Fanny, pulling at her skirt or poking her in bed at night so that at last Fanny had to relent.

'Well, then, I will tell you if you promise never to mention this to another living soul. Behind the door there is a smaller door and beyond that a great big room with a party going on. There is a long table with cake and ice cream and jelly and meringues. Every person who goes in can eat as much of everything as they like. I had three meringues.' Betty was five and it would be two more years before she could go to confession. Each week Fanny added more and more enticing details to the confession-box party. Once she took a silver-wrapped sweet from her pocket and handed it to her sister. 'I saved you that.' And every Saturday when she left Betty in the pew, shivering with envy, she told the priest: 'I lied.'

When Betty's turn finally came her whole life was dominated by the ordeal of confession. If she told the priest she had not sinned he was full of contempt and wanted to know how every man on earth was a sinner but she alone was above reproach. She was introduced to some invisible and unpleasant part of herself called a conscience and compelled to examine it, employing a litany of the seven deadly sins from which flowed all iniquity. Pride, covetousness, lust, anger: she knew she did not possess the extreme emotions necessary for such passionate-sounding weaknesses.

At night she lay awake trying to imagine ways in which her thoughts or actions might be sinful, but when she produced some sins they always seemed too evil and the priest's breath was drawn in in revulsion. She often had to tell the same ones because she couldn't think of any others, and it seemed that even in the dark she was recognized, for the confessor would demand: 'Am I right in thinking you were in here before asking to be forgiven for the selfsame acts of badness? You are turning out very degenerate.' In desperation she would come to confession half an hour early and inspect all the boxes. The confessors' names were inscribed in gold on a wine-coloured plaque above the door and she always hoped that there might be a new one. Sometimes in the dark, while the priest was censuring her, she felt with her fingers the grainy wall of the box, hoping to encounter a little latch or catch which would spring open the door to the big room with the party.

The confession box was constructed like a moth, with a solid central part where the priest wielded mercy behind dusty curtains and on either side of him were spread out two sections like wings where one sinner waited and one confessed. While she waited Betty could hear the murmured vices of other sinners and the priest's disillusioned drone of pardon, but Fanny always came out smiling behind her hands and still Betty imagined that beyond the old priest, waiting like a spider to dissect your rotting soul, the room still waited, the jellies only half eaten, the meringues bloated with sweetened cream.

The two girls grew up. Fanny was a striking, spiky young woman, around whom jealous feuds broke out among men who had not even known they liked her. Betty was a soft, shy, pretty girl who blushed and who was enraptured by romance. When they went to confession now they both had the same sins. Into the dark, musty box they brought with them the fragrance of young women and the provocation of other men's lust. The dim, coffin-like space grew tropical with the scent of their hair and their breathless whispers of tentative carnal celebration. Gone was the pastor's dolorous drone. He quizzed them eagerly, relentlessly. Fanny enjoyed these sessions.

'*Where did he touch you?*'

'On my breasts. My thighs. On my . . . !' And she stopped and gave a little gasp, as if remembering.

'*Was his mouth open when he kissed you? Did you touch his private parts? Did you?*'

When Betty entered the box, even before she opened her mouth, the priest appeared half strangled with rage. She often let boys go a little bit far because it seemed kind, and anyway it was no harm for she had made up her mind that she would not get around to actual sex until she was married. These physical interludes passed in a kind of pleasant blur that stopped her thinking about them too much except when she went to confession and the priest forced her to articulate all the pleasant acts of tenderness in a way that made them seem vulgar and brutal and, in a particularly revolting way, made her feel that she was being forced to do them all over again, but against her will.

There came a time when she knew that she could never, ever do them again. She still dressed invitingly and made little mews when she was kissed, and blushed and flapped her eyelids until her suitors were beside themselves, and then she seemed to turn to ice.

A man told her it was her own fault for driving men crazy and he raped her and then he strangled her. He was haunted by the final look of recognition and, almost, a look of gratitude. The last thing Betty understood was that she had known all along that this would happen to her, and now, at last, she need no longer dread it.

Fanny got married and everyone breathed a sigh of relief. She had a routine sort of life except for a restless phase about ten years after that. There was something on her mind and she was tormented by an urge to tell her husband. She knew the kindest thing was to say nothing, but it was like a thorn in her system and sooner or later it was going to have to work its way out.

'I've been having an affair,' she said to him one night when he wanted to sleep and she wanted to make love. 'Who with?' he said, and she told him it was his friend, his best friend, the man who had been like a brother to him since childhood, whose company he preferred to anyone else's.

There was a period of unpleasantness with accusations and denials, and in the end the two men never spoke to each other again, but there was nothing to be done about that. She did what she had to do and there remained only for her to confess properly, before God, who has the power to wipe away all sins. She had not been to confession since Betty's death. The little brown box looked small and quaint now, like a music box left over from childhood and stored in the attic, and for a moment she felt foolish; but for all Catholics there comes a time when they need to feel once more the pleasant abrasion of total cleansing, so she went inside and bent her bony knees and put her dry red lips up to the little wire grill and told the priest: 'I lied.'

The Kitten

Carlo Gébler

CARLO GÉBLER was born in Dublin in 1954. He was educated at the University of York and the National Film and Television School (which he loved). He has written a number of novels and short stories and is also a maker of documentary films, most recently *A Little Local Difficulty* for BBC 2. His most recent novel is *The Cure*; he is also a playwright, working on his play *How to Murder a Man*. He lives in Enniskillen.

The table was square with an electric light hanging above. The shade was made of raffia. A faint breeze moved the shade and the shadow cast on the wall by the raffia moved in turn. He thought it was like a spider's web.

They were eating their supper at the table below: olives which shone dully; a loaf of bread and peppers, gnarled like roots and bitter tasting, a gift from the Greek family who lived next door and looked after the chalets.

'I'm giving up smoking,' he said.

'I don't think you're ready yet.'

'Why?' he asked.

'I don't think you've found a reason.'

He opened the sliding door and went out on to the veranda. There was sand in the ashtray on the table, butts sticking up from it like a parody of young shoots. He took a cigarette out of the packet on the table and put the end into his mouth. Then he put it back. Martha was moving about in the kitchen. Something fell and smashed on the floor. 'It's all right,' she called.

Martha waved a moment later, a dark shape behind the mosquito mesh.

'Goodnight,' he said.

She padded away. He was sitting out under the veranda; she was going to bed. He shook his head and went tut tut to himself out loud.

He went back into the house, sliding the door shut after himself. What the situation needed was dramatic action.

He found Martha in the bathroom. She was examining her face in the mirror. With her tongue she bulged out a freckled cheek. There was a small blemish on it, a spot. He remembered her asking him not to kiss her there.

'Do you fancy?' he said.

'Oh hon!' she wailed. 'I'm tired.'

In the mirror she caught his eye again and looked upward to the ceiling, infallible signal of irritation. She crossed her hands in front of her chest, took hold of the bottom of her green cotton blouse and lifted. Her breasts were brown and smooth. She pushed her skirt and knickers to the ground, and hung them on the back of the door. He touched the bottom of her back. She slid past him and disappeared through the doorway into their bedroom.

'You've left the top off the toothpaste,' he called.

In the bedroom he could hear Martha sighing as she wriggled into bed. The light in the room clicked off.

The following morning he awoke to find the other twin bed empty.

He looked through the window. He could vaguely remember hearing Martha opening the shutters when she had got up earlier. Outside he could see an empty cloudless sky and the edge of the enormous fir tree at the front. Through the wall came the sound of the shower.

Some time during the night before, after he had climbed into bed and while waiting for sleep, he had come to a conclusion.

Go on, he said to himself. He got out of bed and went to the bathroom. Martha was standing on a towel in front of the mirror, wet and naked. He watched her curl the mascara stick along her eyelashes. She always put her make-up on straight away after washing. She did it, she said, because she didn't like drying herself; and in the time it took, her body dried. It was one of those idiosyncrasies that made Martha Martha.

'You make me feel ugly in bed,' he said.

There was something else that had come to him before sleep and which he wanted to broach, but now he couldn't remember what that was.

The pollinating mascara stick went back into its sheath.

'I'll never mention you're fat again,' said Martha. In the mirror he saw her eye was on his middle, red from the sun but white in the well of the belly button.

After breakfast they bumped into town in the little Fiat they had hired. Martha selected Richard a suntan oil with a high protection factor from a rack outside a shop. He gave her his purse and went off to the bank. The woman who cashed his traveller's cheques was vast, with sweat on her upper lip and a lovely smile.

He returned to the car to find Martha had bought a snorkel, a mask and a lilo. They lay on the back seat, rubbery smelling in the sun.

'Spending my money?' he said.

'Our money,' she replied.

They drove out of town and into the hills. It was hard going for the car. As he changed down, he kept glancing at her beside him, incessantly moving her jaw from side to side.

He touched the cigarette packet lying on the dashboard. The Cellophane had warmed in the sun. He stared at the tarmac, glistening and blue, the white line along the middle and the parapet to the side, the only protection against a fatal descent. He pulled out a cigarette and put it into his mouth and picked up the box of matches.

'I thought you were giving up,' she said.

'If I die at forty from cigarettes,' he replied, 'it won't matter if I've packed in eighty years of living, will it?'

It wasn't an original thought. He'd overheard it at a party. She had too. He was relieved she didn't remember.

'I could be killed by a bus tomorrow.'

Now he remembered suddenly what he'd wanted to say in the bathroom that morning but forgotten.

'When you smoked and I didn't, I never shied away from you,' he said.

'Why have you never said this before?' she asked.

The filter was swelling with his saliva. He put the unlit cigarette and the matches into his shirt pocket.

'I need to reflect on these things,' he said.

They found the turning for the beach and inched down a track of packed mud and white scree. Chalky dust drifted through the window. At the bottom they found a place to park in the shade of the white cliffs.

He got out and walked down to the sea, and when he emptied their basket he found his new tanning oil wasn't there. Damn, he thought.

He got to his feet and started walking back towards the car. She was coming towards him, lugging the lilo behind. Funny to have blown it up by the car, he thought. Probably she'd done it so he wouldn't be able to offer to do it for her.

'Have you got my Ambre Solaire?' he called.

She dropped the lilo and turned back. He returned to his towel and lay down.

At last he heard Martha coming. She sat down with a sigh.

'Well?'

'I couldn't find it. I must have left it in the shop.'

'Well that's bloody marvellous.'

He looked across at her honey-gold limbs.

'You don't know what it's like not to tan,' he added.

'No, I don't.'

He changed into his trunks and walked into the sea. The water was cold for an instant and then it felt warm and milky. He couldn't see more than a few feet ahead because of the chalk suspended in the water.

'I must go in with the snorkel,' Martha greeted him when he returned.

'You won't see a thing,' he said.

She plunged into the sea. He watched the snorkel cutting through the water. A few moments later she stood up and pushed the mask back from her face.

'It's amazing,' she called, 'you can't see a thing.'

The Kitten

'That's what I said, you wouldn't be able to see a thing. Everything's stirred up.'

She came back up the beach and threw herself down on the lilo.

'I was only trying to make conversation,' she said.

He dried himself and went back to the car where he sat in the driver's seat. In the distance he could see Martha as she moved between the water's edge and their towels while behind he could hear the wistful echo of the surf booming from the cliffs above.

The restaurant in the village where they went for lunch had a red awning. It was empty except for two Dutch tourists writing postcards at another table. The waiter came to take their orders. His was swordfish, hers was pork. Neither spoke as they waited for the meal. He looked at the fishing boats in the harbour.

'That looks good,' she said when his swordfish arrived.

He ate slowly. The flesh was strong tasting. Finally, with only two mouthfuls left on the plate he said: 'I'm not going to give you any swordfish unless you ask.'

He forked the last mouthful but one into his mouth.

'I don't want any. If I'd wanted any, I'd have ordered it myself.'

'In that case you've missed a great experience.'

With his fork he ran the last piece of fish around the oil on his plate and put it into his mouth.

The plates were cleared away. Martha ordered a plate of grapes and two Greek coffees. A dog came out of the taverna. He was brown and white with dull eyes.

A man came in, a friend of the waiter, and he began to stroke the dog. The waiter returned with their grapes and put them down on the table. Then the coffees appeared and they began to eat the grapes.

Suddenly there was a sound of running and scratching. In the square in front of the restaurant he saw a scrawny kitten. The dog shot forward and caught the kitten on the steps at the far end. The waiter rushed out of the taverna and began to shout and throw stones. The kitten was thrown into the air. Then it was all over. Richard could see the kitten was lying at the top of the steps, a grey rag on grey stone.

He stood up and went over. The small animal was split along the belly, its intestines spilling out across the stone. They were moving vaguely and he realized the creature was still breathing. You'll have to put it out of its misery, he thought.

He looked at the little neck with its grey ruffled fur. The tiny eyes were half closed and there was a sticky mixture along the edges. He put his foot on the neck and pressed. Through the sole of his sandal he could feel the neck like bird bone. With his other foot he raised himself off the ground. He bounced once. He bounced twice. The third time, there came the shriek of bone. He turned and ran down the steps.

Martha had left their table and was standing on the quayside looking down at the water. He came up behind Martha and stopped. The sun hung just above the hills on the other side of the bay.

He took a step closer and touched her back. She did not move but went on staring down. After standing there for some minutes he realized Martha had started to cry.

He took the cigarette out of his pocket. It was bent and some tobacco had come away from the end. He put it into his mouth and lit a match.

Space Invaders

Elizabeth Berridge

Yes, well, I'm ancient now. And that means old enough to remember when young men got up for you in buses and trains. When running a house and caring for children gave a woman a sort of standing. Of course a wife's duties ran to more than that, I can tell you! Especially in our corner of the world.

My husband, you see, was a publisher. Only in a small way. But there he was, a publisher, and shelves of prestigious books to prove it. That's all water under the bridge now, because when he retired he sold out to an American conglomerate who ruined the business. That killed Justin, I swear. But I'm not dwelling on that. No, for once it's me I'm talking about. Makes a change.

People don't realize what a hard slog it is to be a literary wife. Literary wife. That's funny really. I'm not literary. I've never written anything except letters and postcards and shopping lists. But the meals I've cooked! All that entertaining! Writers can be the very devil at close quarters; my idea of hell is to be shut up with them for eternity. Massaging their egos while you fill their glasses. I could deal with the advances young poets and first-time novelists made to me in the hope that I'd recommend their work to Justin. That's an occupational hazard easily dealt with. Not that Justin ever considered my opinion worth an empty pint pot. I even got used to being invisible at parties. No, what really got to me was the patronizing chat that writers indulged in when they were stuck with me on my own.

317

An American came to dinner one evening, I remember. Over here to sell his novel. While Justin was getting the drinks he said: 'How restful it must be to have such a straightforward, simple outlook on life like yours.'

'How d'you know what my outlook is? I've scarcely spoken to you.' Pretty sharpish my tone was, Justin told me afterwards.

Changing tack, he said easily: 'You have this Madonna-like calm.' But he really meant cow-like, so I escaped to the kitchen to check on the roast. Behind me I swear I heard him laughing.

He smoked between courses. Good food – and I'm a good cook – wasted on a blunted palate. I'll never know if that was why Justin turned down his goddamned novel.

Then there were the women. They thought me simple too. 'Justin's such an intellectual, he needs someone to keep his mind honed.' Who said that? Whoever it was, was wrong. In spite of his prissy name Justin wasn't an intellectual. He had a good mind, a nice sense of humour and a truffle-hound's nose for a book. But he liked people and I don't think intellectuals like anybody except themselves. It's God in the shaving mirror every morning looking back at them.

What was I saying? Oh, women.

There was a couple we used to stay with – weekends in the country, that sort of thing. Mavis used to finger Justin's tie and ask him where he'd bought it. Man-to-man talk. You'll remember her name, she specialized in fly-on-the-wall reminiscences of the nearly-great. I committed the social gaffe of combing my hair in their hallway once, coming in after a windy walk. Justin doted on my long hair. But we heard it was all over London that I had some disgusting habits. See what I mean? If you're the wife of somebody who matters you're at risk.

You could say I still am. The other day I met one of the poets whose career had taken off after Justin launched him back in the fifties. He'd always been a small clenched-up man – I won't give his name – and nowadays runs a sort of literary gossip column about the in-people. There he was, like me, recording memories of those early days for Radio 3. Only he never mentioned that Justin had given him his start. I did, though. Wives who outlive their husbands are useful stand-ins, for women have a natural gift of recall and old trivia is gold dust to pushy young researchers.

'So Dylan stayed with you,' said the producer. 'Well?'

Pause. Digging for dirt. The dry laughter.

'We hadn't any silver for him to walk off with,' I told him 'We played dominoes and shove ha'penny and drank brown ale and strong tea.'

Poor old Dylan! People get remembered for the wrong things.

I suppose I expected us all to go over to the George for a drink afterwards. Not a bit of it. 'Lovely to see you after all these years. You've not changed.' And off they went together.

Not changed! I'm old and grey and full of sleep – trust another poet to put his finger nearly on the spot – and meet most of my friends in the obit columns. So I was pleased a week or so later to spot Fiona Macleod in the food hall at Harrods. I love the food hall, full of gorgeous things I never buy these days. Fiona stopped writing years ago, took up pottery instead, though she was good, really good. Made it into all the literary magazines with no trouble and we published her novel and two collections of short stories. Nice woman, quite barmy. Spent years in analysis. She and Justin would talk for hours, analysing this, analysing that. I used to drift off to sleep.

Anyway, there she was, looking like a bag lady until you noticed her splendid nose and eyes as black and lively as Ratty's in *Wind in the Willows*.

'Let's have lunch,' I said. So I took her along to the Royal Academy, being a Friend of that splendid institution. She whacked into the salads at the buffet and we had a couple of glasses of wine and got quite tiddly. Then she said a funny thing.

'Dear Justin always understood that I liked my own space,' and laughed. 'I did enjoy working with him.'

Justin had given her an editing job when she was stuck between books. Writers don't rest like actors; they're always worrying about writers' block. It was only when I got home that I began to wonder whether dear Justin had ever seriously tried to invade her space, and how. Had they had an affair? It's so dinned into you these days, every biography is a dead donkey without sex. Preferably off-limits.

I didn't really think so, but I was curious. We began to meet now and then for lunch and a drink. I enjoyed our talks, just as I'd enjoyed the letters she'd written to me when she spent a year as a writer-in-residence in America. She came out with some surprising remarks. Once, out of the blue, she said: 'I loved to watch you wake up when Justin and I at last stopped talking.' Then, one early autumn afternoon as we left a pub on the river near Richmond, she said, touching my cheek briefly: 'I must go on by myself now, if you don't mind. We've stirred up so much of the past that I feel that I have to be alone with my thoughts.' And off she went with her plastic bag and tatty old fur.

I watched her go, then walked around the shops, thinking about her. For some time I'd been persuading her to write her memoirs. She'd met most people. She'd known Cowper Powys and his Phyllis. He must have written to her; he wrote to everyone in that slanting hand, sloping like a capsizing boat. She'd laughed at Tom Eliot's jokes at Charleston. She was as old as the world. When I got to the bus station there she was, not ten feet from me. Thinking her thoughts, secure in her own space. Well, I wasn't going to invade it. So I sat, carefully screened, reading the evening paper, waiting for my bus.

Three weeks later I had a shock. There was her obit in the *Telegraph*. I bought the other papers and she was in them all. Heavens, she was into her eighties! As usual, salient bits of info were missing. But there was a paragraph in *The Times* that caught my eye and I wondered who had written it. 'Fiona Macleod never married, but there were rumours that she was deeply in love with a married man for many years and this coloured her fiction. She was at work on a "full and frank" autobiography when she died, so maybe the mystery will be revealed. Like Jean Rhys, her strongest characters were women – betrayed and used by men.'

I was amazed to hear from her solicitor some weeks later. I was her sole beneficiary, and she had left a letter giving me absolute right of veto to her unfinished autobiography. 'I was so struck by your delicacy of feeling,' she wrote, 'in the bus station that day after we'd said goodbye. You saw me and I saw you, but you never attempted to invade my space.' Well, why should I? We'd said all there was to say. It would be like the curtain rising yet again on a half-hearted encore. Let the play go say I, and the audience disperse.

What was Carlyle's remark? 'A well-written life is almost as rare as a well-spent one.' Could Fiona's be both?

Oddly enough, the day it arrived the renegade erstwhile poet rang up, suggesting lunch. Suddenly I'd become interesting. It transpired that he had written *The Times* obit. Did I know anything about the autobiography? He'd heard rumours and we'd been seen about together, Fiona and I. Were we close friends? Was there correspondence? Now, I may be old, but simple I am not. I am blessed with a good memory and sound principles. It gave me a great kick to send him on his way unrejoicing.

I have now looked at the untidy mass of papers and grasped the unlikely truth of Fiona's life and it humbles me. I shall carry on reading it by the fires I light these autumn evenings; old age is full of small pleasures. Good log fires, forbidden in this smokeless zone. I shall read it with care and compassion and take a certain melancholy satisfaction in burning it page by page. I shan't even keep the letters and poems she wrote to me over the years. Let's say I shall be defending my own space as well as hers.

Late Luck

Matthew Sweeney

MATTHEW SWEENEY was born in Donegal in 1952 and lives in London. His work for children includes *The Flying Spring Onion*, a collection of poetry and *The Snow Vulture*, a novel. With Secker and Warburg he has published five collections of poetry including *Blue Shoes* and *Cacti*. He is currently working on a collection of short stories to be published by Cape. He is Writer in Residence at the South Bank 1994/5.

John Jansen stood in the post office queue, thinking of mangoes. Then he noticed the second queue for the stamp desk, behind which was the crossed finger logo of the lottery. On three of the five weeks of the lottery's existence, he'd filled in one ticket – one only, mind you. He was not a gambler, apart from the odd game of poker for small stakes, and besides, he didn't believe in the transforming power of luck. He didn't even want to land the big prize. Who could cope with £15 million and stay sane, quite apart from the hounding by the tabloids, and the very real danger of having wife or children kidnapped, then murdered, as had actually happened in Australia to a lottery winner there? A smallish sum, on the other hand, say £200,000, would help things a little. No big changes, a house somewhere, a private doctor, maybe flying lessons. But if he never won even the £10 consolation prize he wouldn't get gloomy about it.

Things were slow today, and it was no wonder, what with seven of the ten window booths unoccupied. An outrageous situation, Jansen thought, with all these people posting packages of different weights wanting them to arrive before Xmas. He was not a lover of Xmas – well, not since he'd been a child. Xmas clogged the mail, quite apart from all its financial coercions. The package he was carrying had no festive connection. It was his new novel, about to head off to his agent. His headache, earned at last night's celebratory meal, still hadn't lifted.

He got the grumpy man with the ginger moustache again. He

placed his package on the weighing scales. £1.66, the man was asking him for. Jansen always suspected this man of ripping him off, but he paid up anyway. While he was at it, he got a book each of first- and second-class stamps, and a minimum weight stamp for America. He owed his undertaker friend a letter.

He stood impatiently behind a woman who was dipping what seemed like a whole page of stamps, one by one, into the wet sponge. He wanted to get out of here, to go to the market stall by the Tube station to buy mangoes for his hangover, and to get home for two more paracetamol. He wanted to elbow his way alongside her, but instead he picked up a lottery ticket from the nearby holder.

Now he had to decide how to fill it in. The previous week he'd held an old ticket under the table in the train and jabbed with his pen in the dark, then marked those blindly picked numbers on a ticket he bought in Leeds station. Not one of them had come up. The first week he'd opened Yeats's *Collected Poems* six times at random, spinning the book round with his eyes closed, so he wouldn't know if the page number was odd or even, and he'd noted down the numbers. All Yeats's well-known séance activities had yielded no good for Jansen, as again, not a single number came up. The middle week he'd gone for his own and his wife's birthdays, both of which had come up, and he'd got the bonus number as well with 37, which was simply his favourite number. No prizes for that, not even £10, but he'd felt he was finding the range.

The woman was leaving at last, so he plonked his package and his elbows on the counter. He stuck the stamps on in a neat line, first the £1 stamp, then the 38p and the 30p. He looked at the two books of stamps, and at the 42p stamp for America, and he put a short black line through 1, 19, 25, 30, 36 and 42 on the lottery ticket then he joined the by now short queue to pay his pound and get his ticket put through the machine. He folded the printed ticket and put it with the stamps into his shirt pocket.

He had to go outside to post his novel. He held the package in his hand for a minute, as if guessing the weight before dropping it in the slit. Squeezing it in, might be a better way of putting it, the postbox was so full. He could see his package sitting there just below the level of the slit. For a moment Jansen felt like taking his package out again and reposting it later, or standing guard discreetly till the postbox was emptied, but he was too hungover for that. Besides, would the novel do any better than the book of stories or the play, neither of which had exploded into the literary world or into his bank account? Oh, he felt pretty sure this was his best work and last night with his friend Beverly in the Thai restaurant, after copious Singa beers and Mekong whiskeys, he'd been saying it was good enough to win the Booker. Not today, though. His hungover head was filled with doubts about it.

This was some hangover. He'd stayed in bed till midday, then stood in the shower for half an hour. He'd swallowed enough fizzy water and orange juice to keep him going for a week. The two paracetamol he'd taken had had as much effect as two peppermints. His head felt as it had done when he'd gone drinking with the editor of his stories, not so long before, and had fallen down the steps to the loo, head first into the wall. Sometimes he thought about his drinking. It had to be doing him some lasting damage. It didn't square with his hypochondria that otherwise made him careful of what he did. He'd been having a lot of headaches recently. Perhaps it was time he sat out the queue at his doctor's.

His wife kept him from drinking as much as he would do otherwise, but she'd gone up to Scotland, to her Calvinist minister father, a few days ago, and had taken their daughter with her. She was staying there until after the New Year. He had an invitation to join her there of course, and the option was still open, even though he didn't get on with the minister – a dour bastard, Jansen always thought, who didn't drink at all. He did sometimes crack into a kind of black humour, though, and the house was massive, and right on the sea.

Jansen's ostensible reason for remaining in London was to finish the novel, but with his wife and child away, he'd put on a spurt, working ten hours a day, and had finished it quicker than expected.

His wife didn't know this, of course, and yesterday evening he'd thought a week or two of footloose revelry would be a good idea, but now all he could think about was the damage it would do to his body. If he went to Scotland it would be as good as going to a convalescent home. He would sleep on it.

He gingerly crossed at the zebra, keeping an eye out for suddenly arriving motorcyclists. He didn't trust taxis with their yellow lights on, either. He watched for dogshit on the pavement and kept his head down past a *Big Issue*-seller and a young male beggar, before giving the second beggar 40p. He dodged the silk tie stall, and hurried down past the piss-reeking alley at the back of the Tube station, until came to the fruit and vegetable stall. Another queue here, young women buying their fruit or salad lunches. Eventually Jansen could ask for three mangoes that were ripe. After the most perfunctory prodding, the man put the first three mangoes that met his hand into a paper bag. Jansen paid him, knowing that the mangoes would be half-ripe but again he said nothing.

He stuck the mangoes in the freezer for half an hour, while he lay on the bed, waiting for the new paracetamol to take effect. He thought of the novel again. It was a very funny book, blackly funny, of course. At least he thought so. He had often laughed aloud while writing it. He hoped his agent would read it quickly. He was ready for some feedback. Three years he'd spent on it.

He could have easily slept, but he was hungry for the mangoes, so he got up and went to the kitchen. He ran his best knife over the sharpener a couple of times, then took the mangoes from the freezer and sliced their scented flesh into a bowl. He loved their smell and their taste more than any other fruit. He wolfed them down, and washed up the bowl, knife, spoon and board immediately afterwards.

As he took the books of stamps out of his pocket to leave in a desk drawer, he came across the lottery ticket and opened it to look at the numbers. They all looked likely there, printed out on their flimsy paper. He put it away again, and sat down at his desk to write to his American friend. 'I have a headache that won't go away,' he began. The friend enjoyed Jansen's hypochondria.

When he'd finished and posted the letter, he didn't know what to do with himself. The novel had occupied him more completely than he'd thought. He missed it more than he missed his wife and daughter. It crossed his mind to ring his wife but they weren't ones for ringing each other when they were apart. His wife would think something was wrong. His headache would not earn him any sympathy as she had no time for either his hypochondria or his drinking. He wondered whether he could take two more paracetamol so soon after the last two, but he remembered reading somewhere that it damaged your liver, and his liver would be in a delicate enough state today. Despite this, he rang his friend Jasper and arranged to meet him at seven in a South Indian vegetarian restaurant they both liked. Then Jansen went down to lie on the bed in the hope that a siesta would sort him out.

It didn't. He woke when the alarm went at six, and he still had the headache. He swallowed two paracetamol with a pint of water. He thought about ringing Jasper to cancel the meeting, and going to the Emergency Department of UCH instead, but he had pitched up at hospitals before, sure he was dying, only to be told there was nothing wrong with him. Panic attacks were the doctors' term for it. This had the hallmarks of a first-class panic attack, so it was much better to go out and meet Jasper in the restaurant. It was probably withdrawal symptoms from finishing the novel, mixed with early alarm at people's reaction to it. He started to breathe deeply and regularly, and kept it going as long as he could.

Jasper had never seen Jansen like this. The old abrasive humour was gone. The appetite had gone with it – Jansen hardly touched the okra, even, which he loved. He spoke openly and seriously about his hypochondria. He spoke of his worries about the headache. It was as if he was able to think two ways at once. Jasper told him it was normal to have a bad headache after binge drinking and that sometimes the headache stayed put for days, as if wires in the head were jangling. It was the head's way of saying 'Back off the booze, boy,' Jasper said. He tried telling Jansen about the Internet system on his new computer, but he might as well have spoken in Sinhalese. They left the restaurant at nine, and went straight away to their separate homes – or Jansen went to his, anyway. They did not, as was their usual practice, retire to a bar together.

Jansen retired instead to bed as soon as he got in. He didn't even take his clothes off. He tried to set the alarm for ten, but realized it would go off at 10p.m., rather than 10a.m., so he set it instead for 9.30. In the morning he'd think about Scotland, with a clear head. He went over the events of his novel as a way of blocking the thoughts hypochondria sends before sleep.

In the morning the alarm went off until it ran out. There was no other sound until the phone rang on Saturday night. It rang until the ansaphone came on automatically, and it was his wife. She had been watching the lottery draw on television much to her father's disgust. She knew Jansen sometimes bought a ticket, and simply to spite her father, not because she had any real interest or curiosity in the matter, left a message asking if Jansen had any of the numbers 1, 19, 25, 30, 36 or 42. The next message came on Monday morning – his agent saying the novel was wonderful, he could sell it anywhere. When his wife and daughter came home in the New Year they found him lying fully clothed on the bed, the pillow, his beard and shirt soaked by blood. Later, after the body had been cleaned, his wife put the bloody shirt in the bin.

Second Fiddle

Bernice Rubens

B ERNICE RUBENS is the author of thirteen novels. *The Elected Member* won the Booker Prize, and *A Five-Year Sentence* was short-listed. Her latest novel, *Yesterday in the Back Lane*, will be published by Little, Brown in 1995.

Confession is all very well. Forget about it being good for the soul. That's not the point of it at all. Well, not *my* point anyway. I don't have atonement in mind. I'm not sorry for what I've done. Not a bit. I just want to get it off my chest. And now the time is ripe. I've made my little pile. I have done what I set out to do. My ruse has paid off. And handsomely too. Yes. The time is ripe. So listen to me. I am about to come clean. I pick up my pen, or rather, my stubby pencil, which is close, close to the page, with the proximity of true confession, and I whisper to you that which I truly am. You thought I was a woman, didn't you? You were wrong.

Oh yes, I know I made a good job of it. I fooled you, close on a hundred of you. Day after day. For two whole years.

Now the act of confession is meaningless unless it is followed by repentance. For my part, I'm not prepared to go that far. But I will make a small confession. I will offer some explanation for my deception, which is more than generous I think, since not even in the confessional is one asked for that. Indeed in that little box, one can get away with murder. I offer an explanation, not in any cheap plea of mitigation, but simply to satisfy your curiosity. I presume perhaps upon your interest, but frankly, if I had been hoodwinked daily over a period of two years, as to the question of gender, I would bloody well want to know why. So to all those ninety-odd members of the Abergavenny Symphony Orchestra, amongst whose ranks I was the Token Woman, I offer without excuse,

333

without apology, and certainly without remorse, the reasons I was forced to frock myself.

I play, as you all well know, a pretty mean fiddle and I may add, a rather meaner fiddle than most of the Abergavenny rank-and-file. My graduation from the Royal Academy was profoundly ill-timed, for it coincided with the flowering of the Women's Movement. By that time, the Movement had forced the male establishment to mend its ways, and we were into the season of tokenism. I applied for auditions to almost every orchestra in the land. Believe me, I played like an angel. But talent had little to do with success. Invariably some scratching, scraping Veronica, Fiona or Sally pipped me to the post. I became so disillusioned that I no longer read the advertisements. But money was running low and I was bound to seek employment.

Out of long habit, I returned one day to the advertising columns of the *Musical Times*, and found therein a plaintive request from Abergavenny. Abergavenny is my home town. I was born there, and that made me Welsh, which I hoped would give me an edge over non-Welsh applicants.

Now, I know that Abergavenny might not boast the greatest Symphony Orchestra of all time, but at least they are a band of honest men, for they actually specified in their advertisement that application for the violin vacancy was restricted to women. It crossed my mind to report them to the Sex Discrimination Committee, or whatever they call themselves. 'If you can't beat them, join them,' my mother used to say when I returned bloodied from school, as I did often enough, being of small and fragile stature. What I decided to do on seeing that advertisement did not strike me as deception, but as a manoeuvre of the utmost logic. I made my application in the name of a lady who, at the age of ninety-seven, had died that morning in *The Times*. Her name was Agnes Morrow. Have you noticed that people who die in *The Times* die old? It's all that wealth I suppose, and private medical care. Anyway, I thought it would be quite a nice little memorial to Agnes to take her name. She might well, as the paper stated, be deeply mourned in Mayfair,

334

but I would resurrect her in Abergavenny and blazon her name with honour.

I went shopping. I gathered together a wig, two frocks, some blouses and petticoats. I said I was shopping for my dear wife who was bedridden. I needn't have bothered with that little deception for the assistant was not fooled. She actually winked at me, and asked, in a whisper, whether I would like to try them on. I was indignant and insisted on my ailing wife. One owes a certain loyalty to one's lies, and to abandon them when their backs are to the wall is to betray a sad lack of character. I hovered in the evening-dress department, but decided to postpone that purchase until the result of the audition. I am not one to tempt Providence. When I reached home I tried on my gear. I am not of the hirsute persuasion and, with a little make-up, the deception was foolproof. I looked pretty good. Well, you know I did. I fooled you, didn't I? Why, some of you even made a pass at me. Yes, I looked good all right, and between you and me, I *felt* rather good, too. You should try a frock sometime. It might even improve your playing.

I wore jeans to the audition, to be on the safe side. But the blouse and curly wig proclaimed my gender well enough. Again I played like an angel and, secure in the job, I sallied forth to buy a black evening frock for my still ailing wife. The rest is history.

Mind you, there were some dicey moments. D'you remember, Dowi, when you followed me into the Ladies' room? You said you mistook it for the Gents'. My God, Dowi, after twelve years with the Abergavenny band, you should have known your way about backstage. I was in the process of adjusting the padding of my bra which had become dislodged during the last frenetic movement of Mahler One. I saw you through the mirror and I reddened in fear of discovery. You took my colour for a blush of modesty and mercifully withdrew, but it was a close shave.

And then there was that terrible moment in the supermarket. Among other buys, I'd picked up a packet of razors from the shelf and you, Alan, happened to be behind me in the check-out. We exchanged greetings as you eyed the contents of my basket and I distinctly saw an eyebrow raised at the sight of my razors. I pre-empted your question. 'For my legs,' I said. I hoped I was blushing. Not only did my explanation satisfy you, Alan, but it seemed to turn you on. 'I'd give a lot to be your barber,' you said. I *must* have blushed then, if only out of shame for my true gender.

And Gareth, d'you remember the Eisteddfod? We were the guest orchestra, though God knows there must have been better bands in Wales than the Abergavenny Symphony. But one of our Board had a brother who had a friend on the Eisteddfod panel. That's how we landed the invitation. We went to Bangor by bus, d'you remember? I used to dread those bus-journeys. It was all right *going* there, but coming back was a nightmare. Drunk you were, the lot of you, and you, Gareth, were the drunkest of them all. And you started a sing-song. Everyone joined in. Even the driver. Except me, of course. I could achieve a reasonable lightness in my speaking voice, round about the contralto level, but in singing I was barely at home in a tenor. Baritone was my natural singing level and had I opened my mouth to join in, I would surely have been rumbled. So I held my tongue and pretended to sleep. But you weren't having any, were you, Gareth? You nudged me awake and told me to join in. Then in your loutish and drunken fashion, you started to tickle me. I needed to laugh but I dared not, because my laughter, like my singing, was baritone. I twisted away from your groping and I was close to tears. Then some good man, I'm not sure who, dragged you off me and I felt an arm of comfort on my shoulder.

Maybe it was you, Norman. You were different, and when I look back on it now, you were the only one I feel sorry I deceived. Because you respected me. All the time. You behaved like a proper gentleman. D'you remember when my E-string snapped when I was tuning up in the band-room? You came over straight away and offered to re-string it for me. And you did, there and then, with one of your own spares. And you asked for nothing in return. You just smiled. 'It's my pleasure,' you said. I'll never forget that.

There were good moments and bad, but the worst occurred during our midsummer concert. We were playing the Beethoven Fourth

Second Fiddle

Piano. During the cadenza, I chanced to look into the audience. And there, slap in the middle of the front row, sat my mother. I trembled, and had difficulty in pulling myself together in time for that final trill and our entry. The second movement was murder for me. It was impossible to concentrate. I just couldn't understand what my mother was doing in Abergavenny. She hadn't lived there in years.

It was not until the final movement that I recalled that she had often spoken of an old school-friend, who had never left this benighted town. No doubt it was that austere lady who sat by my mother's side. It did not occur to me that they would be at the reception after the concert. But it seemed that my mother's companion was a regular patron of our band and, as such, felt obliged to greet each member of the orchestra with patronising patting. She dragged my mother in tow. Mere rank-and-filer though I was, my turn was unavoidable. I gave her my most girlish smile, simpering yet wide, wide enough to embrace my mother as well. And do you know, my mother actually smiled back at me with that undisguised condescension that she had possibly caught from her friend. But on her face was no flicker of recognition, no wrinkle of hesitation, and her unastonished eyebrows were still. I turned quickly and went straight away to the dressing room. I was actually weeping. My mother's total lack of recognition had hurt me deeply, and I wondered how she who had carried me, suckled me, bathed me, and presumably loved me, did not know me from Eve. It was a terrible blow, but I soldiered on and took care never to look into the audience again.

And I would be amongst you still, had it not been for Mrs Williams, our founder's widow. She had every right to come on tour, of course. Her late husband had funded our band since its inception. But I had not reckoned on sharing a room with her. I tried all manner of argument. I offered my insomnia and my restless nocturnal pacing, but nothing short of leprosy could promote my claim to a private room. I bowed out with grace and packed my frocks away.

I shall now seek a profession in which gender is irrelevant. And not only gender, but presence too. I seek a post in which it makes absolutely no difference, frocked or trousered, whether I am there or not. I shall don a beard, I think, and take up conducting.

Performer, Performance

William Palmer

WILLIAM PALMER was born in 1945. After a bewildering variety of jobs he is now a full-time writer and the author of three novels: *The Good Republic* (Secker & Warburg, 1990), *Leporello* (Secker & Warburg, 1992) and *The Contract* (Jonathan Cape, 1995). His stories and poems have appeared in many magazines. He lives in the Midlands with his wife and daughter.

Snow fell into the club entrance. The warm air from inside died before it reached the edge of scarlet carpet. McKendrew leaned out to look up the street.

At last a car turned from the orange glow of the main road and moved down. The wheels hobbled on crusts of ice. It stopped at the entrance.

The driver got out. He read the neon sign high on the wall, smacked the top of the car, and called across to McKendrew: 'Hide yourself away a bit up here, don't you?' He came around to open the rear door and bent to look inside. 'We're there,' he said.

The passenger got slowly out, drawing a long brown leather case after him.

In the club's foyer a large photograph on an easel showed a broad-shouldered, middle-aged black man, his arms cradling a saxophone, a faintly malicious smile on his huge handsome face.

But the man on the pavement seemed barely to fill his clothes. He was bald, with a few wisps of white hair straggling to his collar; the heavy lidded eyes were thinned to slits, his skin yellow. He shivered and folded a long, opulent, ancient fur coat about him.

'I'll have to have a signature.' The driver had brought out a tattered duplicate book. The passenger had gone into the entrance and stood, looking round slowly; at the carpet, the walls, the ceiling.

341

'To prove you've had him,' said the driver. 'They get lost sometimes on these out-of-town jobs. Or just don't turn up. This one hasn't said a word all the way up.'

McKendrew signed and tore off his copy. He ground it in his fist and let it fall to the snow.

The driver was getting back into the car. 'I'll pick him up at about one,' he said. 'Wants to go back to London. Can't say I blame him.'

In the foyer, the old man stood in front of the easel, the case clutched in one hand, the long fingers of the other stroking his cheek as he looked at the photograph.

McKendrew strode past him and opened one of the double doors into the club. 'Come in,' he said. With an odd, shuffling walk, the man followed him.

Heavy drapes hung down the windowless walls of the converted warehouse. Between the drapes were pasted huge black-and-white photographs of famous jazz musicians; after five years they had turned a dingy, nicotine-stained grey-yellow. A false ceiling extended as far as the bandstand. To the side, steps led to the mezzanine dining area, 'The Bistro'.

'Mr Alex asked me to look after you till he got here,' said McKendrew. 'He'll be late. I'll show you to the office.'

An hour later the phone rang.

'Mr Alex. Half past six when he came,' said McKendrew. 'OK. No, nothing to eat. Just sat down in the office and put the fire on and asked for a bottle of brandy. Rémy Martin. That's all he said. So I got him that. I made a bill out but he just put it in his pocket. Eh? All right. If that's all right with you? Yeah, yeah – we'll look after him.'

The phone must have rung and rung up in the office; McKendrew had been called at last to the extension in 'The Bistro'. The little restaurant, with Chianti bottles hanging from the blue-lit fishing nets on the walls, was empty.

But the club floor was filling up rapidly. Wednesday night was usually dead, but not this one.

And the crowd coming in were older than usual. They were dressed in sports coats and cords, or smart suits a few years out of fashion. There were not so many women, and they weren't young either. McKendrew made his way through them all, proud of the way the swagger of his broad, powerful body made them part, amused as one of them bumped into him and spilled a spot of beer froth on his shoe and then began apologizing profusely as McKendrew stared hard down at him.

Passing the bar, he nodded to the girls serving. They laughed at him, he knew that. At his belly and balding crew-cut. They didn't know what a man was . . .

He went up the uncarpeted stairs to the office.

The old man sat on a straight chair, hunched over the electric fire. On the wall above him the calendar had only one month left, December 1967. McKendrew looked at his watch. After nine. Mr Alex had said he was on his way over. Time to work. He coughed loudly and took a step forward.

'Is it time?' the slurred, thick, American voice asked. 'Give me that, will you?' He pointed to the case on the desk. Beside it, the brandy bottle had about an inch left in it.

Opening the case, the man took out the shining trunk and neck of a tenor saxophone. His hands were steady as he assembled the instrument, putting on the mouthpiece, mulling over a box of reeds, then screwing up the ligature with strong fingers. He pushed out his lower lip, his thick tongue wetted the reed. He reared his head back and regarded the mouthpiece. He adjusted it slightly, then applied his lips again, twiddled a couple of keys exploratively, and gave out a great, sudden blast of sound.

'Christ,' said McKendrew. 'Makes a hell of a noise, don't she?'

Alex had arrived. He was a disappointed man. It had always been his dream to bring great jazz names – the names he had learned off record sleeves in his youth – to play in his club. He'd kept a jazz policy going as long as he could, but lately fees had been too high, attendances sparse, the artists unreliable. The rock boom was sweeping everything else out of the clubs.

'What's it like?' he asked McKendrew.

'Full,' said his doorman.

Surprised by the crush, Alex eased his way to the front.

The rhythm section had started to play already. A long, long introduction to a blues. The great tenor saxophone player hugged the crook of the hired grand piano, smiling to himself, eyes hooded, swaying slightly, disinclined to join in.

Alex was shocked by the man's appearance. Of course he'd heard rumours – of drink and illness, that he wasn't playing well on this tour with local scratch trios, and the man was in his sixties – but the rumours didn't prepare you for the fall, for the once powerful body shrunk in the too large suit, the shirt collar awry, the loud painted silk tie falling out of the buttoned jacket.

In Alex's head, in the heads of the audience, were all the legends of this man. He had played with Bessie Smith and Billie Holiday, Ellington and Basie, Charlie Parker and Coltrane. He had invented the saxophone as a jazz instrument the same way Armstrong had invented the trumpet. And all their heads rehearsed his old solos . . .

He cradled the saxophone in his arms. His head nodded in and out of time to the music; the pianist kept looking up at him, waiting for, and not getting, some sign. At last, with infinite weariness, the man lifted the saxophone to his mouth.

The sound faltered and wheezed; for a terrible moment Alex feared that his performer was not going to be able to play at all. Then the notes fattened and grew rich, until it was as if a huge, extraordinarily beautiful rose had unfurled, filling the room. In Alex, the music spread along his veins like another blood. The old man disappeared; there was only the great, soft sound that whispered, boomed, cried out, sang and, above all, spoke of love. Then it stopped, and the old man was looking at the ecstatically applauding audience as if it did not exist.

In the office, Alex counted money into the outstretched hand. He tried again to put his thanks into words. 'Wonderful. Absolutely wonderful. Thanks so much for coming . . .' words which seemed utterly inadequate as repayment for the two hours of power and beauty which had been given tonight. The player simply grunted, stowing the money carefully in an inner pocket of the fur coat. Alex was ashamed to feel relieved when McKendrew came in to say the car was here. The old man drained the last of his glass slowly.

'The case,' he said.

McKendrew carried it down the stairs, feeling resentment at having to do this thing. What in God's name Mr Alex saw in these old black geezers he couldn't guess.

He stowed the case in the back of the car and held the door open. The driver yawned.

'Thank you again for coming,' said Alex. 'It was wonderful. Truly wonderful . . .'

The old man's handshake was brief and slack. He sat in the back of the car and stared straight in front.

The car started forward; the rear wheels raced in the snow, the driver spinning the wheel to turn in the narrow street. It lurched forward up to the main road. At the top it hesitated, turned again, and went away from the town.

Alex dropped the empty brandy bottle into the waste paper basket. Marvellous night; but he had still lost money on it. Jazz sold too much beer; too much attention given to the artist. You sold far more with the movement and youth of the disco.

So that one was the last. The jazz was over. He felt suddenly depressed; he could do with a drink himself. A large Scotch. He sat behind the desk. On the cassette player was a tape of the great saxophonist. He switched it on. It had been recorded some time in the fifties. The tune was fast, the saxophone lunged and flashed arrogantly through a barrage of riffing brass. For some reason the very vigour of the playing was profoundly dispiriting. Alex turned it off abruptly.

In the bar McKendrew heard the music start, charge forward for a minute, then stop. He pulled the bar shutters rattling down. He came out and locked the door, leaving one light shining weakly on the mirrored bottles. The empty floor was scuffed and dirty. Moving his powerful arms easily into the swing, he began to pile chairs up on tables, whistling tunelessly as he worked his way along to the dark bandstand.

Vermin

———— ❧❧ ————

David Profumo

DAVID PROFUMO was born in London in 1955. A former teacher, he is now a freelance writer and columnist with the *Daily Telegraph*. His books include *The Magic Wheel* with Graham Swift (1985), *Sea Music* (1988), and *The Weather in Ireland* (1993). He was awarded the Geoffrey Faber Memorial Prize in 1989.

At the time of the exodus I was just eight, for Heaven's sake, but still they come and pester me with their lousy questions – minstrels and tattlemongers mostly, wanting my tale *gratis* for their repertoires. 'I understand, *Lehrmeister*, you were the only surviving . . .' Well I'm getting too old for this modern rage for story-telling: what's past is past, and there'll be no more interviews.

They just embellish it, anyway, to satisfy their mooncalf audiences – one version has me as a cripple, complete with stump and bloody clout, and in another they've got it hopelessly mixed up with that later business at Lorch, where the charcoal-burner made off with all the sheep (or was it the famous fiddler of Brandenburg? I'm beginning to muddle it all, myself). Any rate, if I had collected a gylder for each different account of what happened that summer I'd be the richest baker in Saxony.

People believe what they want, of course, and sometimes the truth is not quite colourful enough (though it can work the other way round). Take the central character – they've got him completely wrong. It was over sixty years ago, I grant you, but even then a man would hardly have roamed Westphalia dressed up in red and yellow like some zany. In fact, he looked like a vagabond, with matted hair, dingy attire and an old felt hat. We were used to the place being full of foreigners then, but he stood out by being immensely tall and dark-skinned. (The image of a youthful prancer is misleading, too: he must have been pushing fifty, and had only one good eye.)

He first showed up that spring in a barge carrying currants from the Levant. It may be hard to imagine now, but in those days Hameln was a thriving port, a byword for prosperity and order; several generations of its burghers had grown rich from the great weir on the Weser, which meant all cargoes had to be unloaded and held in staple for two days, during which time they could be compulsorily purchased. Business was good because it was tightly regulated, and those who made the rules (not my family, by the way) lived in sandstone mansions with golden roofs and elaborately carved rafters. There were liveried bailiffs to protect the citizens, monthly assizes, and ferries that ran to a timetable. It was not really a place that welcomed unkempt strangers.

For some reason the local merchants were suspicious of this visitor, and refused to do business with him. If your face didn't fit, you got ignored. They were an arrogant lot at the best of times – especially Burgomeister Hoffmann, who was absurdly fond of the chain around his neck – and I expect by now their names would only be remembered from some family plaque on a wall in St Boniface's, had it not been for the rats.

It was claimed in retrospect, of course, that the infestation coincided exactly with the arrival of the 'piper' – he had been disgruntled and somehow introduced the pests to undermine the reputation and efficiency of the township (well, he managed that, one way and another). The fact that there was obviously a population of rats established long before the evil trader arrived only goes to prove the point, according to the badger-bearded chroniclers whose quills scratch to ascribe blame: it was all nicely under control until he came, so they say.

The scale of the problem was dramatic, that I do recall. Seemingly overnight the rodents proliferated and became bolder, lolloping around in broad daylight, gnawing like beavers at our woodwork, pissing in the kitchens, and occasionally leaping into cradles. They got run over by cartwheels, making a dreadful stench, and their screeching at night became intolerable. It was an awful insult to our civic pride.

Vermin

I remember my mother saying: 'That something so filthy should happen here, of all places,' and my Aunt Maria, who then lived with us, tutting indignant assent from her shawl, in the corner.

Hoffmann did his best. Experts were summoned from all over the Empire (or so he claimed), and dogs, smoke, nets, poisons, cats, charms, traps and systems of mirrors were all brought to bear. In the meantime, the townsfolk lashed at what they could with brooms, and lit votive candles. Clean food and snug sleep were becoming precious commodities. Charlatans and bounty-hunters appeared, and were dismissed. The number of boats logging into port during May fell way below expectations – and I suppose that's when the deal must have been struck.

On the night itself there was an early curfew, well before dark. My widowed mother and I had lodgings at number five Papenstrasse (it's been renamed since the atrocity), so we were well placed to see what happened; word had spread that our brave burgomeister had organized some drastic action, and there were curious neighbours leaning out of every window in the street.

It began with a whisper, like the rustling of leaves, and then the tatty foreigner walked slowly round the corner apparently playing a set of bagpipes. But instead of making a noise like a roasting cat, his instrument seemed to us quite silent; the only sounds we could hear were the clack of his hobs on the cobbles, and the growing, hissing whisper, with now a rhythmic creaking, like rope stretched around a capstan. The vermin burst suddenly into view and began pouring down the hill towards the river in a great, grey stream: I suppose there must have been millions of them, for this spectacle lasted half an hour (there were various domestic animals too, including useless cats, swept along in thrall to the inaudible tune). That night the town slept deeply in the new quiet, as if cupped of all its foul blood.

There are conflicting accounts, naturally, about what happened the next morning. It seems that Hoffmann had offered an absurd sum as a reward, and thought the old man gullible; the jubilant councillors first demanded proof of his deed, then accused him of sorcery, and finally made the mistake of haggling with him. This broke all the basic rules of business. Three times the 'piper' registered a claim for his gylders – some say he was promised as much as 10,000 – and would settle for nothing less than the full amount. In the end, they had him escorted outside the town walls under threat of imprisonment if he should commit any further nuisance (they had no idea whom they were up against).

On Sunday, June the 26th, Feast Day of Saints John and Paul (those unknown martyrs), there was a special service of thanksgiving at High Mass, and most of the adults attended. It was to be followed by a celebratory banquet in the Corn Exchange – jugged hare with ginger, turbot in almond milk, the works – but that was one meal the townsfolk never got to enjoy, because (I need hardly remind you) when they returned from their devotions there was not a single child over the age of four left in Hameln.

One minute I was playing soldiers around the pump with Otto, the bell-maker's son, and the next – so it seemed – I was on that hillside. People always want to know what the diabolical tune sounded like; but it's hard to say, except that it had pictures in it. All at once we were caught up in a dream, surrounded by notes of stained glass, honey music, fragrant visions of orchards in the air and distant, sugary landscapes. We sung our way over the slow green river, dancing like boughs in a rising wind. I remember being helplessly happy, feeling quite safe, because the one-eyed showman was conjuring a story shot through with beauty and colour.

As we ascended the first foothill of the Kuppenberg I must have slipped and broken my ankle. I don't recall any pain, but it slowed me down so much that I only reached the rocky pass just as the last child was disappearing into the mountainside, and the stones closed for ever.

At first, no one would believe me (it's not easy being an eye-witness); then the cross-questioning began, and in a way it's never stopped since. Their immediate reaction, on realizing this was not some prank, was to grab staves and tools and form a furious search party. Later, I was accused of cowardice for not having prevented it (they blamed me for my very survival). The aftermath was quite terrible.

Despite having lost two daughters, Hoffmann was hounded out of office and his wife had her coach stoned as she crossed the bridge. Officials came from Hannover with a team of miners, who set about fruitlessly excavating the hill. Some blind old gypsy was tracked down to his hut in the Reinhardswald and strung up, by way of reprisal. The bishop delivered a sermon of consolation, assuring us they had gone to a better place – and I'm certain he started those rumours about the hundred or so blonde children being rescued from a hillside somewhere deep in the eastern territories (I know for sure that was a load of dreck).

They began to date all public documents in Hameln from the year 1284, 'na user Kinder uthgang', out of respect.

The rest of my childhood was strange and lonely, and as soon as I could I secured an apprenticeship and moved here to Kassel, where I've made myself busy baking bread ever since (I was about to say 'man and boy', but I never did manage a family of my own). Here, I'm famous for my biscuits. Life needs to appear dull, in order to continue.

People believe what they want, and long ago I stopped describing the moment I crested the final hill and saw him outlined there, in the mouth of that furnace. The gaping rockface behind was filled with what must have been hellfire, like a huge oven, and his whole figure was framed in its light: he had thrown down his pipes, and there was no more music spinning lies. The last child to go was my friend Otto, swung by his hair into the flames.

Why I was spared, I do not understand – some speak of Providence, but I leave such ideas to the young.

Like all survivors, I am plagued with disbelief.

Sea Lion

————◆————

Douglas Hurd

DOUGLAS HURD was born in 1930 and educated at Cambridge. He has written six books: *The Arrow War* (1967), *Send Him Victorious* (1968), *The Smile on the Face of the Tiger* (1969) and *Scotch on the Rocks* (1971) (in conjunction with Andrew Osmond), *Truth Game* (1972) and *Vote to Kill* (1975). A book of stories, *A Suitcase Between Friends*, was published in 1993. He is married with three sons, and has been a Member of Parliament since 1970.

It wasn't working. It wouldn't work. This was his last week in the Islands. Perhaps one more conversation with the sea lions would do the trick.

Richard was allowed to use the motorbike on which old David Macgregor visited his sheep. He drove it brutally through the colony of penguins about half a mile from the knoll on which the farmhouse and hotel stood. A dirty cloud of their own droppings enveloped the birds as they waddled indignantly away. In his present mood the extraordinary tameness of the wild life was an affront to Richard's sense of reality. Why couldn't penguins and elephant seals and sea lions learn to protect themselves like ordinary creatures? Why couldn't David Macgregor and his like recognise that they lived next door to Argentina and thousands of miles from Scotland? But in both cases they didn't and wouldn't.

Richard made for the bluff at the end of the island and the memorial to HMS *Sheffield*. Somewhere out there, to the south of the most southerly of the Falklands, her bow line had finally snapped 14 years ago, and the work of the Exocet had been accomplished.

Richard could not afford to repay the publisher's advance, but knew he would have to. George Schonbrum could hardly reclaim the return air fare as well, but that was small consolation. It had seemed such a good idea over lunch at the Savoy, just the thing to revive his flagging reputation. Brilliant young historian turns the

357

Douglas Hurd

tables on his own Tory past and exposes the falseness of the Falklands War. Secrecy, of course, was essential. To Lady Thatcher, to the Foreign Office, to the Governor and to Mr Smith, the Curator of the Museum in Port Stanley, he had presented himself as working on a straightforward account of the war, updating the quick book put out at the time by Max Hastings and Simon Jenkins. They had all been most helpful. Richard had kept his good looks and could deploy plenty of boyish charm. Only Schonbrum the publisher knew that Richard had reached the answer before he started asking the questions.

Richard liked the company of the sea lions. They did not fuss like the penguins. They were not as gross or familiar as the elephant seals. They lay, a mix of tawny and black, on the rocks beneath him, economical with their movements and their grunts. There were eight of them on that particular stretch, more than usual, and looking along to the next bay Richard saw the reason. The French marine botanists were at it again, photographing through the glass bottom of their boat. They occupied all eight small white bedrooms of the hotel, which was why Richard was lodged with the farmer, David Macgregor. They were, he understood from Macgregor, making an immensely intellectual film, based on the ripples of the floating local seaweed or kelp, which they repeatedly photographed in all lights and all weathers.

Richard was one of those Englishmen who shuns the French for fear that they might be more intelligent than himself. He had made no contact with them. Macgregor had, however, told them with satisfaction the story of the young Frenchman who had mysteriously committed suicide on the island forty years earlier. Macgregor's uncle had had to pull down a partition in the farmhouse to provide wood for his coffin. The four puny conifers struggling in David Macgregor's garden were still the only trees on the island. Though the Falklands were not as cold as Richard had expected, the wind was incessant.

Richard sat in the lee of a huge mound of tussock grass. Its roots were exposed by the wind, and he could see the black layer of ash from the time when the island had been on fire. The peat had burned for several months, set alight, it was supposed, by

358

castaways in search of warmth. The Islands were full of such stories. Those of the 1982 war fitted well with the tales and emblems of earlier drama – skulls, masts, whalebones, the prows of abandoned vessels, and now the wreckage of crashed Mirages.

Richard heard the air taxi before he saw it approach the mown grass strip. The autumn light was fading and the Cessna did not linger. Within ten minutes it was in the air again. A tall girl was carrying a suitcase to where David Macgregor was waiting in his Land Rover. Of course, his daughter Laura, back for Easter from Southampton University. 'She talks a bit,' David had said. Since David himself was monosyllabic, it was hard to say what the comment meant. David, a widower for twenty years, disliked any intrusion on his sheep and his solitude. Soon the airstrip would close for the winter, 'and there'll be an end of all this noise and pother,' David had remarked, as if he lived in Mayfair. Against this background Richard's evenings in the farmhouse had not sparkled. He had read and reread his research materials, but the answer lay dozing in front of the peat fire. There were no powers of force or charm which would turn David Macgregor into an Argentine citizen.

With Laura the evening was certainly different. She spoke at once as if they had met often before.

'How did you vote?' she asked.

Richard had forgotten it was election day in Britain.

'I voted by post. The ballot is secret.'

'Don't be tiresome. I need to know for my thesis on political communication. How did you vote?'

'I voted Labour for the first time.' Richard was 29. He spoke as if a lifetime of electoral experience weighed upon him.

Laura passed him the mint sauce. The lamb was home-bred. She had bought the mint sauce at Tesco's in Southampton on her way to the airport, together with the Cadbury's Fruit and Nut which her father particularly favoured. She was tall and freckled, too thin for Richard's taste, but with direct blue eyes which could not be ignored. As the evening passed and she moved about the kitchen and dining table in her tight jeans his first disappointment passed.

'How on earth did you turn Left? All those articles of yours belong to the sour Right.'

Richard wished she had mentioned the book rather than the articles. His biography of Sir Austen Chamberlain, published five years ago, had been well researched, well received, earned little. But it had opened the columns of the right-wing press to him, editors paid well and Richard found he could earn more from bitter topical articles than from attempting another book. The more caustic the article, the higher the fee paid on behalf of Messrs Murdoch and Black. He carried a folder of recent articles in his suitcase to reassure him as necessary of his own cleverness.

'The Government is so awful,' he answered her question lamely. 'Anything would be better.'

'Then why did you try so hard to get selected for places like South Hants?'

'How the hell do you know that?'

She refilled his Nescafé.

'I told you. I am reading politics. I follow these things.'

She was getting warm. That had been the most humiliating year of his life. Handsome young historian, darling of the *Spectator*, constantly compared to the slashing early Disraeli – full of his own future, he had trailed round constituency selection committees being rejected by old women, estate agents and seedy councillors. He had conceived a fierce hatred of the present Conservative Party which neglected such obvious talent.

'That's all over now. I'm working on another book.'

David Macgregor had mumbled his way upstairs to bed. Outside the wind, never still, was rising and rattling the windows.

'You could cheat on the book, I suppose. I mean, you could decide after all that the Argentines offered us a good deal and Margaret Thatcher insisted on war to fix the '83 election.'

He stared at her again. His years as a columnist had taught him not to blush.

'I've given up wondering how you know what you know,' he said after a pause. 'It must be the second sight of the Macgregors.'

'It's John Wilson at the Museum in Stanley. He rang me in England to say you'd been nosing around the archives. Asking slanted questions. Trying to suggest that we were an unreasonable bunch. Or else a lot of fools exploited by electioneering politicians at home.'

'But it won't work!' Richard found himself saying to the girl what he had said to the sea lions.

Despite all those tendentious column-inches, he had started as a scholar and still believed in evidence. There were therefore still limits to what he could write. Unfortunately there was no evidence in London, or New York, or Buenos Aires or Stanley to support the thesis which he and Schonbrum had tossed around over lunch at the Savoy.

'I'm glad,' she said. Reaching out, she touched his hand. 'It would have been bad if you had come out against the Islands.' She paused. 'Maybe we can do you a good turn one day.'

'You have already,' he said, lightening the tone. 'The lamb was delicious, and . . .'

But she was already up the stairs.

The next morning he had time before the Cessna came for him. He went with Laura to see the Slipway. The wind was still stiff. Yesterday's clouds had blown away, and the waves sparkled as they formed, rose high and toppled in white explosion upon the rocks. The Frenchmen had wisely pulled their boat ashore. There was no harbour on Sea Lion Island. Before the days of the air taxi, supplies came to the farm three times a year and were hauled almost vertically on an iron pulley up a wooden slipway to a ledge of tussock grass fifty feet above deep water. The crew would scramble up the rocks to help David Macgregor and his father before him to work the pulley.

'Grief, look at that!'

Laura had reached the ledge first. Below them, exactly where the lighters had once bobbed and scraped against the rock face, was a smart white launch tossing furiously but tied to a rusty iron ring set in the rocks. It was empty.

'The French must have brought in a second boat.'

'No, look at that.'

Because of the lie of the land they now saw for the first time the cruise ship out in the bay which formed the southern shore of the island. In the sun it, too, shone white, and through her binoculars Laura could see the Greek flag.

'Greek, Russian, Japanese – they come quite often nowadays, but usually only to Stanley.'

Richard heard the footsteps before she did. 'Down,' he whispered loudly, pulling hard at her sweater. They lay side by side on the ledge, concealed by the long wiry hummocks of grass from the upward path which sailors had once made and which the sheep preserved. A young man, dark and wiry, was near the top. He carried a hand-held TV camera. Behind him followed a girl, looking exactly like him, carrying what seemed to be a canvas gun-case slung over her shoulder.

Long ago sailors had built a small cairn to mark the top of the Slipway. The couple paused at the cairn, and spoke together. They were too far off for Richard to know more than that they were speaking a language he did not understand. The young man began to organize his camera. The girl opened the long tubular canvas case and took out the contents. A couple of neat movements and she had achieved her purpose. The camera made it immortal.

'Grief!' said Laura again.

'*Bellissimo*,' shouted the young cameraman.

On the day when the new British Government was formed, the blue and white flag of Argentina, rooted in the cairn, flew bravely over the southernmost of the Falklands.

Without a word or gesture to Richard, Laura charged across the open space straight at the flag. She shoved the amazed girl aside, snatched the flag, and threw it down the Slipway. Without any concern for her own safety, she watched it rattle down between the parallel ridges of wood into the sea, and spread lazily in the waves. When she turned round she faced the young man's pistol.

'That was not an intelligent action,' he said in excellent English. But that was all. Afterwards Richard often asked himself why he had acted as he did. No calculation, no thought, just an impulse which changed for ever his view of himself.

Richard was in reasonable training. Vague memories of the rugby field produced the perfect tackle.

'It wasn't loaded,' he said, picking up the gun. The Argentine sat on the grass, nursing his knee.

'Of course not. We are not bandits.'

'At least we have the picture,' said his sister, 'which is what we came for.' The young man got up. 'Permit me to introduce ourselves. We are Roberto and Susanna Tuzman, partners in the public relations company of that name, based in Buenos Aires.' He broke off, and in a different tone shouted at Laura: 'Stop that! It is not yours.' But Laura had already thrown the camera down the Slipway. Its descent was noisier than that of the flag, and ended dramatically with a combination of crash and splash.

'Better go while you can,' said Richard. 'I don't suppose the Greeks will wait forever.'

The two invaders took his advice.

'It would be better if you did not mention this to anyone,' said Roberto Tuzman.

'*Viva las Malvinas*,' said his sister.

Then they were down the path, and three minutes later the launch was on its way.

L aura gave him a kiss just before he boarded the Cessna. But that was that. No shared comradeship after victory, no discussion of what had happened or why.

'Not much point,' was all she said when he began. 'It's all pretty obvious. A PR stunt which went wrong. Lucky we were there. I've sent a radio message to Stanley, with the gist of it.'

Richard never knew what that message of hers contained. The Cessna came down at Mount Pleasant, and Richard was put without explanation into an Army helicopter. Within ten minutes he landed on the grass between Government House and the elegant new comprehensive school.

The Governor was there, with his red London taxi, also the Commander British Forces, Mr Smith, the curator of the Museum, elected councillors and the chief executive. Four police officers saluted. A television camera flashed.

'You didn't give us time to get the Marine band organized,' said the General.

'Stout work,' said the Governor. 'You'll stay overnight with Hilda and myself, I hope. A lot of people will want to hear from you direct.'

The next twenty-four hours were a splendid muddle. John Major had been re-elected with a majority of twenty. The British press linked this with the repulse of a second Argentine invasion of the Falklands. Lady Thatcher sent Richard a telegram. He broadcast repeatedly. He held a public meeting in the hall at Stanley, attended by a high proportion of the town's inhabitants. He tried to get in touch with Laura, but in vain. He ate a huge celebratory lunch with much Chilean wine at the Upland Goose Hotel. He had a few minutes of final packing before he left in the Governor's red taxi for the airport.

He would never see Laura again, and would hardly think of her. But he remembered what she had said about the Islands doing him a good turn. He thought of that rugby tackle on Sea Lion Island. He took out of a drawer his research material and first notes for his book *The Falklands Falsehood*, together with a folder of his recent press articles.

Slowly but without regret he tore them up and dropped them in the crested wastepaper basket of the spare bedroom at Government House.

The Roman Candle

Donna Tartt

The little girl has a red parka and white mittens. She is small – three years old – and happy to be outside in the cold and dark and Christmastime. A tree glows ember-rich through the living-room window. From the white house, gold squares of light slant across the packed snow; and, across the yard, sharp cut-outs of the Chinese magnolia, the tall hedge, stand black against the frosty stars.

The girl is very small and she has not seen snow before. The ground-glass sparkle is new to her, and its smooth luminescence; the waffled crunch her red galoshes make and the softness when she falls backwards like a chopped tree to make white angel-wings with sweeps of her arms. 'What do you want for Christmas?' the Santa Claus at the Otasco store asked her as she climbed on to his knee on his gold throne amidst all the green tinsel and the refrigerators and washing machines.

Wings, she whispered in his big ear.

Wings? What sort?

To fly with.

What colour?

Little red ones.

This is a night of first things. She has never seen snow and she has never seen fireworks. Nor has she ever been outside so late at night. She is alone with her father, and this is unusual, too. Her father is a busy man. His presence is not comforting like her mother's but electric and unfamiliar. He has black hair and eyes the icy blue of the German Shepherd dog down at the lumberyard, the one that jumps snarling at the fence and that everyone says is part wolf. He pulls her along by a mittened hand and her neck hurts with craning to look up at him, he is so high above the ground, his big, handsome head majestic in a cloud of cigar smoke and his cigar's red ember burning high in the dark like the red star on top of the Christmas tree. He walks fast, and does not look down. A paper bag of fireworks is tucked beneath his other arm: black cats, Catherine wheels, fire with beautiful names. Humbly, she trots after, trying to keep up. She is his puppy, she knows, she takes not after Mother but after him: his dark hair, his Arctic eyes, his knife-bright quickness. Though he is godlike to her in his absence and his grandeur she senses the dash of his fierce blood in her own veins and the rasp of his breath as he sucks hard on the cigar, is the amplified music of her own small breath. When he barks, or cuffs her, she takes it humbly, rolling over with a whimper to show her tummy to his teeth.

Mother has not come to see the fireworks but is in the house: lying on her bed with her shoes and stockings on, a flag of light spilling into the darkened room from the hall corridor. She went upstairs and lay down not long after Father let himself in the front door and came inside without saying hello to anybody and turned on the ball game on television. She herself – feeling lonely after Mother's disappearance – lay down on the floor behind his chair, but he didn't answer when she tried to show him the picture she'd drawn except to say 'That's nice' and then, more sharply, 'Later', without looking either time. After the game was over he galloped upstairs, bellowing to Mother in a certain cheery way he has sometimes, while she scrambled up the stairs behind him unnoticed. But Mother didn't answer, and didn't answer when he knocked at the door: in a jolly way at first, and then with his fist.

He went in anyway and slammed the door behind him. Angry voices. She waited for them on the landing: on her back, waving her arms and legs in the air, pretending to be a bug. After she got tired of being a bug, she grabbed the tips of her toes with both hands and made them go back and forth like that while she sang to herself, a song she'd learned from a detergent commercial.

When the door flew open, her father was alone, and he came out of the dark room fast without bothering to shut the door behind him. When he saw her – fallen on her side now, still holding her toes, and not singing now but watchful because she was uncertain of his mood – his voice was loud and friendly in a way that surprised her, like he was talking to a client on the telephone or a grown-up he didn't know that well. Unexpectedly he swooped and grabbed her up so she laughed aloud. Over his shoulder, as he ran with her down the stairs she can see her mother's legs, on the dim bed through the open door, very still.

Now alone in the snow and dark with him, her mother's absence worries her; but it also makes the night seems dangerous, like a movie or an adventure on TV. Stumbling fast beside, she tries to catch her father's eye so that she can show him by her raised eyebrows and happy expression how exciting she thinks this all is, but his hearty joking manner from the landing has vanished; he looks into the dark distance and as he pulls on the cigar so the red tip glows brighter he squints, painfully, as if somebody's making him listen to a noise that hurts his ears.

When they stop, at the cleared gravel road that runs down the high bank behind the house, he sets off the firecrackers: carelessly, a pack at a time, lighting them with his cigar and flinging them into the road. She shrieks with delight and claps her mittens over her ears as he throws them faster and faster, the whole road dancing with sparks as firecrackers twist and jerk upon the ground, five packs at a time, six: fresh ones bouncing off the gravel and exploding in white machine-gun fire until the last pack spends itself, and pops far apart, like popcorn in the pan when nearly all the grains have burst and then there is nothing but a ringing in her ears and a flat blanket of white smoke hovering three feet above the lonely road.

Now the volley has stopped, she has lots of questions. 'How far does the sound go?' she asks, and then: 'Do you think Mama heard it back at the house?' She watches her father carefully as she asks this, because if she talks to him when she shouldn't he will sometimes growl, or grab her upper arm and shake it, or sometimes even slap, and when this happens it is nobody's fault but her own.

But her father only takes a swig from the little bottle in the pocket of his coat, the one he calls his Christmas Cheer. Like he's answering somebody else's question, not the ones she's asked, he says: 'Come on. Let's shoot some Roman candles, Tiger.'

Rome, she knows, is a town in Italy, and all her life long she will connect it in her mind with the smell of gunpowder and balls of pink and green fire. A city of coldness, shattered crystal, explosions. Her father points the striped cylinder away from him, like the garden hose: *whoosh*, his face lights up; *whoosh* it lights again. She is breathless with the beauty of it, each spatter of light against the black sky hits her like a blow between the ribs: 'Daddy,' she cries, and then again, 'Daddy', hardly knowing what she says when her father, stooping beside her with the candle, says: 'Here you try it, honey.'

She scarcely knows what happens next. The pain shoots through her left hand and spits white on her optic nerve like the after-image of the fireburst, sparklers on a birthday cake: the white mitten is melted, her ring and pinky fingers are stuck together and the scream, when it tears through her, is white and like fire and does not stop.

Her father is fumbling at her wrist, trying to peel the mitten off: 'Oh, God,' he says, and 'Shut up, shut up, your mother will hear you, *shut up*, I said', and an instant later his slap rings across her face. But the pain in her hand is such that she cannot feel it, nor the slap that comes after, nor the one that comes after that.

The stars are needle-pricks in black velvet. She is lying on her back in the snow while her father kneels above her, one knee on either side of her ribcage, frantically heaping snow on her hand. And she is still screaming because the snow burns as much as the fire did, because she cannot help it, even in her terror when her father's face swoops down practically to touch her own and she is screaming through his leather glove: 'Shut up,' he says, breath hot and teeth close to her cheek; 'shut up, you're gonna get us both in trouble, let's don't tell Mother about this, OK?' But she is beyond shutting up, the pain crackles across her eyelids in a white wire, like sheet lightning in a black sky, and even though she is thrashing, half-suffocated from the glove clamped across her mouth, the screams seize her again and again. This is her gift from the dark fairy: this will be her first memory, and all her life long all cobwebs and chains will wind her back here, to this snow-banked hillside – this smoke, this ice, this artificial fire, these first singing-lessons in the coloratura of pain.

A selection of quality fiction from Headline